D1596918

Zenobia

The Patriot Way

By Bob Adamov

Other ***Emerson Moore*** Adventures by Bob Adamov

Rainbow's End	Released October 2002
Pierce the Veil	Released May 2004
When Rainbows Walk	Released June 2005
Promised Land	Released July 2006
The Other Side of Hell	Released June 2008
Tan Lines	Released June 2010
Sandustee	Released March 2013

Next ***Emerson Moore*** Adventure

Missing

This book is a work of fiction. Names, characters, places and incidents are either products of the author's imagination or are used fictitiously. Any resemblance to actual events, locales or persons, living or dead, is entirely coincidental.

The following publication provided reference material:

Anatomy of Deceit by Jerry Blaskovich, M.D.
Copyright 1997 Dunhill Publishing Company

"They that wait upon the Lord shall renew their strength; they shall mount up with wings as eagles; they shall run, and not be weary; and they shall walk, and not faint." – Isaiah 40:31

ISBN: 0-9786184-4-0
978-0-9786184-4-5

Library of Congress Number: 2014931226

Cover art and Dustjacket by Lange Design
www.langedesign.org

Submit all requests for reprinting to:
BookMasters, Inc.
PO Box 388
Ashland, Ohio 78735

Published in the United States by:
Packard Island Publishing, Wooster, Ohio

www.bookmasters.com
www.packardislandpublishing.com
www.BobAdamov.com

First Edition – May 2014

Printed in the United States

Acknowledgements

For technical assistance, I'd like to express my appreciation to Detective Pete Swartz with the Toledo Police Department, Tasha Perdue of the Lucas County Human Trafficking Coalition, Toledo Judge Connie Zemmelman, U.S. Customs Agent Ernie Corpening, Arnie Sutter, owner of the *Western Basin* magazine, Captain Bob Lewis and Lieutenant Mark Cherney from the Collier County Sheriff's Office in Naples, Denis Lange at Lange Design and trucker David Hummer. Special thanks go to my long-time friends Gary Mazey, Larry Evans and Sandy Evans Huffine for their coaching.

I'd also like to acknowledge the dedication to creating awareness about human trafficking by Celia Williamson, professor of social work at the University of Toledo, as well as recognizing her numerous and outstanding white papers.

I'd like to thank my team of editors: Cathy Adamov, Peggy Parker, Hank Inman of Goldfinch Communications, Andrea Goss Knaub, Jackie Buckwalter, Mike Steidl and the one and only Joe Weinstein.

Dedication

This book is dedicated to my beautiful, loving and caring sweetheart of a wife, Cathy, and to the victims of human trafficking.

Donations

The Lucas County Human Trafficking Coalition and Second Chance will receive a portion of the proceeds from the sale of this book.

If you would like to help support the following organizations, please send your donation to:

Lucas County Human Trafficking Coalition
        Or
Second Chance

c/o The Toledo Area Ministries.
3043 Monroe Street
Toledo, OH 43606

The Free2BMe Project
3540 Seaman Street
Oregon, OH 43616

The Daughter Project
PO Box 255
Perrysburg, OH 43552

For more information, check these sites:

www.ohioseagrant.osu.edu
www.MillerFerry.com
www.cusslersociety.com
www.Put-in-Bay.com

Foreword

For a number of years, I had been contemplating a novel about the Serbo-Croatian war. Part of this was due to my being half Serbian (my father) and half Croatian (my mother). My Serbian relatives resided in Croatia in Tenja and Bobota, not far from Osijek and Vukovar, the scene of the most ferociously devastating battle.

My father moved to Vukovar after his retirement in the United States, but returned to the United States before the war broke out. I had visited my relatives and Vukovar before the war started.

Many of my Serbian and Croatian friends in the U.S. were saddened by the ravages of the war. We abhorred the atrocities on both sides and the inability of the people to live peacefully with each other. The haunting seesaw battle for power and payback between the Serbs and Croats over the years seemed to deter a life of harmony.

As I researched the war, I read Dr. Jerry Blaskovich's *Anatomy of Deceit* that detailed his first-hand encounters with the war. He painted a vivid and graphic picture of the atrocities committed. When I tried to contact Dr. Blaskovich in California, I learned that he had died four months earlier. I did talk with his son, Matt, who gave me permission to use his father's book for part of my research.

The idea for centering the novel on human trafficking originated with Mark Cherney in Naples, Florida. I had finished a day with the sheriff's department SWAT team leaders and was brainstorming with Mark in his office. He brought up the human trafficking idea based on what he had seen in Collier County. I was aware of trafficking that had taken place during the Serbo-Croatian war and decided to explore the possibilities of using it as a thread to tie together the plot in *Zenobia*.

As I researched, I was stunned to learn about the high levels of trafficking in Toledo, Ohio. It was primarily due to the city's proximity to the crossroads of the major highways of Interstate-75 and Interstate-80/Interstate-90. I was also shocked by how prevalent trafficking was and the abuse of the victims, especially the teens. I decided to use *Zenobia* as a means to create additional awareness about the evils of human trafficking.

Over the years, I'd drive along Ohio State Route 250 to catch the ferry to the Lake Erie islands and pass a street south of Norwalk. The street's name was Zenobia. I loved how the name rolled off my tongue and thought I'd use the name for a novel one day. Zenobia is also the name of a Masonic chapter in Perrysburg, Ohio; a restaurant in Canfield, Ohio; and a ferryboat that sunk off the coast of Cyprus on its maiden voyage. It's a great diving spot. Zenobia also was the name of an Egyptian warrior princess, who defeated the Romans and married a Roman general.

The Patriot Way part of the title I'll leave to you to decipher as you read the story.

Human Trafficking – You Can Make a Difference!

By Tasha R. Perdue, MSW
Co-chair of the Lucas County Human Trafficking Coalition

Although Lady Liberty stands at the coast, we are a nation where not everyone is free. The Emancipation Proclamation, a decree against slavery, was supposed to ensure freedom for all. Despite this document, some people living in the United States are enslaved without the essential liberties that the United States guarantees. Human trafficking, a form of modern day slavery, is responsible for the unjust treatment of individuals across the United States. It is happening here, in the land of opportunity, and includes foreign nationals and our domestic citizens.

The federal Trafficking Victims Protection Act established human trafficking as a federal offense. The Trafficking Victims Protection Act of 2000 (TVPA) defines "severe forms of trafficking in persons" as follows:

Sex trafficking: the recruitment, harboring, transportation, provision, or obtaining of a person for the purpose of a commercial sex act, in which the commercial sex act is induced by force, fraud, or coercion; or in which the person induced to perform such act has not attained 18 years of age; and Labor Trafficking: the recruitment, harboring, transportation, provision, or obtaining of a person for labor or services, through the use of force, fraud, or coercion for the purpose of subjection to involuntary servitude, peonage, debt bondage, or slavery.

There are some important components included in the above definition. Under federal law anyone under the age of 18 is automatically a victim. There is no need to prove force, fraud or coercion. For anyone over the age of 18, these are necessary elements. Force can involve physical or sexual violence or the use of confinement. Fraud involves deception where traffickers may lie to individuals about employment opportunities to get them to a different country or area and can include things like modeling, waitressing or even domestic work. Coercion involves the threat of harm or use of intimidation to get the victim to believe that harm may occur if they fail to comply with what the trafficker wants.

When individuals hear of human trafficking they may immediately consider the Hollywood version of trafficking. Although Hollywood is raising awareness that trafficking is an issue, it may also be promoting false assumptions about trafficking. It is important to realize that people do not have to leave the United States, nor even their own neighborhood, to be trafficked. Movement across borders is not a necessary element under the federal trafficking law. People can be trafficked in the town where they were born and raised; or they may be sold in various cities around the U.S., or, on rare occasion, outside of the U.S. Trafficking victims are both men and women, as well as adults and youth.

All youth are vulnerable to trafficking; and traffickers know and recognize this vulnerability. Traffickers prey on youth who demonstrate this vulnerability to a greater degree, but all youth by the very nature of being young are vulnerable. In addition, adults may also be vulnerable to sex and/or labor trafficking, including both domestic citizens and foreign nationals. However, the United States Department of State estimates that our domestic born youth are the largest population trafficked in the United States. Approximately 100,000 U.S. born children are trafficked for sex, within the United States, in a given year. In Ohio, it is estimated that over 3,000 youth are at-risk for trafficking and over 1,000 are successfully trafficked.

Human trafficking is a global issue but you can help make a difference. You are one person, but one person can get another person involved who can then inspire another. That is how movements are started. We encourage you to find out about local trafficking initiatives in your area. Then if you are able, join a local coalition. If not, follow them on Facebook or Twitter and share these resources with your friends and family. Attend events that local programs and coalitions hold in your community. If your area does not have a coalition, then start one.

Support victim services. You can do this in several ways. Attend fundraisers that the victim service programs may have in your community. Find out what they are in need of locally and make monetary donations or donate the items needed. If you are unsure what to donate, most victim service programs can always use personal hygiene products. Let other people know about victim services in the area. If you are on a board, be creative and recommend that you adopt a victim service agency for a month to a year. Sophisticated boards can offer technical assistance, space for events, strategic planning, grant writing and other resources; smaller boards can offer items, cover printing costs, partnership in fundraising and more.

One of the most important things that you can do to engage our youth is to let them know about this issue. It is a difficult conversation to have, but it is important to start the conversation. Education is key to prevention and knowledge is power. If you are uncomfortable initiating the discussion, you can check into having a youth group or organization schedule a theme around trafficking for some peer led support and discussion. It doesn't matter how the education happens as long as it does indeed occur.

Consider your own choices. We are an increasingly global society. Consider where your purchases are coming from and how they arrive at your location. There are several websites and phone Apps that can assist with this understanding. The Free2Work App allows you to examine the companies you shop from. You can compare companies in different categories and see how they rank in their treatment of employees and fair labor practices. The App makes it easy to see the grades that different companies get for their labor practices. You can also visit "How Many Slaves Work For Me," to see how your normal daily routine may have an impact on others around the world. The website provides a glimpse of what impact your products and choices may have on others. In addition, you can replace the unethically made materials with survivor made and fair trade items.

Critically analyze media that you and youth around you are consuming. Really listen to the song lyrics of your favorite artists. Examine what the shows, movies and internet content is promoting. Begin a dialogue to encourage youth to consider why they may be drawn to a particular theme and have a discussion over what that really means. For example, we have allowed the word "pimp" to become watered down. However, when people say "pimp", they do not realize that the word really means someone who is enslaving and taking away the rights of another. Fewer people would allow their young children to dress up as a "pimp" for Halloween if they took time to consider the reality behind the costume.

Let your voice be heard! Take time to write or call your representatives to let them know that you support anti-human trafficking initiatives and that they should as well. Write letters to the editor to help educate others. You never know who might read your article and become inspired to make a difference. Talk to your friends and family. Let them know about the issue of human trafficking and encourage them to tell others. If we can get everyone to commit to telling at least two people and then encourage them to commit to telling at least two people, we can really make an impact. The time to stand against human trafficking is here and now. No effort is too small to help make a difference. In the words of Margaret Mead, "Never doubt that a small group of thoughtful, committed citizens can change the world; indeed, it is the only thing that ever has."

Coalition Name	Counties Served
Northwest Ohio Rescue and Restore Coalition	Williams, Fulton, Defiance, Henry, Putnam, Paulding, Van Wert, Mercer, Auglaize, Shelby, Hardin, Hancock, Allen
Lucas County Human Trafficking Coalition	Lucas, Wood, Ottawa, Sandusky, Seneca
Northern Coalition Against Human Trafficking	Geauga, Portage, Cuyahoga, Carroll
Human Trafficking Collaborative of Lorain County	Lorain
Northeast Ohio Coalition on Rescue and Restore	Ashtabula, Trumbull, Mahoning, Columbiana
Southeast Ohio Human Trafficking Coalition	Guernsey, Noble, Morgan, Washington
Central Ohio Rescue and Restore Coalition	Marion, Richland, Morrow, Logan, Union, Delaware, Knox, Champaign, Madison, Franklin, Licking, Pickaway, Fairfield, Ross
MidEast Ohio Rescue and Restore Coalition	Coshocton, Muskingum
Abolition Ohio Miami Valley	Miami, Montgomery, Clark, Green, Warren, Clinton
End Slavery Cincinnati	Butler, Hamilton, Clermont, Brown, Adams

ADDITIONAL RESOURCES

State Websites:

http://www.publicsafety.ohio.gov/ht/index.html

https://www.facebook.com/NorthwestOhioRescueRestoreCoalition

http://lchtc.org/

http://collaborativeinitiative.org/

http://www.centralohiorescueandrestore.org/

http://www.itcouldbemelorain.com/

http://neocorr.org/

http://www.endslaverycincinnati.org/

https://www.facebook.com/abolitionohio

National Websites
National Human Trafficking Hotline:
1.800.3737.888

Human Trafficking Certificate Program:
www.traffickingeducation.com

Polaris Project
http://www.polarisproject.org/

Shared Hope International
http://sharedhope.org/

Not For Sale
http://www.notforsalecampaign.org/

Free to Work
http://www.free2work.org/

Slavery Footprint
http://slaveryfootprint.org/

Lake Erie Islands

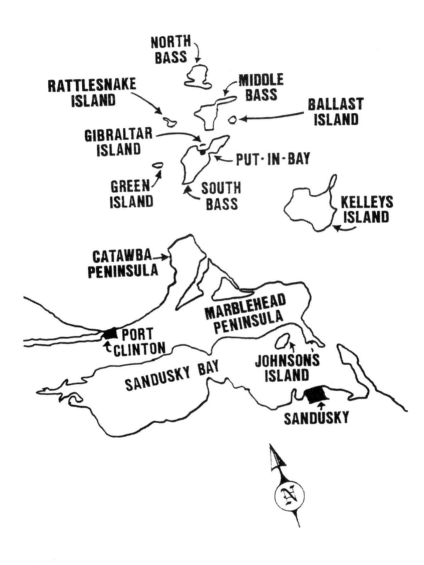

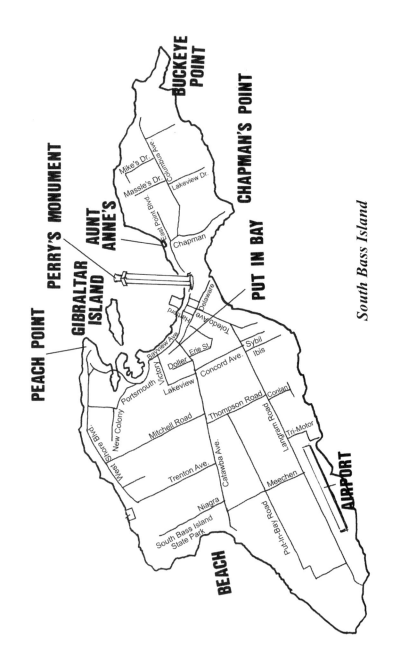

South Bass Island

Book One
Destruction
1991

Early November 1991

Vukovar, Croatia

The rocket-propelled grenade hit the small truck on the left front fender as it drove through the night, sending it careening into the ditch. The Croatian driver, who a few minutes earlier had been chatting amicably about the beauty of his country before the war had started, was now slumped against his passenger. The driver's lifeless eyes stared into oblivion.

"Mihailo, Mihailo. Are you okay?" rookie *Washington Record* reporter Emerson Moore asked as his vision cleared and he looked at the driver. Moore shook the driver before he saw the piece of shrapnel projecting from the driver's temple.

Visibly shaken by his first personal exposure to the brutal reality of war, the twenty-three-year-old pushed the dead body away from him. In a shocked daze, he forced himself to concentrate on his survival as he heard a vehicle approaching. He grabbed his duffel bag and scrambled out of the badly-damaged vehicle through the rear window.

Quickly, he jumped off the truck and into the ditch where he crouched. Under the cover of the night, he moved a hundred yards through the ditch. Behind him he heard a vehicle stop and the sound of several Serbian soldiers walking over to the truck. If he understood Serbian, he would have heard them congratulating each other for finally killing the Croatian courier, who had evaded them for the last two months.

The Serbs flashed their lights around, searching for the passenger whom they saw when the truck drove by their hiding spot.

When Moore saw the flashlights searching for him, he knew that he'd have to make a break for the forest. Cautiously, Moore raised his head to look across the road to ascertain whether any of the Serbian soldiers were close. Seeing none, he bolted out of the ditch and into the forest.

After walking for thirty minutes, he spotted a large overturned tree in a pine grove. It would be his home for the night. He decided to continue his journey to Vukovar in the morning. For now, he chose rest and reflection on his first exposure to the horror of war.

After graduation from college, Moore landed a position as a reporter at the *Washington Record* although his eyes had been focused on a job at *The Washington Post*. He covered a number of local stories and helped investigate politicians. When a rumor circulated that the newspaper was considering sending someone to cover the Serbo-Croatian war, Moore rushed into the managing editor's office and pleaded for the assignment. She gave it to him.

Moore had quickly caught a flight to Zagreb in Croatia where he took a train to Osijek. There, he hitched a ride with Mihailo, a courier, for the twenty-two kilometer drive southeast to Vukovar, which had become the strategic focus of the war.

The war for Croatia's independence from Yugoslavia began in July. By October, the Serbian-dominated Yugoslav army had virtually surrounded the prosperous and provincial eastern Croatian city of Vukovar. It sat along the banks of the Danube River where the Vuka River emptied into it.

The Yugoslav army had amassed 36,000 troops around the city of 31,000 people. Vukovar, which saw the majority of its Serbian citizens flee, was defended by 2,000 militia members, some of whom had served previously in the Yugoslav army, and civilian volunteers. Despite the pleas for help, the Croatian government in Zagreb had refused reinforcements to save Vukovar.

Newspaper reports characterized the siege as the worst since World War II's Stalingrad, with shells and rockets blanketing the city daily. Some compared it to the heroic stand at the Alamo.

The distant sounds of an artillery barrage in the early dawn awoke Moore from a fitful sleep. He crawled from under the fallen tree and stretched as he breathed the pungent pine scent. Standing and looking around for any danger in the dead-still forest, Moore saw shafts of the early morning light penetrating the tall trees, casting a peaceful glow in steep contrast to the battle raging nearby.

Moore grabbed his duffel bag and hiked farther into the forest. An hour later, he heard his name being called by someone with a light accent.

"Emerson Moore! Emerson Moore, are you here?"

Quickly dropping to the ground, Moore found partial concealment behind some large ferns and beneath the low-hanging bow of a hemlock. He raised his head to identify the caller.

Making his way slowly through the forest and toward Moore was a seventeen-year-old boy with a medium build and close-cropped black hair. He was wearing jeans, a black tee shirt and a black Adidas track jacket. Two white stripes ran down the jacket's arms. He wore an orange watch cap on his head. In his mouth, he clenched a cigarette. Even though he moved slowly, there was an air of cockiness about him.

"Emerson Moore," he called again. "I'm here to help you."

Moore hesitated a moment and decided to take a chance. Who else but a few Croatians knew his name, he thought to himself. He stood up. "I'm Emerson Moore."

The boy's face broke into a smile. "I found you. I told them I would find you."

"Who's them, and who are you?" Moore asked.

"I'm Blago," he smiled with an air of defiance. "I told them I'd find you. No one gets things done like Blago can.

"When you didn't arrive in Vukovar last night, your reporter friends were worried something had happened to you. They know how much the Serbs dislike reporters. We Croatians, on the other hand, we love you. You need to let the world know what is really happening to us in Vukovar," he said before taking a long draw on his cigarette.

"I'm glad you found me," Moore said with an obvious sigh of relief. "And I'm glad you're here, Blago. Mihailo's truck took a round and we crashed into a ditch last night."

"Yes, I know. I rode by there this morning and saw his truck. When I pulled over to see if you two were there, I found Mihailo. He was dead." Blago said. There was a sadness in his voice as he spoke. "Then I started searching for you."

"I'm sorry. Was he your friend?"

"Yes. We were school classmates. When the war started, we both volunteered as couriers."

"Sounds dangerous."

"It is," Blago acknowledged. Then he added, "It was deadly dangerous for Mihailo."

Nodding his head, Moore asked, "What should we do about his body?"

"Nothing now. The Serbs are looking for you and will be watching for you to return to the truck. I have some friends who can sneak over there tonight and get his body."

"How did you know where to find me?" Moore asked.

"Anyone escaping from the truck would have naturally run into the woods. So, I came looking for you." Blago looked over Moore's shoulder and into the woods. "We must hurry. The Serbs will be looking for you, too."

"Where are we going?" Moore asked as he picked up his duffel bag.

"Back to my bike," Blago answered as they walked.

"Your bike? You rode out here on a bicycle?"

Grinning, Blago replied, "No, no. I have a dirt bike. It's a 1988 Honda XR600." There was a tone of pride in his response. "There are several dirt roads that run through the woods. Easy for me on my dirt bike."

Within ten minutes, they arrived at the dirt bike which had been hidden at the edge of the woods and along the little-used road. The bike had been spray-painted a dark green.

Standing the bike, Blago said, "I'd suggest you hoist your duffel bag on your back. It'll give you a little more protection in case any bullets are fired at us as we ride."

"Good idea," Moore agreed as he followed through with the suggestion and slung the bag over his back.

Blago started the motorbike and Moore settled behind him for the ride to Vukovar. As they rode, Moore had a hollow feeling in his stomach. He hoped it was due to hunger and not a precursor of what was to come. He wasn't sure.

Within twenty minutes, they paused on a small rise and looked at Vukovar below. Moore looked with disbelief. Rounds of mortar and heavy armament cascaded down upon the city. Smoke billowed from burning buildings as uncontrolled fires reaped their damage. Many of the buildings were nothing more than hollow shells.

A water tower stood proudly on a hill as it overlooked the carnage below. It was pockmarked from the impact of countless shells. It was becoming a symbol of the Croatians' stand against the Serbian invaders' bombardment.

Moore swayed from side to side with a gaping mouth and a panic-stricken look on his face. The reality of the situation hit him. "This is horrific," he said as he stared.

"This is nothing," Blago said. "Wait until we get there and you see and feel it first-hand. You'll smell death in the air. Then you can say how truly horrific it is."

"Smell death?"

"Mostly from dead cows and horses. Some pets. It's too dangerous to try to haul them away and bury them. It's dangerous enough when we risk our lives at night to retrieve the bodies of people who've been shot during the day or have been hit by incoming rockets and shells. Then we bury them."

From their vantage point, Moore could see the Serbian lines and artillery emplacements. "How do we get through the lines?" he asked with a bewildered look on his face.

"There's one road that my cousin guards. He's half Serbian and Croatian like me," Blago said with a proud grin.

"That's got to be difficult."

"What's that?"

"Being half Serbian and Croatian," Moore replied.

"Intermarriage. That's what happens in Vukovar," he said with a shrug of his shoulders. "There are a lot of us like that. It's going to happen when your population is split almost evenly between Serbs and Croatians. Although not as much these days."

"Why?"

"Most of the Serbs packed up and left before the bloodshed began."

Moore had a perplexed look on his face. "How did you decide which side to fight on?"

"Every one of us has to wrestle with that decision. For me, my family lived peacefully here with all of our neighbors. There was good-natured teasing, but we got along. I chose to defend my home from the invaders. They are the ones who disrupted my life. I'll tell you more one day."

"But…" Moore didn't get to continue as Blago gunned his engine.

"Enough talk for now. Let's see if my cousin is working today," Blago shouted as they continued their ride toward the devastation.

"I hope he's on duty," Moore yelled back with a worried look.

"Oh, he always is. He's a sergeant in the army. He's always there. Sometimes, he puts on a show of shooting at me, but I can count on him always missing," Blago grinned.

I hope the others can be counted on to miss, too, Moore thought quietly to himself.

Five minutes later, they approached a Serbian checkpoint on the road to Vukovar. Two soldiers leveled their rifles at the two riders. The rifles were quickly lowered when a sergeant walked around the back of a large truck that blocked the road. He waved and yelled at the driver to move the vehicle forward a few feet so that the dirt bike could drive by.

"That's my cousin," Blago yelled as he gunned the Honda and

they rode through. Blago waved at his cousin as they rode.

As they rode into Vukovar, Moore saw the devastation first-hand. Incoming rocket rounds and bombardment had taken its toll on Vukovar. Buildings were crumbling. No roof appeared intact. It seemed as if every structure had some level of damage. Broken glass from windows littered the small yards, which had once been well-kept.

Most of the facades were pitted with various-sized indentations and gaping holes. The size of the holes and indentations indicated the caliber of the weapon which made the damage.

The Honda slowed several times to make its way around rubble and dead animals in the streets. The stench from decaying cows and horses permeated the air as Blago had warned.

A Small Gas Station
Vukovar, Croatia

With bullets zipping by their heads, the dirt bike abruptly turned left from the road and raced through an open garage door into the gas station. Laughing, Blago brought the Honda to a stop near the rear wall. "Those Serbs think they can kill me. I'm like Superman. Bullets bounce off me," Blago boasted.

Moore stepped off the Honda and looked for cover. He wasn't as comfortable with the current circumstances as his new friend. His nervousness showed on his face.

When a bullet embedded itself in the wall next to Moore, he dropped to the ground.

His action was greeted by a round of laughs from the two veteran reporters, who were seated in a corner behind a wall of sand bags.

"Better get used to bullets zinging by. They're more plentiful than mosquitoes around here," one of the reporters said as he walked over to Moore and helped him to his feet.

"You must be the newbie, Emerson Moore," he said as he looked at the six-foot-two inch, dark-haired, brown-eyed young man.

Extending his hand, Moore responded, "That would be me." He cast a wary eye toward the garage door opening and to a number of empty buildings which he could see across the street. They had been severely damaged from Serbian shelling.

"Fresh out of grad school I hear."

Moore nodded his head. "June graduate."

"Well, Mr. Emerson Moore, welcome to Croatia. It's where the blood runs red and the rest of us just run. I'm your newly assigned mentor, Buck Andrea, with the Associated Press." Andrea was six-foot tall, medium build and in his early fifties. His thick graying hair highlighted his deep blue eyes, which were beginning to show the first hints of crow's feet. He had the beginnings of a pot belly from his years of beer drinking.

Another bullet whizzed by, sending Moore to the ground.

Andrea stayed on his feet, daring the shooters to take him out. "It doesn't matter if it's from a Serbian or Croatian weapon. They can both kill you," he laughed. "Grab your gear and bring it inside the station." Andrea walked toward the garage's corner and spoke to his companion. "I don't think that boy has seen any combat. Why do I always get the ones who're still wet behind the ears?"

"Maybe this one will last longer than the other one," his companion joked as he passed the bottle of slivovitz, locally-made plum brandy, to Andrea.

"Me first," Blago said as he grabbed the bottle from Andrea's hand, took a quick swig and returned it to Andrea.

"Want a drink, kid?" Andrea asked Moore as he held out the bottle.

"Sure," Moore said as he tossed his duffel bag in the corner behind the sand bags and took the bottle from Andrea. He took a pull and began to cough as he handed the bottle back to Andrea.

"Strong stuff, kid," Andrea chuckled. "First time you tried slivovitz?"

"Yes." Moore coughed twice more.

"You'll get used to it. We expected you last night and when you didn't appear, we sent Blago out to find you. He has a nose for finding things and news for us to report on."

Blago grinned. "I get the job done," he boasted.

Moore quickly explained what had happened the previous night and his encounter with Blago.

Andrea smiled as he looked at Blago. "That's our Blago."

The noise of something hitting the floor caused the three of them to look down. Two grenades were rolling on the floor toward Moore.

"Grenades!" Andrea yelled as Moore jumped over the sandbags and to the floor on the other side. When he landed he found himself on top of a man, who reeked of alcohol and was laughing uncontrollably.

Andrea walked over to the two. In his hands were the two grenades. "Emerson, they don't work unless the pin's pulled," he laughed. "It's kind of a ritual here whenever we get a new guy in."

He tossed the grenades to Moore, who caught them.

"I don't need these."

"Oh, yes you do, Emerson," said the man with a British accent, who was pulling himself from under Moore. "They're smoke grenades. You throw them to cover your escape when you get in a jam. That smoke screen makes it harder for them to target you as you run."

Nodding his head, Moore said, "I see. Thank you."

"I'm Fitzgibbons. Peter Fitzgibbons with the U.K.'s *Guardian*."

"We call him Fitz," Andrea interjected.

"Hello, Fitz. Sorry about knocking you over," Moore said as he shook hands with the medium height journalist, who had red hair and a fair complexion. He looked to be in his late forties.

"It's no problem at all. Welcome aboard." He paused as he looked at Moore. "You wearing a Kevlar vest?"

"No. I don't have one."

"Here's an extra," he said as he tossed it to Moore. "Keep it."

"And be sure to wear it," Andrea warned.

"Thanks, I will," Moore responded.

"See that red stain on the chest?" Fitzgibbons asked Moore.

Moore looked down at the vest and saw the stain. His eyes widened. "That's blood!" he deduced. "Didn't it work for somebody?"

"Nope. He's not with us any more," Fitzgibbons said as he put his two hands together and looked toward the heavens. "He made the mistake of carrying it on his back with his backpack rather than wearing it. Took one in the chest and bled like a stuck pig," Fitzgibbons said as he rolled his eyes over to stare at Moore.

Andrea was chuckling. "That's a ketchup stain, Emerson. Fitz is just trying to make a point so you wear it."

"Yeah. Yeah, Buck. I get it," Moore said as he looked at the ornery Fitzgibbons, who was taking another swig of the slivovitz.

A figure appeared at the rear doorway which led to the owner's small quarters and a storage area. "What's all the laughing about?" a heavily-accented voice asked.

"That's Pajo. He owns the place and is our ever-so-gracious host," Andrea explained.

"I'm the new guy, Emerson Moore," Moore said as he shook hands with the seventy-two-year-old owner. Pajo was wearing an old sweater and a fedora which had seen better days. He walked with a limp, incurred years earlier during a hunting accident.

Andrea corrected Moore. "He's the new *kid*."

"Buck, I'm not a kid," Moore stormed.

Andrea just smiled. "You bring a mobile phone with you?"

"Yes, I have a Nokia in my gear bag."

"Leave it there."

"Why?"

"Won't work. The towers are down."

"I see." Turning to Pajo, Moore asked, "Do you still sell gasoline here?"

A smile crossed Pajo's weathered face. "Yes, but very carefully. The Serbian shooters wait for people to pull in for gas. They are perfect targets. Very dangerous." He shrugged his shoulders. "We try to sell gas at night but the Serbs have those special glasses."

"Night vision," Andrea explained.

"That's it," Pajo remarked. "I also have a pump inside and we sell them liters of gas in gas cans so they can sneak them home. But there's no real place to drive here. It's too dangerous unless you are trying to get out of Vukovar."

"And that's quite dangerous," Fitzgibbons commented. "It's running a gauntlet of bullets and shells. You were lucky to get through safely, lad."

Moore nodded and thought to himself that coming here may not have been such a wise decision.

Andrea lit a cigar.

"Crikey, the bloke has to smoke us out with one of his cigars," Fitzgibbons complained.

Ignoring him, Andrea spoke to Moore. "These are quite good. Cuban. Want one?"

"No, no." Moore responded. "I agree with Fitz. You're going to smoke us out. Besides, the slivovitz did enough damage to me."

"And listen, kid. If you are out in the open and you see planes approaching, take cover. The Croats don't have any planes. Only the Serbs do. Those Serbian MIGs are either strafing the Croats or dropping bombs," Andrea warned.

"Thanks. I'll remember that."

"This is a bloody sad war," Fitzgibbons observed.

"Aren't all wars?" Moore asked.

"They are. There was an incident near here where the Croats destroyed a Serbian tank. In turn, the Serbs retaliated by massacring fifty-five villagers. Blago, tell Moore about you finding your family and what happened to them."

Blago exhaled blue smoke from his cigarette. "My father and family were slaughtered by the Serbs. I don't want to talk about it."

Moore caught a movement out of the corner of his eye and turned toward the rear doorway to catch someone disappearing from it.

"Who was that?"

"Tatiana," Fitzgibbon answered.

"Tatiana?" Moore asked. "Is that Pajo's wife?"

The men broke out in laughter with Pajo laughing the loudest.

"No, not at my age," Pajo said between laughs. "That's our house guest."

"Sort of like our mascot," Andrea explained. "We're sheltering her and, in some ways, protecting her."

Before Moore could ask another question, Andrea called toward the doorway. "Tatiana? Tatiana? Come join us. He's a friend of ours."

A sixteen-year-old girl appeared in the doorway between the garage and the back room. Her face was dirty and she was wearing a soiled gray sweatshirt and torn blue jeans. Her long brown hair was pulled back. Despite her appearances, she was an attractive teen.

"Could you get my friend here a Pepsi?" Andrea asked as the girl disappeared into the back.

Pajo commented when she left the garage. "She's an orphan now. Her house was two doors down. It was destroyed a week ago by an incoming shell. It killed her parents. Now, she lives here and tries to help me."

The girl returned with a cold Pepsi and delivered it to Moore. "Thank you," he said. As he reached into his pocket for his money, he noticed that one of her beautiful, dark brown eyes was blackened. "What happened to your eye, Honey?" he asked.

"A brick hit me in the face when the walls to my home crumbled," she answered.

There was a sense of emptiness about her. Moore guessed it was due to the death of her parents and he understood.

"She doesn't talk much. Hasn't talked much since the shelling of her house," Pajo said.

"I think she's in shock," Fitzgibbons suggested as Moore handed her money for his drink.

"Here, I think I have something for you," Moore said as he walked over to his duffel bag and opened it. He withdrew a Hershey bar and held it out to the girl. She smiled shyly and took the candy, then disappeared into the back room.

"So, what really happened to her eye?" Moore asked as he looked at the four men.

"We think it really happened when the house collapsed around her," Pajo said as he began to close the garage doors.

"Pretty girl," Moore observed.

"Before the war, she won several beauty contests in Vukovar. Her beauty is well known through the countryside," Pajo offered.

"Oh, come on, Pajo. She's hotter than my first wife in the month of July," Andrea stated boldly.

Ignoring the comment, Moore looked at Andrea. "You mentioned you're protecting her. From what?"

"It's more who than what. And that who is Marko Marinkovic."

Moore noticed Pajo twitched at hearing the name. "Marko Marinkovic? Who's that?"

"They also call him the Vuk, sly like a fox but as dangerous as a hungry wolf. He's the head of a Serbian paramilitary unit. Vuk means wolf in Serbian and his unit is the wolf pack," Andrea explained.

"Are they part of the Serbian army?" Moore asked.

"Yes, but they have a lot of freedom."

"More like a bloody gang of thugs," Fitzgibbons offered grimly. "You need to be very careful around them. They're Serbian hardliners. They kill whenever they want and with no repercussions. They've made several forays into Vukovar."

"He's right. They have hair triggers," Andrea warned. "And they don't like reporters."

"None of the Serbs do," Fitzgibbons added.

"Why is that?" Moore asked.

"They're concerned we'll report the rapes, mass murders, pillaging and human trafficking they're involved with," Andrea answered.

"Two reporters, Danny Johnson from the States and Loren Wells from London, disappeared after stories appeared in their newspapers and they encountered Marinkovic and his wolf pack. Of course, Marinkovic denies he had anything to do with their disappearance," Andrea added.

"Where does Tatiana come in?" Moore asked.

"Marinkovic is looking for her," Andrea replied as he puffed on his cigar.

"And any other especially attractive woman," Fitzgibbons added. "When they find them, the women disappear. Never to be heard from again."

Moore had a puzzled look on his face. "Rape?" he asked.

"More than that. He's also involved in human trafficking. Provides women for whorehouses in Yugoslavia and outside its borders. We believe the army also sets up rape camps for their own use. We can't prove it, but we're trying to run it down."

"No respect for women," Moore observed.

"No respect for anybody is more like it," Andrea said. "There are all kinds of human rights violations taking place. The atrocities and massacres are what we're after. If we can expose them to the world, we hope international pressure will put a stop to the atrocities and ethnic cleansing we see. "

"Marinkovic has been here twice, looking for the girl. He thinks we have her, but can't find her."

"And he won't find her," Pajo said with a twinkle in his eyes. "I have a hidden trapdoor in the floor. She hides below the floor when he makes a raid here."

"We also hide our sole laptop there. That bugger Marinkovic destroyed our other one during one of his visits," Fitzgibbons chimed in.

Moore nodded his head. "And he doesn't bother either of you?"

"Not so far. He pushes us around, but he hasn't harmed us," Andrea said.

"At least not until we get a ball-buster of a story developed and placed," Fitzgibbons replied. "Then bloody hell will break loose. He'll be after our arses."

"I'd like to help," Moore eagerly interjected.

"Easy there, sonny boy. This is a new frontier for you. You watch what we do and keep your head low. We don't need to lose our young protégé here," Andrea cautioned.

"Unless he starts drinking too much of the slivovitz," Fitzgibbons teased.

Andrea continued with educating Moore. "Let me give you a little history lesson, kid. Yugoslavia was a recipe for disaster. It was multi-ethnic and multi-religious with four distinct languages and two alphabets."

"Sounds like the diversity we have back home," Moore offered.

"To a point. But other than our Civil War, which wasn't really an ethnic issue, the diverse nationalities didn't fight each other. In this region, there's been a long history of one or the other ethnic group being in power and repeating the atrocities the other committed on them. It's been an endless cycle of payback."

"And don't forget the Ottoman Turks ruled this area for 500 years," Fitzgibbons commented.

"Right," Andrea agreed. "The Yugoslav president, Milosevic, divided Yugoslavia on ethnic lines by putting Serbs in the most influential positions and whipping up nationalism and hatred. He had the state-controlled TV stations run wartime footage of atrocities committed against the Serbs by the Utashe. That was the government installed in Croatia by Nazi Germany during World War II."

Pajo interrupted them when he shouted from the back room, "I've got lamb stew and bread for lunch."

That interruption got the attention of the three men and they walked into the back room.

"Bring your gear with you. You can toss it in the back," Andrea said to Moore.

Moore grabbed his gear and followed the men into the back room with boarded up windows and sand bags. It was sparse with a kitchen stove, sink, a small refrigerator and a worn wooden table with four benches around it. A single bed was against one wall. Pajo slept in the bed. Tatiana slept on a few blankets in front of the wood-burning stove.

"Throw your gear over there," Andrea said as he pointed to one side of the room where two sleeping bags and duffel bags were on the floor. "This isn't the Hilton, but it does quite nicely for us."

Moore followed Andrea's instructions and joined the others at the table. Starting the meal with toasts of slivovitz, the men began to dine as Tatiana served them.

As the men discussed the events of the war, Andrea turned to Moore and said, "There's a good story about Fitz here and his train ride from Belgrade to Vukovar before hostilities opened."

"Oh?" Moore asked.

"You're going to love this story," Fitzgibbons interjected with a twinkle in his gray blue eyes as he leaned back to hear Andrea retell one of his favorite stories.

"There were four people standing on a train which ran from Belgrade to Vukovar. There was Fitz, a Croatian baba…"

"What's a baba?" Moore interrupted.

"That's the Serbo-Croatian name for grandmother or older woman," Andrea explained before continuing. "A pretty, young Croatian blonde and a Serbian soldier. When the train went through a tunnel, everything went dark. Then you heard this big slap."

Fitzgibbons began chuckling.

Andrea continued his story. "When the train emerged from the tunnel, the Serbian soldier was rubbing his face. It had a large red mark on the cheek."

"Yeah, he tried to get fresh with the blonde," Moore deducted.

"Hold your britches, sonny boy," Andrea said as he held up his hand to the eager Moore. "Things aren't always what they seem. The blonde was probably thinking the soldier tried to grope her, but groped the baba by mistake and the baba hauled off and slapped him."

Moore nodded his head and listened.

"But that's not what happened. The baba thought the blonde slapped the soldier as any good Croatian girl would do when he tried to grab her." Andrea paused, and then continued, "The soldier was thinking Fitz here fondled the blonde in the dark and she thought it was the soldier and hit him by mistake."

Moore had a puzzled look on his face.

Andrea, who was now snickering, turned to Fitzgibbons and asked, "Would you like to finish the story, Fitz?"

With tears of laughter streaming down his face, Fitzgibbons responded, "I was just hoping there was another tunnel coming up so I could slap that bloody Serb again."

Moore joined everyone in laughing at the story. He sensed he was going to enjoy his companions in spite of the war raging around them.

An Inn
Southwest of Vukovar

Surrounded by a grove of pine trees, the inn seemed to be an oasis from the fighting in Vukovar, three kilometers away. It was here that many of the Serbian fighters would converge to boast of their kills or the destruction they rained upon the Croatian town.

The inn had a wood-beamed ceiling, wooden floor, and several wooden tables and chairs. At one end of the room, stood a wooden bar. Behind the bar were three shelves. They held a handful of bottles containing various types of alcohol.

Seated at a table and facing the doorway was a swarthy man with a stout build. His dark hair was topped with a black beret, set at an angle. He was wearing a stained khaki shirt, brown leather vest and black trousers. He had on black combat boots and a .45 hung from the holster on his belt.

The innkeeper cautiously approached him. "Is there anything more I can serve you, Colonel Marinkovic?" he asked nervously, hoping he wouldn't unleash the man's highly volatile temper. There had been stories about Marinkovic destroying inns when his anger was triggered.

"More slivovitz," Marinkovic growled.

"Right away. Right away." The innkeeper scurried away to secure another bottle of slivovitz. When he returned to Marinkovic's table, he asked, "Would you like me to pour it?"

Laughing, Marinkovic snatched the bottle from his hand and lifted the bottle to his mouth. Pulling the cork out of the bottle with his teeth, he laughed as he forcibly poured the liquid into the mouth of the terrified Croatian waitress he held on his lap. He had been fondling her for ten minutes.

He then took a long pull from the bottle. Continuing to laugh, he turned to the struggling female and started to kiss her. His advances were interrupted by two soldiers walking into the inn. They were dragging a third Serbian soldier between them.

"Colonel," one began as he addressed Marinkovic.

Marinkovic spun around as he pushed the woman off his lap. She quickly disappeared into the kitchen, looking for a safe refuge.

"What is it? You've interrupted me," he glared at the two, and then focused on the Serbian soldier, who was barely able to stand between the two. He had been severely beaten.

"What's going on here?" Marinkovic stormed.

"We caught Dimitrivich trying to hide a Croatian family when we searched their farm."

Cocking his head to the side, Marinkovic eyed Dimitrivich. "Hiding Croatians are we? Why would you do that?" Marinkovic stood and walked in front of the prisoner.

"Dimitrivich was one of their neighbors. We think he was trying to protect his friends," the one soldier offered.

With the speed of a rattlesnake strike, Marinkovic slapped the soldier who had spoken. "I didn't ask you. I'm talking to Dimitrivich," Marinkovic said angrily.

The soldier stepped back and looked at his prisoner.

"Are you going to answer me? Is it true you were trying to hide your friends?"

Marinkovic's questions were greeted by silence.

"You know I have ways to make you talk."

When the prisoner didn't respond, Marinkovic's anger grew. "Take him outside and stretch him from a tree limb."

The men walked out of the inn and to a tree across the street from the Croatian Catholic Church. There, the two soldiers hung the prisoner by his arms from a tree limb.

"Stake his legs," Marinkovic ordered.

The two soldiers produced two steel rods which they pounded into the ground. They then tied the prisoner's dangling legs to the stakes so he couldn't kick.

Marinkovic walked to his Jeep and withdrew a chain saw. Starting it, he gunned it several times as he approached the young soldier whose eyes were wide with terror.

"Do you want to tell me where they're hiding?" he challenged as he walked around the soldier, gunning the engine again as a number of soldiers gathered in a semi-circle to watch Marinkovic's brutal interrogation.

The prisoner looked from Marinkovic to the church and the nearby pigsty. He saw his Croatian friends escaping and running towards the woods. He knew he needed to keep the Serbs' attention on him.

"No. I have nothing to say to you," he said. Then, he spat on Marinkovic who had stopped in front of him.

Anger flared in Marinkovic as he wiped the spittle from his face. "Brave man. Let's see how brave you are."

He toyed with the soldier as he lifted the chain saw and slowly eased its deadly blades toward the dangling prisoner. Several times, Marinkovic brought the blade close to the prisoner's face without cutting him, playing a deadly game of cat and mouse.

Pulling the chain saw back from the prisoner, Marinkovic asked in a taunting tone, "This is your last chance. Do you want to talk?"

The prisoner's forlorn silence was the only answer Marinkovic received.

Gunning the chain saw, Marinkovic lightly touched the side of the soldier's face. He sliced his face several more times as the soldier screamed.

"Want to tell me now?" Marinkovic whispered to him as he watched blood ooze from the facial cuts.

The soldier's eyes had a defeated look. He knew his future would end within minutes. "I have nothing to say to you."

"So be it," Marinkovic pronounced as he suddenly twirled and extended the chain saw, amputating one of the soldier's legs from his body.

The prisoner's agonizing shriek completely drowned out the sound of the chain saw. The terror that now gripped the very depth of his being was prolonged as his entire body strained and it expelled its last vestiges of life.

His dying screams echoed throughout the forest, displacing birds from their roosts and causing the assembled soldiers to look away in horror.

Not stopping, Marinkovic moved quickly and severed the other leg. Then he stood back and watched as blood poured from the prisoner's torso into large puddles on the ground. The prisoner had fainted and wouldn't be aware of the final torture.

With a wild look in his eyes, Marinkovic moved in for his coup d'grâce. Starting from the bottom of the torso, he cut upwards, chain-sawing the soldier in half. When he was finished, he shut off the chain saw and set it on the ground.

"Cut him down and burn the body." As two soldiers began cutting down the body, Marinkovic turned to the gathered soldiers. "Let this be a lesson to any of you who want to protect Croatians." He left the assembled witnesses and walked back to the inn.

With the help of several of the onlookers, the body was doused with gasoline and set afire.

Pajo's Gas Station
Vukovar

"Emerson! Wake up!" Blago shook the sleeping Moore. "You've got to come to the edge of town."

Despite his fatigue from spending the previous night in the forest, sleep had not come easily that evening for Moore. Shaking his head as he raised to his elbows, Moore asked, "Why?" He could hear sporadic explosions and gunfire in the background.

"Soldiers in trucks are pulling people from their homes."

"Here?"

"No, at the edge of town. Hurry, we must go."

"Okay, I'll come."

Moore jumped up fully clothed and followed the boy outside. They hopped on his motorcycle and raced toward the edge of town as shells crashed into the streets and buildings, setting them ablaze. Parachute flares and machine-gun tracers ignited the sky. People with plaster dust in their hair and fear in their eyes ran through the streets in search of safe shelter.

As the two riders neared the edge of town, the boy cut the engine and they coasted toward a number of buildings where they hid the motorcycle. Cautiously, they crept through the darkness to one of the one-story stucco houses where they could hear voices.

Blago translated the conversation between the captain and the two old homeowners.

"You have ten minutes to grab your valuables and get in the truck outside," the captain ordered.

The old man, with disheveled hair and wearing a yellowed undershirt and torn pants, asked, "Why do we have to leave our home?"

"Orders," the captain responded curtly.

"Where are you taking us?" the old man asked nervously.

"You'll see."

"Will we be allowed to return?"

"No. Now get moving!"

"What?" the old woman asked. "You want me to leave this house and this stove? I cooked food on this stove for my eight children. I don't want to leave our home!"

The captain looked at the old woman and used the Serbian term for grandmother. "Baba, you now have seven minutes."

The old woman looked back at him in shock.

Her husband placed his arm around her and pushed her toward the bedroom. "We must do as he says, or we might end up dead in our home."

"Or dead wherever he takes us."

"We don't know that. Grab your things. Time is running short," he urged her.

Within five minutes, they had returned to the front of their small house. Each was carrying a suitcase, filled with their valuables.

"Good," the captain said. "Outside and into the truck."

This scene was repeated at the twenty-some homes in the area where two trucks were loaded with families and their worn suitcases filled with their valuables.

Once everyone had boarded the trucks, the small convoy drove out of town. Blago and Moore followed at a safe distance on the motorcycle. When they were two kilometers away the trucks stopped near two pickup trucks parked alongside the road. The families were ordered out of the vehicles.

Blago drove the motorcycle off the road and hid it in some bushes along the side of the road. Then, Moore and Blago crept closer to the scene where they could watch.

"Leave all of your luggage here," the captain commanded. "We will have it delivered to you when you arrive at your destination."

"But, why can't we just keep it with us?" one man asked.

A soldier stepped forward and aimed his weapon at the man. The man understood the message and placed his suitcase on the growing pile.

"Thank you," the captain said with an evil grin. "Back into the trucks. You'll have more room now."

Mumbling, the families climbed back into the trucks and the trucks continued their journey.

Before Moore and Blago returned to the motorcycle, Moore asked, "What's this all about?"

"They are stealing all of these poor peoples' valuables."

Nodding his head in understanding, Moore commented, "Pretty smart. They don't have to search the homes to find them. They let the homeowners pack them up for them."

"Right. But don't let appearances trick you."

"How's that?"

"Some are wise enough to have sewn valuables into a set of clothes. Women stuff their bras with small valuables. Some of the men are probably wearing money belts under their shirts."

"I see," Moore said.

Blago pushed the Honda through the woods and past the parked pickup trucks. When he felt they were far enough away, he pushed the motorcycle back near the road and started it. They moved quickly to catch up to the trucks loaded with families.

Ten minutes later, the trucks stopped by a large, moonlit field. The families were ordered off the trucks and to stand along one side of the road. Soldiers holding automatic weapons took up positions on the other side of the road and faced them.

Blago pulled the bike off the road again and hid it. The two raced to watch what the Serbs had planned.

"Strip," the captain ordered.

The crowd stood in shock. A murmur arose as the group prepared to resist. A man in his seventies stepped out of the crowd. He stared defiantly at the captain. "We will not!"

Without hesitating, the captain raised his weapon and fired two shots point-blank at the man's chest, dropping him to the ground.

"Next?" he asked as he swung his weapon around at the crowd.

The crowd, with many of them crying, began to strip while the captain watched.

Once the assembled Croatian families finished stripping, the captain asked, "You want your freedom from us Serbs?" Not waiting for a response, he continued, "Then I will give it to you."

The soldiers raised their weapons and pointed them at the families.

"On the other side of this field, your Croatian soldiers await you. Run to them!"

The families were stunned and distrustful as they looked at the weapons pointing at them. They anticipated being mowed down under a fusillade of bullets. Instead they were being given their freedom. Or so it appeared.

"I said to run!" the captain shouted as he produced a handgun and fired two shots into the air.

Panic and fear spread through the families as they had no choice but to do what he said. With many of them crying, they turned and ran naked across a small ditch and into the field. Some looked over their shoulders from time to time, expecting to see a hail of bullets directed at them.

Halfway across the field, three Croatian soldiers emerged from the forest. They were waving their arms for the families to stop.

From their hiding place near the trucks on the road, Blago said, "This is very cruel."

"I don't get it. What's going on?" Moore asked as he took pictures.

"The Croatian soldiers are stopping them. They are running through a minefield. The Serbs are using them to clear the minefield!"

An explosion filled the air as a fleeing man stepped on a hidden mine. From the roadside, the Serbian soldiers laughed. The Croatian soldiers yelled louder and the families stopped running.

The Croatian soldiers ran out and began to lead the families through the minefield as the Serbian soldiers loaded the discarded clothes into their trucks and headed back to meet their friends in the pickup trucks filled with valuables. They would split their night's pickings.

"You see what they make innocent people do? You see how they steal?" Blago asked with rising anger.

"Yes."

"This is what you need to write about. Tell how our people are being treated."

"I will, Blago. I will."

As the trucks disappeared around a bend in the road, Blago flicked on a small flashlight.

"Our evening may get more interesting."

"How's that?"

Shining the light on his fuel gauge, he answered, "Looks like we are near empty. I meant to fill up at Pajo's and forgot."

Moore looked around in the darkness. "I'm not sure this is an area where we would want to be in the daylight."

"It isn't," Blago agreed. "Feel like a little adventure?" he asked with a raised eyebrow.

"What are you thinking?"

"I need gas. The Serbs have gas in those trucks." He nodded his head in the direction the Serbian trucks had driven.

"You want to go after those trucks and siphon the gas? What are you? Nuts?"

Blago grinned with a sense of bravado. "We can do it."

"Not sure that's a wise thing to do."

"It's a lot wiser than being found out here by the Serbs, unless you're thinking about walking through the minefield to see if our Croatian friends have any gas for us."

Moore looked toward the minefield and back to Blago. "You're probably right."

"If a mine didn't get you, the Croatian soldiers might shoot you," Blago laughed.

Moore shook his head from side to side. "I'm not sure there's a good choice in this matter."

Blago tried to reassure him. "The trucks will be parked and all of them will be focused on splitting their loot." Blago patted a small saddle bag on his motorcycle. "I keep a hose and collapsible container in here for emergencies like this."

"I don't know," Moore said uncomfortably.

"Come on, Emerson. Live a little. Around here, we live for today because there may be no tomorrow. Go for it," he urged.

"I guess we really don't have a choice. Okay, I'm on board."

"Good. Let's go."

Moore climbed on the back of the motorcycle and they rode to catch up with the trucks.

Eight minutes later, Blago shut off the Honda and the two jumped off. They pushed the Honda into the nearby woods and emerged within minutes. They were carrying the siphon hose and the container.

Making their way carefully along the side of the road, they soon saw the two large trucks and the pickups parked next to each other. Loud voices and laughter could be heard from the other side of the trucks as the Serbian soldiers celebrated their good fortune in the glow of the headlights. They were drinking slivovitz as they ransacked their way through the treasure horde of valuables in front of them. Their attention was fully focused on their task at hand.

Seeing this, Moore relaxed. He knew that they would be too busy to be watching the trucks.

The two crept up to the fuel tank of the closest large truck. Blago twisted off the fuel cap and set it on top of the tank. He then inserted the hose in the tank. He placed the other end of the hose between his lips and sucked. Within seconds, he spat out a mouthful of fuel, and stuck the hose into the container which Moore was holding. The gas began filling the container.

Less than a minute had elapsed when Emerson heard a noise. It sounded like approaching footsteps. He looked underneath the truck and saw someone walking in their direction. Within seconds, the person would be on their side of the truck.

He hurriedly motioned to Blago, who quickly pulled the hose from the fuel tank. He rolled under the truck to join Moore, who had already ducked under as he clutched the quarter-filled container to his chest.

The soldier walked to the cab of the truck and opened the door. He reached in and withdrew a pack of cigarettes, then turned to face the side of the road. He pulled down his pants' zipper and began to urinate.

Moore was stunned when he saw a knife appear in Blago's hand. He tapped on Blago's shoulder and gave Blago a concerned look when Blago turned his head. Moore hadn't planned to be involved in killing anyone that night.

Blago slowly raised his finger to his lips, signaling Moore to be quiet.

When the soldier finished urinating and zipped up, he turned to walk away. Suddenly, he stopped as he noticed the gas cap on top of the fuel tank. He quickly pulled out his handgun and looked toward the woods as his eyes searched for any intruders. He stood quietly for three minutes, listening for any sound which didn't belong there.

Hearing nothing, he walked to the truck, replacing the cap onto the fuel tank. He then began to walk away, but suddenly stopped. With his service revolver extended in front of him, he dropped to his knees and peered under the truck. Seeing nothing, he stood and began walking back to his comrades.

From where he stood behind the front tires of the truck, Blago motioned to Moore, who was standing behind the rear tire of the truck. The two moved quickly under the truck just before the soldier walked by that side of the truck. It was fortuitous that they had taken positions on the other side of the truck.

They waited a few minutes to make sure no alarm was raised. Moore was grateful to have the waiting time. His heart was racing from the near encounter.

"We can go now," Blago said cautiously as he moved out from under the truck and stood. He quickly twisted off the gas cap and began siphoning gas again.

"That was too close," Moore said quietly.

"A little danger adds spice to your life."

"I think I'm allergic," Moore said weakly.

"To spice?" Blago asked.

"No, danger."

"This is nothing. You'll get used to it."

"But, I'm a noncombatant," Moore said.

"Bullets don't care who you are, Emerson," Blago said as he withdrew the hose from the now-filled container.

As Moore started to walk away, Blago said, "Not yet. I told you to live a little."

"What now?"

Blago slowly opened the cab door and reached in. When he turned around to face Moore, he was holding a soiled rag in his hand. "Now for some fun. Let me have the container."

Moore handed Blago the container and watched as Blago poured gasoline on one end of the rag. He then stuffed that end into the gas tank filler tube as Moore watched in disbelief. Reaching into his pocket, he produced a cigarette lighter and lit the end of the rag which protruded from the gas tank.

"We should go now!" he urged as he began running down the side of the road to where they had hidden the motorcycle. Moore was close on his heels.

When they reached the motorcycle, they quickly added the fuel. No sooner had they finished than a large explosion was heard as the truck's gas tank ignited and exploded, interrupting the Serbian soldiers' celebration.

The motorcycle roared to life as Blago and Moore made good their escape. Shortly thereafter, Moore found himself crawling back into his bedding. His last thought before falling asleep was thinking about what the next day would bring. He hoped his first twenty-four hours in Vukovar would not be indicative of his next twenty-four hours.

Pajo's Gas Station
The Next Morning

The next morning, Moore awoke to the sounds of incoming artillery rounds. He jumped to his feet and looked for a hiding place.

"Nowhere to hide from those shells, kid," Andrea said as he sipped his morning coffee. "When it's your time to go, it's your time," he said in a matter-of-fact tone.

Moore nodded. "I guess you're right." He looked around the room and saw Tatiana was pouring a cup of coffee at the stove. She looked a little better this morning. It appeared she had spent some time cleaning herself up. Her hair was washed and hung straight to her shoulders. Her eyes had a sparkle in them Moore hadn't noticed the prior day. She was also wearing makeup to help cover her black eye.

Moore turned his attention back to Andrea. "Where's Fitz?"

"He and Blago got wind of a story. So they ran off to cover it."

"I see," Moore said as he took the cup of coffee Tatiana had offered him. She gave him a warm smile as he took a sip, then walked back to the stove.

Andrea noticed the smile. "I think she's interested in you."

Moore looked towards Tatiana as he drank his coffee. He set the cup on the worn wooden table and looked at Andrea. "I don't think so. I'd guess she was just being appreciative since I gave her a Hershey bar."

"I could use a little appreciation, too. Got any extra candy bars?" Andrea teased as he winked good-naturedly at Moore.

"I do, but I sell them at a high premium."

"What? No friend's discount?" Andrea kidded. Then, he turned more serious. "By the way, Emerson, Blago told me about last night's adventure before he left this morning."

"It's despicable what they did to those poor people," Moore started.

"Yes, it is. The true victims of war are the poor civilians who, for the most part, want to live in peace. But I want you to know one thing and I've already lectured Blago this morning. And this isn't the first time I've lectured him on this!"

"What's that?" Moore asked.

"No one leaves here without telling us where he's going. If something happens, we need to know where to send the cavalry to the rescue."

"I didn't know."

"It's common sense. You youngsters will get it one day. Over here, you'd better get it pretty fast. Otherwise, the only getting you'll get is a bullet in your brain – and I'm not kidding," Andrea said seriously.

"It won't happen again."

"If we're not here, tell Pajo. He's always here." Andrea looked around the room and back to Moore. Standing he said, "Finish your coffee and you can come with me to the hospital. I'm writing a story on it."

Moore gulped down the coffee and took a large chunk of fresh bread that Tatiana brought to him. "Thank you," he said quickly as he stood and ran to follow Andrea.

Andrea was standing next to the back door of the building. "Listen closely if you want to have a chance to live."

Moore was all ears.

"We're going to cut behind these buildings. Keep that young head of yours low and run from cover to cover. Otherwise some Serbian sniper is going to blow off that full head of hair you have." Andrea peered around the corner of the building. "And we have a sniper out there today."

"How far is it to the hospital?"

"I'd say about a mile. It's not as bad when we get closer to the hospital as far as snipers go. Then, all we have to worry about are the incoming artillery rounds. In either case, if one hits you, you won't know the difference. You're gone."

Moore didn't realize how worried his face looked, but Andrea did.

"Come on, kid. You'll do just fine. You're younger than me and should be able to outrun me as we hustle through the real dangerous part."

"That's real comforting," Moore retorted sarcastically. "Not sure my age difference will help me outrun a bullet."

"Let's go," Andrea launched himself through the doorway with Moore close on his heels. They ran bent-over to the ruins of a house next door and walked to the far corner. Andrea cautiously peered around the corner and then ducked back behind the safety of the building.

"See a sniper?" Moore asked.

Andrea's head whipped around and he stormed, "You don't see snipers! They see you! The other thing you've got to worry about are the Serbian soldiers making forays into town. The last thing you want to do is to run into a bunch of them. Remember, they are not particularly fond of the press corps."

Moore nodded his head.

"Let's go," Andrea said as they ran towards the next building, which was nothing more than a shell. It had been hit by several rockets a few days earlier.

As he ran, Moore tripped and fell to the ground. He heard something whiz over his head and began to crawl to where Andrea was waiting in safety.

"Get up and run," Andrea yelled. "You're in the open. Easy pickings for any sniper!"

Moore jumped to his feet and ran to the next building. As he reached its relative safety, a bullet ricocheted off the brick above his head.

"That's what I'm telling you, kid. You don't want to make it easy on them by crawling across open ground." Andrea was more frustrated than angry with his young charge.

"I'm a quick learner," Moore offered with a weak grin.

"I hope so." Then, Andrea added, "For your own sake." Andrea looked down the stretch of small backyards. "It should be easier from here. The buildings are closer together and we'll be exposed for only a few seconds as we run between the buildings. The snipers haven't worked this far into town yet. But you just never know."

The two started their dangerous run again and twenty-five minutes later approached the remains of what had been Vukovar's hospital. It had been targeted by Serbian artillery and was heavily damaged.

"I can't believe anyone would target and destroy a hospital like this," Moore said, stunned by the damage he saw.

"This is nothing, kid. The atrocities of war are mind boggling." Andrea found the entrance to the basement. "Follow me."

They descended the stairs, leading to the basement. Moore wasn't prepared for what he saw in the basement. It was lit by a combination of candles, lanterns and flashlights.

Moore saw bloodied and wounded patients of all ages and both sexes lining the floor. The room was filled with moans of agony. As he followed Andrea, Moore saw that some of the patients had open, gaping wounds and others had lost limbs; most were swathed with bandages caked in dried blood.

Walking carefully through the maze of damaged bodies, Moore felt a sense of loss for the wounded and dying. The seriousness of the situation touched Moore's soul.

The two men walked to the rear of the basement where an underground, makeshift surgical theater worked to full capacity, but it couldn't keep up with the ever increasing stream of incoming casualties.

One of the doctors saw Andrea and stepped away from the operating table. She stuck her hands into a bucket of cold water to wash the blood off.

"Shouldn't she be washing in hot water?" Moore asked, dumbfounded.

"Where's she going to find it? These doctors are doing what they can with basically nothing to try to save lives. There's no electricity. No gas. Water has to be carried in by volunteers." It was obvious Andrea was very disturbed about the hospital's needs.

"Did you bring us any supplies?" the doctor asked as she approached the two.

"No, but we may be able to help obtain them. We're writing a story to show the world the poor conditions here." Andrea introduced himself and Moore. The doctor's name was Irina Gabric.

"We need your help. Tell your readers we have virtually no medical supplies. We have to operate without anesthesia."

A scream rose from the operating table. When Moore and Andrea turned their heads in that direction, they saw an amputated leg being thrown into an old plastic laundry basket.

"It's not a pretty sight, is it?" Gabric asked. Her dark brown hair had streaks of gray and was pulled back. Her face seemed weary. She took off her long medical coat. It had once been an immaculate white. Now it was soiled and stained with blood.

"No, I can't imagine what you and your doctors go through," Moore offered as he looked back at her.

"Don't try because you're right. You cannot imagine. Not only can't you imagine the futility we face with our patients' situations, you can't imagine the depth of their pain."

Moore was silent.

She continued. "Medical supplies are running so short we remove the bandages from the dead and wash them in cold water. Then, we reuse them on the living. The disposable items which were intended for single use, we clean and reuse over and over again."

"I am sorry," Andrea said as he looked up from his note taking.

"Sorry. Don't be sorry for me. Be sorry for our patients. They are the ones who are paying the cost of the war – with their lives."

"Are the Red Cross trucks able to make deliveries?" Andrea asked.

"No. They are stopped before they enter Vukovar. The supplies are hijacked by the Serbs and taken to sell on the black market in Belgrade."

Andrea and Moore spent an hour with her as she showed them around the eerie basement facility and gave them additional insight into the hospital's needs.

Promising to do all they could publicizing the gravity of the dire situation, the two men began to leave the basement. They had to pause twice on the stairs to allow people carrying the wounded to bypass them on the stairway.

The two reporters carefully made their way back to their home base at the gas station. When they stopped before making their dangerous run in front of the sniper by the gas station, Andrea groaned.

"What's wrong?" Moore asked.

"Look in front of Pajo's place."

Moore looked and saw two Jeeps parked in front. "Trouble?"

"See the Jeep with the two flags on the front fenders?"

"Yes."

"That belongs to the Vuk. He's probably looking for Tatiana. We better go and help."

They made it safely across the open space and ducked into the rear of Pajo's. Cautiously, they walked to the front where they could hear someone moaning. As they walked through the doorway, they saw Pajo being held by two soldiers as another one worked him over. Marinkovic the Vuk was sitting in a chair, laughing as he watched the old man being punched.

"Is there something I can help you with?" Andrea asked as he entered the room. He was closely followed by Moore.

Surprised by his entrance, the two soldiers dropped Pajo and produced weapons that they aimed at Andrea and Moore.

The Vuk stood from his chair and casually eyed the intruder. "Andrea, isn't it?"

"That's right."

The Vuk looked behind Andrea at Moore. "Who's the fresh meat?"

Moore responded. "I'm Emerson Moore. I'm with the *Washington Record* and I'm working on a story to expose your atrocities to the world." Suddenly Moore found himself sitting on the floor as Andrea shoved him.

"Not a smart thing to say, Emerson."

Moore slowly returned to his feet as the Vuk laughed. "He's so fresh; he just came out of the slaughterhouse."

"Yeah, and you're the one who puts people into it." Moore unexpectedly found himself sitting on the floor again.

Andrea tried to shrug it off. "New kid. They just don't learn quickly, do they?" he asked as he tried to defuse the situation.

"You be sure to teach him well. And I don't think you have long to do that," the Vuk said with a depraved look on his face.

"What can we do for you?"

"Where's the girl?"

"Girl? What girl?" Andrea feigned ignorance. They had all agreed earlier to deny she lived with them.

"Tatiana. The beauty of Vukovar." The Vuk appeared to be salivating as he mentioned her name.

"I've heard of her beauty, but haven't had the pleasure of meeting her."

"You know her home was accidently destroyed by our shelling."

"Accidently. Of course, all of your shelling accidently destroys homes and hospitals," Andrea retorted.

Moore had walked over to Pajo and helped him into a chair. The two were watching the exchange between the Vuk and Andrea.

Marinkovic the Vuk produced a .45 caliber pistol in his hand and approached Andrea. His eyes narrowed as he placed the business end under Andrea's chin. "Be very careful in trying to taunt me. I cannot and I will not tolerate it."

Andrea didn't flinch. He stared boldly into Marinkovic's eyes.

Suddenly from the rear doorway, a voice cried out. "Bollocks! If it isn't the Vuk! Doesn't that rhyme with puke?"

Everyone in the room spun their heads toward the rear. Standing in the doorway was Fitzgibbons.

Andrea shook his head slowly from side to side as a warning to Fitzgibbons to be cautious. The Brit ignored him.

"Piss off, why don't you!" Fitzgibbons said as he walked into the room. His approach was a mistake.

Marinkovic the Vuk ordered his men to grab Fitzgibbons and they rushed to obey his command. They restrained Fitzgibbons' two arms as Fitzgibbons stared defiantly at Marinkovic.

"You're quite the big shot, aren't you? You're nothing without the help of your henchmen here."

"You think so?" Marinkovic asked. He looked at his two men and motioned for them to release Fitzgibbons. He then turned his back to Fitzgibbons.

"Well, now. That's more like it," Fitzgibbons grinned.

Suddenly, the Vuk spun around, took three steps to close the distance between the two men, and struck Fitzgibbons with a right hook to the jaw. When his back was turned to Fitzgibbons, the Vuk had slipped on a set of brass knuckles. As Fitzgibbons reeled from the blow, the Vuk closed in with a flurry of blows to Fitzgibbons' head and stomach.

Fitzgibbons dropped to the ground as the Vuk stood over him. He slipped off the brass knuckles and returned them to his pocket. "Anything more you want to say?"

From the floor, Fitzgibbons moaned.

"Take him out and shoot him," Marinkovic ordered two of his men as his fury began to quiet and his blood pressure began to lower.

Andrea intervened. "Can't we be reasonable here? Fitz just gets a bit feisty. He didn't mean anything by what he said. You know how those Brits can be at times." Andrea knew Marinkovic had spent time in London and the United States.

Marinkovic looked at Andrea and then his men. "Take both of them out and shoot them," he ordered.

Two more of his men quickly secured Andrea in their arms as the first two jerked Fitzgibbons to his feet.

Moore, who had been silently observing the confrontation, spoke. "Wait a minute!"

The Vuk spun around to face the youngster. "You want to join them? Sure, we can arrange that," he smiled evilly as he looked at Moore.

"No, no. I don't. And I don't think you want to kill either one of them," Moore began.

"You're right. I don't think I want to kill them. I know I want to kill them!" the Vuk laughed at his own joke. His men laughed with him.

Inadvertently, Moore's intervention triggered the right response from the Vuk and the ensuing laughter helped ease some of the tension in the room.

"Listen. I've really been sent here to make sure our reporting is fair. That we accurately report both sides of what has been happening in Vukovar."

The Vuk raised his eyebrows in disbelief. "They sent a youngster to do this when these experienced reporters can't get the news correct?"

"Yes."

"I don't believe you. How many wars have you covered?"

"This is my first," Moore replied, somewhat embarrassed.

"And just like that," the Vuk slapped his hands together, "you're going to change the way war reporting is handled!" The Vuk started laughing and was quickly joined again by his men.

"My father owns the *Washington Record*," Moore bluffed. "That's why I can make sure reporting is fair and accurate."

The Vuk stopped laughing and turned to his men. "I give this idiot credit for speaking up. Let them go."

The soldiers released their grips on Andrea and Fitzgibbons. Fitzgibbons dropped back to the floor.

"But I am warning you all. Next time, I may not be so forgiving. Next time, I may return and have you all tied and surrounded by cans of gasoline. Then, I'll light you all up and watch you burn alive. And if I find out you know where Tatiana is and didn't tell me, I will disembowel you before I torch you." The Vuk turned to his men. "We go."

They all left the gas station as Moore and Andrea checked on Pajo and Fitzgibbons.

"That was bloody stupid of you, kid, to speak up like that. You didn't need to get involved, but thank you," Fitzgibbons said as he was helped to a chair.

"Are you okay?" Moore asked as he heard the Vuk's vehicles leave.

Fitzgibbons rubbed his jaw. "I may have a hairline crack, but I'll recover from the beating. The Vuk and his bloody wolf pack are nothing more than a highly trained band of recreational killers."

Andrea was helping Pajo to a chair. "Thanks, kid. Fitz is right. You shouldn't get involved. We're old codgers so to speak. The sand is running out of our clocks. You still have plenty of time to live."

"I couldn't stand there helplessly and not do something. It was worth the risk," Moore offered.

Andrea looked at Moore. "I didn't know your father owns the *Washington Record.*"

Moore grinned. "He doesn't. But I thought it might sound plausible to Marinkovic."

"Plausible but risky," Andrea said as he and Fitzgibbons chuckled at Moore's audacity. "You just might fit in."

Moore grinned at their acceptance. He was going to enjoy working with and learning from the two veteran reporters. "Where's Tatiana?"

"In the kitchen. There's a small trap door in the floor with a hiding space below it. You can't tell it's there," Pajo spoke as Moore helped him to his feet. "I should go and let Tatiana out of her crawl space. It's a very small hiding place," he said as he walked to the living quarters.

"There's nothing more that would tickle the Vuk's fancy than having Tatiana in his harem," Fitzgibbons commented.

"He'd keep her awhile, then either send her to one of the rape camps or sell her into the sex slave market," Andrea suggested.

"It sounds like they're in the business of hunting down women," Moore said.

"It's a sideline business to the war," Andrea said.

"The Serbs use the rape camps to destroy the Croatian culture," Fitzgibbons added. "It's the most humiliating form of genocide. The women are stigmatized and are reluctant to return to their families."

"You'll see many of the women suffering from post-traumatic stress disorder, some become depressed and attempt suicide," Andrea said. "Rape camps have been used for years. The Japanese had them back in World War II for their troops."

"The women are subject to physical maltreatment and abuse. Most of the stories are too shocking, too clinical and too painfully graphic to publish," Fitzgibbons said as he slowly stood from his chair and began to stretch.

Andrea watched Fitzgibbons and spoke. "There's one instance where a woman was gang raped by four Serbian soldiers. Then, she asked for her crying baby so she could breastfeed him. The soldiers laughed and brought her the baby. Only, it was the infant's severed head. When she cried hysterically, they executed her."

Moore shook his head in shocked disbelief. "The atrocities of war. Why? Why?" he asked sadly.

"Rape and pillaging. It's been around for centuries. I'm not making excuses for it and I'm not sure how you prevent it during a war," Fitzgibbons said.

"Afterwards, you have the war crimes tribunals. But even then, they don't atone for the damage to people who have been ravaged," Andrea said.

"I don't think anything can," Moore commented.

Andrea continued, "The archbishop in Zagreb issued a pronouncement stating that raped women have not lost their dignity. They are worthy of our deepest admiration and must be treated with respect by the family, society and the Church."

"That's something the whole world should heed," Moore offered.

A noise from the doorway in the back of the building caused them to turn. When they did, they saw Tatiana. She brought the three men cups of coffee, which they savored as they drank.

"Where's Blago?" Moore asked when he realized, in all of the confusion, he hadn't seen him.

"He'll be along shortly, I'm sure," Fitzgibbons said. "The Vuk would love to get his hands on Blago."

"Yeah, and Blago knows he wouldn't get a reprieve from Marinkovic," Andrea added. Turning to Fitzgibbons, Andrea asked, "So, what did you two turn up?"

"False lead. There was a report by the Serbian media that Croatian forces had slaughtered a number of innocent Serbian civilians ten kilometers from here. They said the bodies of a hundred Serb men, woman and children had been mutilated. We rode out to the site to investigate further. It turns out it was a fabrication. The media were duped on that one," Fitzgibbons said.

Andrea turned to Moore. "There's a lesson here for you. Be sure to check your facts."

"Especially if you get it from the Serbs," Blago said as he entered the room.

"Our job is to report the news as accurately as possible. You've got to be careful of both sides pulling a hoax on you," Andrea cautioned. "We're culpable for failing to investigate the story's source."

Blago appeared in the doorway and walked into the room. Andrea gave Blago an overview of what had transpired with the Vuk. Then, Andrea and Fitzgibbons, between shots of slivovitz, took turns on the laptop writing and printing their daily report from the frontlines. When they finished, Moore wrote his story on what he had witnessed the prior evening.

The printed reports were then sealed in a large envelope and given to Blago so he could deliver it to another courier near Osijek, who would deliver it to Zagreb. There, it would be faxed to their respective editors for the next day's newspaper.

When Andrea finished, he walked over to Moore who was standing near the open door to the garage bay. "Be careful you don't get in some Serb sniper's scope," Andrea cautioned.

"I will," he replied as he watched a baba working in her yard across the street as bullets whistled overhead and artillery shells landed randomly in the area. "That looks dangerous."

"Right on. She's stubborn, that one is. When we sent Blago over to talk to her, she said no one was going to keep her from tending to her flowers and vegetables."

"How did you know this morning there was a sniper set up across the street?" Moore asked.

Andrea pointed to the baba. "She told me."

"What? I was with you. How could she tell you?" Moore asked.

"See her house?"

"Yes."

"Do you see anything in the first floor windows?"

Moore looked. "Yes, the window on the left has a lamp in it."

"That means the sniper is in her attic."

Moore looked up and saw a small window on the second floor. It was open.

"If the lamp is in the window on the right, then there's no sniper."

"Brilliant!" Moore said. "So, that's how you knew we had a sniper there this morning!"

"Yeah. She thought it up. Her son was one of Vukovar's defenders and was killed. This is one way she can help us."

Moore nodded.

Near the Outskirts of Vukovar
The Next Afternoon

After concealing his Honda nearby, Blago led Moore between the remains of a number of homes. He stopped when they approached an open area which had once been a beautiful, treed park. Most of the trees had been destroyed by incoming artillery rounds. The grounds, which the locals had once groomed and maintained, were filled with craters from incoming shells. At night, the Croatians would bury their dead in the park.

Blago pointed to a grave. "That was one of my cousins. He was a Croatian soldier. His bride-to-be buried him here in the park. This is where they walked and spent time together. He proposed to her here."

"I am sorry, Blago," Moore said.

"The story gets worse."

"Oh?"

Pointing to the grave next to his cousin's grave, Blago explained, "She buried him during the early evening hours. After she buried him, a Serbian sniper shot and killed her. We found her body lying across the grave and buried her next to him."

Moore was stunned.

"Come with me," Blago said as he led Moore to a small hill.

As they crested the hill, they saw below a steady stream of trucks and cars with Belgrade registrations. Filled with booty from looting Croatian homes, they were returning to Belgrade to sell their stolen goods in the thriving black market.

Slowly, the two made their way down the other side of the hill to a small farm. They walked through the house which had been ransacked and out a back door. Seeing a small shed, they walked to it and entered. There, they found the bodies of a middle-aged man and woman, likely a married couple.

"This is what Marinkovic does to people." He pointed to the wife's head. There were four, almost identical lesions on the scalp – all were straight with extremely sharp borders. The apex of the wounds penetrated the skull bones and extended deeply into the brain tissue; all the underlying bones were fractured.

"This is tragic," Blago said.

Not hearing a response, Blago looked behind him and saw Moore vomiting in the corner.

"It's not pretty. None of this stuff is. It's the horrors of war, my friend."

Moore stood straight up. He could taste the last remains of vomit in his mouth. "I expected it to be bad, but not like this."

Moore looked away from the carnage. As he did, he spotted an axe on the dirt floor. He walked over to it and saw the dried blood. "Looks like we found the murder weapon."

Blago joined him. "Serbian pigs!"

They approached the husband's body, which had been stripped

of all clothing. The victim was bound with double-knotted loops of linen cloth on the left wrist and ankle. There was also a linen cloth noose wrapped twice around his neck. It was cinched with a single knot and used to garrote the victim after he was forced to watch his wife's torture.

Moore bent over and could make out two small stab wounds at the height of the left nipple, close to the sternum. The first stab wound penetrated the lung, resulting in massive internal bleeding. The other stab wound pierced the heart.

The sound of vehicles stopping redirected their attention to the shed's doorway.

"It's Marinkovic!" Blago said softly as he looked around the shed for another exit. Soldiers poured out of the two trucks and ran through the house. "We've got to get out of here!"

Moore opened a window at the rear of the shed. "Here we go," he said as he jumped out and waited as Blago quickly followed.

Keeping the shed between them and the soldiers, they ran to the woods and concealed themselves in the underbrush so they could observe Marinkovic.

Two Croatian police officers were dragged out of the truck and behind the house. They were pummeled as Marinkovic interrogated them. When Marinkovic didn't get a response from the officer, he pulled his .45 from his holster.

Moore watched as Marinkovic approached the first officer and fired his weapon. He repeated the action with the second officer. Marinkovic pointed to the pigpen, next to the shed where Moore and Blago had been. Moore heard Marinkovic yell something in Serbian and then saw several of the soldiers dragging the two bodies to the pigpen where they dumped them.

Blago interpreted. "Marinkovic told them to feed them to the pigs. Pigs eat anything."

From the woods the two watched the men return to their vehicles and drive away. They waited a few minutes. Then, they cautiously left the safety of the woods and walked to the pigpen to examine the bodies.

The officers had been executed with one bullet below their right eye. The bullet's pathway had turned the brain to mush and exited in the back of the head, leaving a gaping cavern with clots of blood, bone and brain tissue.

"Help me, Emerson," Blago said as he began to lift one of the bodies. "We'll not let them be food for the pigs."

The two worked together and pulled the two bodies out of the pigpen and found a worn tarp to cover them.

They jumped back into the shed when a truck full of soldiers drove slowly by the house.

"We won't be going back tonight. It's too dangerous out here. They have too many patrols out," Blago said as Moore nodded his head in agreement.

"Where to?" he asked as the twilight hour began.

"We'll find an abandoned house," Blago replied as he began to run in a crouch. "Follow me."

Within five minutes, they had located a house nearby with the front half destroyed. They crept into the back and checked it to be sure it would be safe.

"Let's sleep here," Blago said.

"I can't see anything," Emerson said as he pulled a pack of matches from his pocket and extracted a match. Before he could light the match, Blago knocked the match from Emerson's hand. "You want to get us killed?"

"Snipers around?"

"No! Worse!" Blago stood and walked to the kitchen stove. He examined it in the darkness and then called softly to Moore. "Come here."

Moore joined him. "What is it?"

"Hear the hissing?"

Moore lowered his head to the gas stove. "No." After a moment, he said, "Yes, I do."

"Gas. The Serbs will turn on a gas stove and leave it on. They know that anyone returning to a house at night would light a match. Big explosion. No more house. No more Emerson."

"But I didn't smell gas," Moore said with a bewildered look. "We'd smell gas in the U.S."

"Not here. We don't put an odor in our gas like you do. Too expensive," Blago explained. "Come on. We'll check the house next door."

"It looked in worse shape than this one. Half the front was destroyed," Moore said.

"It's easier for the gas to escape," Blago grinned. "Let's go."

The two left and entered the remains of the house next door. They found some bedding in one of the back rooms and put it on the floor behind some overturned furniture.

"Just like a Hilton," Blago said as he lay down on it.

Moore shook his head from side to side. "Your perception of a Hilton and mine are quite different," he commented as he dropped on the bedding.

The two lay there, listening to incoming rockets in the distance.

Moore turned to Blago. "Blago, do you still have any family here?"

His question was greeted by silence.

"Do you still have any family in Vukovar?" he asked again.

"No," he responded quietly.

"Where are they now?"

"Gone."

"Gone? Where did they go?"

"I thought I told you they were killed by Marinkovic and his wolf pack."

"That's right. You did. I am so sorry." Moore felt bad he had forgotten Blago telling him earlier.

"They are all better off now. They killed my brother, too."

Moore saw a blank look in Blago's eyes as the boy stared at the wall in the darkening room. "I arrived as Marinkovic was pulling away with his team of murderers. They didn't see me. I ran into the house to find my family. I was worried because Marinkovic had been after my father to make a choice."

"A choice?"

"Yes. My father's parents were Serbian and Croatian. Marinkovic wanted my father to choose the Serbian side and join the fight against his neighbors. Marinkovic stopped by our home several times trying to persuade him. My father couldn't turn against his friends and told him so. This time was the last time.

"I didn't find my family in the house. So, I ran toward the shed. That's where I found them, or what was left of them. My father, mother and fourteen-year-old brother had been bound together with chains and burned alive."

Moore's eyes widened in horror. "Blago, I am really sorry. I can't imagine the trauma you went through."

Blago continued to speak in a monotone, almost as if he were in a trance. "Their bodies were still smoking. My nostrils were filled with the smell of burnt flesh as I dug a large grave next to their bodies and pushed them into it. After filling the grave, I sat on the ground and wept." He turned to look at Moore. "I think I sat there through most of the night. That's when I made my decision to join the Croatians.

"The Vuk keeps an eye out for me. He wants to kill me, too. But, I'm waiting for my opportunity. I'll kill him first," Blago said with determination. "I'm not good with firearms, but I have these." He reached into his pocket and produced two hand grenades which he showed Moore before returning them to his pocket. "These aren't the smoke grenades you carry. They're the real thing! I just need to get close to him."

Moore nodded his head as the two listened to the surrounding sounds and eventually fell asleep.

The Next Morning
Pajo's Gas Station

After retrieving Blago's motorcycle, the two returned to Pajo's gas station. They parked the Honda in a small shed behind the station and entered the rear living quarters where they were greeted by a sobbing Tatiana. She was seated on the floor next to the stove with her head buried in her arms.

Moore knelt next to her and began to put his arm on her shoulder. She immediately pulled away.

With a look of concern, Moore asked, "What's wrong, Tatiana?"

She continued to sob.

From the doorway, Andrea spoke, "I doubt she's going to say anything."

Before Moore could ask a question, Blago asked. "Why is she crying?"

"Pajo."

"Pajo?" Blago asked.

"Sniper got him when he went outside." Andrea looked down at the floor. "He's dead."

Moore stood to his feet and faced Andrea. "Didn't he check the lamp in the window?"

"I'm sure he did. I checked it and it didn't indicate we had a sniper," Andrea said.

"Have you seen the baba this morning?" Moore asked.

"That's a bit strange. We haven't seen her. She's a creature of habit and she's always outside," Andrea responded.

"We should go see if she's okay." Moore impetuously started for the door.

Blago grabbed his arm. "Just like that? You're going to walk over there and see if the baba is okay?"

"Blago's right," Andrea said. "Blago's younger than you, but he's got more street smarts than you do, Emerson."

Moore relaxed. "I wasn't thinking."

"Like I told you when you first arrived. Not thinking gets folks killed around here. You're in a war zone, not going for a cup of coffee in Georgetown."

Moore nodded his head.

"We'll go tonight," Blago said.

"You two can help me bury Pajo out back," Andrea said.

The three men entered the front of the gas station where Pajo's body was lying. Fitzgibbons was seated nearby; a half empty bottle of slivovitz was in his hand. "This is bloody awful. Poor bugger never had a chance."

"Fitz dragged his body in here. Lucky he didn't catch a bullet himself," Andrea said.

"This whole scene in Vukovar is futile," Fitzgibbons said as he took another swig from the bottle. "People like Pajo don't deserve to die."

"They don't," Andrea agreed as he pointed to a nearby wheelbarrow. "You can use that, Blago."

Blago walked over to the wheelbarrow and brought it next to the body. He then motioned to Moore to help him lift the body into the barrow. Next, they pushed the barrow through an open door in the rear of the station and into the small courtyard.

Spying a couple of shovels, Blago grabbed them and tossed one to Moore. Neither of them spoke as they began to dig the grave. When they finished digging, they were joined by Andrea, Fitzgibbons and a sobbing Tatiana.

Moore and Blago carefully lifted Pajo's body from the barrow and lowered it into the freshly dug grave. It was then that Tatiana approached the grave. She knelt on the ground and covered Pajo's body with a large bath towel. She stood and stepped back to stand with Andrea and Fitzgibbons.

"Somebody should say some words, now," Fitzgibbons slurred. Before anyone could speak, he continued, "Pajo, you were a good bloke. That you were, all right."

"Thanks, Fitz," Andrea said somberly before looking toward the heavens. "God, he was an honorable man and we commit his soul to you." Andrea looked around the group. "Anybody else want to speak?"

No one spoke as the seriousness of the moment overwhelmed them.

"Okay, then. Fill in the grave."

Blago and Moore began shoveling the recently excavated soil into the grave as the others returned to the building.

Later that night, Blago eased over to Moore. "Ready to go check on our baba? She hasn't been out at all today."

"Let's go," Moore said.

"Take one of these." Blago handed Moore a flashlight. The lens had been covered with black electrical tape in such a manner as to allow a small stream of light to show when flicked on.

"Thanks," Moore said as he followed Blago out the door.

The two zigzagged their way across the street to the baba's house. In contrast to other nights when they could see a small light turned on in the house, there were no lights on this night.

They raced to the front door and tried to open it. It was locked. They went to the side of the house where they found a window. It was unlocked. Blago raised the window carefully and slowly stuck his head through its opening. He listened quietly for a couple of minutes and then boosted himself through the window. Moore closely followed him.

They had barely taken three steps when they heard the crunching of broken dishes under their feet. They were in an eating area. Blago placed his hand on Moore's arm to stop his forward progress. He then turned on his flashlight to survey the room and just as quickly turned it off. The light had revealed broken dishes and overturned tables and chairs. It looked like a fight had taken place in the room.

Cautiously, the two moved to the front room. This time Moore bumped into something on the floor. It was his turn to stop Blago.

"There's something at my feet," he whispered.

"Check it out," Blago responded in a hushed tone.

Moore flicked on his light and aimed it at the floor. It was the signal lamp. It had been broken. Moore flicked off his light and stepped sideways. When he did, he bumped into something hanging from the ceiling. He flicked his light back on. Then he shuddered at what he saw.

The baba was hanging from the ceiling light. The lamp's cord had been wrapped tightly around her neck. She was dead.

"We need to cut her down," he whispered to Blago.

Before Blago could respond they heard a noise overhead. It came from the second floor where the sniper would lie in wait for his prey. The noise repeated followed by someone swearing in Serbian.

"What was that?" Moore asked as he quickly shut off his flashlight.

"I'd say that someone upstairs just farted," Blago grinned. "Stinking Serb!"

"Our sniper?"

"That would be a good guess," he said as he sniffed the air. "He's upwind." Turning serious, he said, "We'll take care of him."

"How's that?"

"Patience. You'll see."

The two disappeared into the rear of the home where they cautiously flicked on their flashlights and rummaged through several drawers until they found some string. Then, Moore followed Blago to the base of the narrow steps to the second floor.

Blago crouched down and extracted one of the hand grenades from his pocket. He tied the grenade to one end of the railing. Then, he carefully pulled the pin partially from its position and tied one end of a second piece of string to it.

Turning to Moore, he quietly instructed, "Hold this taut. But not too taut as we don't want the pin to come completely out. If it does, we go up. Understand?"

"Yes," Moore said as he very carefully held the string while Blago tied the other end to the other railing.

Returning to the piece Moore was holding, he took it from Moore. He made a couple of adjustments and stepped back. Looking around he clicked on his flashlight, examined his work and flicked off the flashlight.

"See how that works?"

"Yep. When the sniper walks down the stairs and into the string, the pin pulls out completely," Moore responded.

"Exactly. We are safely away from here and we just paid him back for what he did to the baba and Pajo."

"Speaking about the baba, what are we going to do about her body?"

"Nothing yet. Once our sniper is dead, we can come back and cut her down. Then, we'll bury her."

"She was a brave woman," Moore said as he followed Blago to the window through which they had entered the house.

"Yes, she was. I'm sure she saved a lot of lives with her signaling," Blago said.

The two zigzagged back to the gas station and entered it through the rear door. An hour later, they were rewarded with an explosion in the baba's home.

"Got him!" Blago said triumphantly.

"Nice work, Blago!" Moore congratulated his new friend.

The two watched for an hour to see if any Serbian reinforcements appeared. When none did, they raced across the street and reentered the house. They saw the dead sniper sprawled on what remained of the staircase.

They walked into the front room where they quickly cut down the baba and carried her body out the back door. They dug her grave next to a flower garden behind the house and buried her. Then, they raced back to the relative safety of the gas station.

When they entered the living quarters, Moore bumped into Tatiana. "Are you okay?" he asked as Blago retrieved his sleeping gear and lay on it near a snoring Andrea and Fitzgibbons.

"I can't sleep," she replied.

In the darkness, Moore could still see a forlorn look on her face. "It's Pajo's death, isn't it?"

"Yes," she replied as Moore placed his arm around her to comfort her. She turned her face into his chest and cried softly. Moore felt compassion for the teen for whom he had a growing fondness. She was like a little sister to him.

"Sit over here with me," Moore said as he guided her to his sleeping gear and the two sat down. Moore's back was to the wall as he continued to hold her and gently stroked her hair. After twenty minutes, he heard her crying stop and her breathing signaled she had fallen asleep. Within a few minutes, Moore fell asleep as he held her.

The Next Morning
Southwest Side of Vukovar

Having hidden Blago's motorcycle, Blago and Moore carefully made their way through several of the destroyed homes. Blago would call softly as they looked for survivors.

"Many times, you'll find survivors hiding in their homes. They live in the basements with only candles providing light," Blago said.

"Why don't they leave their homes?" Moore asked.

"A couple of reasons. One, it's their home. Some of them will defend their homes with their hunting rifles. Secondly, where do they go? You've seen Vukovar. No place is safe."

"Especially where you are!" a voice said in a menacing tone.

The two spun around and saw one of the Vuk's wolf pack men in front of them. He held an AK-47 in his hands and it was pointed in their direction.

"Step outside," he ordered.

Blago and Moore walked through the debris-filled room into the yard where another one of the Vuk's wolf pack waited for them. He also pointed a gun at them.

"What were you doing? Looking for things to steal so you could blame it on us?" the first one asked.

"No," Blago replied. "We're looking for survivors to help."

"We're looking for survivors, too. Especially of the female type," the first one cackled as he shot a quick glance at his comrade.

"Very pretty ones," the second one added before taking a drink from his half-full bottle of slivovitz.

Moore had noticed alcohol on the breath of the first one and knew they were not in a good situation.

"I thought you'd taken them all. That's what I heard," Blago said trying to defuse the situation.

"The Vuk has taken all the pretty ones. We get the leftovers," the first one said.

"And there is nothing wrong with leftovers unless they're spoiled," the second one chortled at his quip.

"And when we're finished with them, we kill them," the first one said.

"After we torture them a little," the second one added. "We are experts at torture," he said as he leaned toward Moore.

Moore looked from the two soldiers and to Blago. He was becoming more and more uncomfortable.

Blago spoke in a low voice to Moore, "We're dead."

"What do you mean?" Moore asked.

"Think about it. Do you really think they'd brag about their murders and then let us live?"

"Oh," Moore said somberly. He realized Blago was right.

"What are you two whispering about?" the first one asked as he moved closer to Blago. He was now holding a knife in his hand.

"About that Croatian with the rifle pointed at you!" Blago pointed behind the two Serbs. When they turned their heads to look, Blago made his move on the Serb in front of him.

He kicked, connecting with the Serb's kneecap, and caught the Serb off guard. With his left hand he grabbed the Serb's knife hand and jabbed his right fist into the Serb's stomach. When the Serb doubled over, Blago quickly raised his knee into the Serb's face, breaking his nose. In pain, the Serb dropped the knife and Blago ran him headfirst into the side of the house.

While this was happening, the second Serb looked at Moore.

"I'm a noncombatant," the wide-eyed Moore shouted as he shrank back in fear. "I'm a reporter."

The Serb grunted at Moore and turned his attention to helping his friend. He pointed his weapon at Blago, who was standing over the first Serb.

Before he could pull the trigger, he sprawled to the ground as the result of a blow to his head. Standing behind him and holding a board in his hand was Moore.

"Guess I'm not a noncombatant anymore."

"Good decision, but don't wait so long to make it next time," Blago said as he looked at the two men on the ground.

Moore grinned sheepishly. "I hope there's no next time."

A burst of gunfire streamed across the road from a number of approaching Serbs.

"Let's go," Blago said as he took the lead and the two sprinted through the back yards of a number of homes and eventually made their way back to the hidden motorcycle. Once they retrieved it, they rode directly to the gas station.

From the top floor of a nearby building, the Vuk had been observing the fight between the four men through his binoculars. He recognized Moore and planned on paying another visit to the gas station.

November 20, 1991
The Fall of Vukovar

After twenty-four hours of intense shelling by Serbian forces, Vukovar was captured. The battle by its citizens and soldiers had held off defeat for eighty-seven days. Serbian forces overwhelmed the town. The streets were filled with Serbs and their vehicles as they conducted house-to-house searches for any remaining resistance. Drunken Serbian thugs roamed the rubble of Vukovar randomly shooting people point-blank.

At the gas station, Blago rushed into the room. "Where's Buck?"

"He's out," Moore responded.

"How about Fitz?"

"He's out, also."

"You need to come quick!" he said urgently. "They took 300 people from the hospital."

Moore stood. "Where did they take them?"

"Outside of town about four kilometers to the Ovcara farm. Hurry. We must go. Bring a camera!"

Grabbing his camera, Moore followed Blago and joined him on his motorcycle. Its motor roared to life and the two rode through the maze of traffic to an area near the farm where they dismounted and hid the Honda.

"I was at the hospital this morning when they came in," Blago spoke in a hushed tone as they looked down on the farm.

"When who came in?"

Blago pointed. "The Vuk and his men. They had everyone leave the building. Doctors, patients and visitors. I was able to slip away unnoticed. They walked them down the street two blocks and had them board those buses. About fifty people per bus and they didn't care about what age the people were."

Below them, they saw six buses unloading people in front of their raging captors.

"They said they were being evacuated, but I didn't believe them. Not when the Vuk is involved. Now look, they're prisoners."

They watched as the passengers were ordered to strip naked and then run through a gauntlet of wild-eyed members of the Vuk's wolf pack who beat each passenger with sticks, bats, rifles and their own hands. Some couldn't take it and dropped to the ground where they died. The elderly and children were the first to die.

Screams filled the air while blood turned the ground red. Pools of blood collected in small depressions on the ground.

Those, who had survived staggering through the deadly gauntlet, collapsed to the ground to rest. But they found themselves facing a new threat when the Vuk walked over to them.

He yelled, "I am conducting a military court and have found you all guilty of organized treason against the state." He paused as he heard the approaching sounds of diesel motors. When he turned he saw two bulldozers drive into view.

One of his men pointed to an open field and the two dozers began pushing earth as they dug out a large trench. It would be used as a mass grave.

The Vuk turned back to the nude people gathered in front of him. "I'm sentencing you to death by firing squad!" he snarled.

A collective moan went up from the survivors and most of them began to cry as they clenched their loved ones. The two on the hill watched in disbelief.

"But out of the kindness of my heart, I'm allowing you time to say your good-byes to each other."

Fifteen minutes later, the bulldozers had completed their work and began pushing the bodies from the gauntlet area into the mass grave. The Vuk ordered his men to stand in front of the survivors, and then ordered them to open fire. With a withering gunfire, they quickly mowed down the survivors. A few, who tried to escape by running, were also cut down.

The Vuk commanded the bulldozers to push the remaining bodies into the trench. Then, he had them cover the bodies with the dirt which had been excavated.

A very somber Moore snapped photos of the entire massacre. "They won. Why would they do this?" Moore asked no one in particular.

"More ethnic cleansing! You have direct evidence of this atrocity, Emerson. You are a witness and you need to tell our story."

"Vukovar has been a complete maelstrom for me," Moore said as he took one last look below. "We'd better go before they discover us."

The two made their way back to the hidden motorcycle and rode quickly to Pajo's gas station. They were stopped a few times by Serbian soldiers, but Blago identified himself as a Serb and the two were allowed to continue.

When they arrived at the gas station, Blago spoke as they were getting off the Honda, "This is getting more dangerous. I didn't like us being stopped and questioned."

"Me neither. Now they know we were out there," Moore said as the two walked into the house where they were greeted by Fitzgibbons.

"Where have you lads been? Out for a joy ride in the country?" Fitzgibbons asked as he sat at the table drinking a cup of hot tea. An opened bottle of slivovitz stood next to his tea cup.

The two quickly recounted what they had witnessed.

"I've got it all on film," Moore said as he set his camera on the table.

"This is serious business, all right. And you say you were stopped several times coming back?"

"Yes, but we made it through," Blago smiled, although he wasn't quite as cocky as he usually was.

"But don't you think word would get back to the Vuk? Don't you think he'll check with his men to see if anyone was in the neighborhood? Crikey, he's going to be on to you faster than you can say Bob's your uncle." Fitzgibbons was obviously irritated at the risk Blago and Moore had taken.

"I hadn't thought about that," Moore said.

"And with you two lads being witnesses, don't you think he'll be coming here? How many Honda motorcycles like yours do you think are in Vukovar today? One. And I bet they know it's right here."

Neither Moore nor Blago spoke.

"Bollocks, the damage has been done!" Fitzgibbons looked around the living quarters and saw Tatiana had been listening. "Now, we've made her culpable because she heard it all. You two may have really botched this up!"

Tatiana turned around and busied herself at the sink, but she had heard everything they had discussed.

Fitzgibbons played with a spoon as he thought. "Wait until Buck gets back. He'll work this out."

The noise of screeching brakes stopped Fitzgibbons from going further with his tirade. He stood and quickly walked over to the door to the garage bays. He could see through the doors and didn't like what he saw.

He turned his head back into the room and said, "I may have found a new calling. I'm a blasted fortune teller. The Vuk and his men just pulled up in front of here. There's going to be hell to pay, lads."

He started to walk into the bay, unconsciously carrying Moore's camera in his hand, and then paused. "It'll be for keeps this time. They'll tear this place apart so I'd suggest taking the girl and holing up a few doors down until I'm done dealing with them."

"I'll come out with you, Fitz," Moore said.

"I'll be having none of that. Now, on with you. Make sure the girl is safe. That's your priority right now."

Moore, Tatiana and Blago ran out the back of the gas station and not a minute too soon. As they cleared the next building, Moore looked back at the gas station and saw the Vuk's men surround it.

The Vuk and ten of his men with weapons drawn entered the garage bay from the front.

"I guess I should say a cheery congratulations to the victors!" Fitzgibbons said. "That's why you're here isn't it? To get my congratulations? Sort of like the blessing from the Pope. Oops, I should say the Serbian Orthodox Patriarch, shouldn't I?"

The Vuk fired his weapon, catching Fitzgibbons in the left shoulder. "You Brits have been a thorn in my side too long." He looked around the garage bay. "Where are the others?"

"On a bloody picnic, you Nancy boy!" Fitzgibbons quipped painfully as he looked at the wound in his shoulder.

Vuk didn't smile. He raised his weapon and fired again, hitting Fitzgibbons in the right shoulder, causing him to drop the camera. The Vuk walked over and picked up the camera. "What have we here?" Before Fitzgibbons could make another quip, the Vuk yelled, "Search the building. Tear it apart. I want the rest of them found."

Half of the men ran into the living quarters and began searching while several of the others looked around the bay and the small office.

"Been taking pictures, have you?" the Vuk snarled as he saw there was film in the camera.

"Yes, I have. Took some snaps of my wonderful stay at this beautiful war-torn vacation paradise to send home to the family." Fitzgibbons was feeling his oats and the effects of several pulls of slivovitz earlier.

"Get these developed," the Vuk said as he tossed the camera to one of his men, who disappeared with it.

The men returned from the living quarters.

"Anything?" the Vuk asked.

"Nothing," one responded.

"Where are your friends?" the Vuk asked as he approached Fitzgibbons and ran the gun's barrel along the side of his cheek.

"I told you they were on a bloody picnic!"

"Restrain him," the Vuk ordered.

Two men grabbed Fitzgibbons' arms and pulled. Fitzgibbons winced in pain, but managed not to give the Vuk the satisfaction of hearing him scream.

The Vuk approached Fitzgibbons and stuck the end of his gun barrel into the bleeding gunshot wound on Fitzgibbon's left shoulder. Fitzgibbons couldn't hold back. He moaned.

"Now, do you want to tell me where your friends are picnicking?"

Fitzgibbons didn't respond.

The Vuk called one of his other men to his side and whispered in his ear. The man ran to the living quarters and returned a minute later. He handed an object to the Vuk. The Vuk stepped closer to Fitzgibbons. "One last chance to tell me where your friends are."

Fitzgibbons maintained his silence.

"Then, you give me no choice. I want you to see what I have in my hand because it may be the last thing you see." The Vuk raised his hand to show Fitzgibbons what he was holding. It was a tablespoon.

"I'm going to have the pleasure of scooping out your eyeballs with this simple eating utensil."

Fitzgibbons eyes widened in terror and he shrank back as much as he could while being restrained.

The Vuk raised the spoon to Fitzgibbon's left eye and placed it firmly below his eyeball. He began to apply pressure and Fitzgibbons screamed out.

"Andrea is walking the streets. He's covering your victory. Moore, the kid, is down by the river and covering Vukovar's defeat."

The Vuk eased up on the pressure. "Do you know why I'm here?"

Fitzgibbons wanted to make a quip, but decided it wouldn't be wise. "No," he responded.

"It's because I went on a picnic today. It was on a farm not too far from here. And I heard your young reporter friend may have been out there, too – and spying on me! I heard from two of our checkpoints he was seen on the back of a motorcycle which was allowed to proceed through those checkpoints."

"I don't know anything about it. All I know is he was going to the riverbank to cover a story. Maybe your men are mistaken."

"I don't think so." The Vuk stepped back from Fitzgibbons and eyed him. "I really don't think you know where he is – at least now." The Vuk started to walk away.

Relaxing, Fitzgibbons felt his bravado returning. It was a fatal mistake. "When the dust on all this clears, they'll be coming for you. You'll end up in a war crimes trial, you Nancy boy," Fitzgibbon said boldly.

The Vuk whirled around and, without hesitation, fired at Fitzgibbons' chest. "You won't live to see how I avoid it," the Vuk said as he walked over and looked down at Fitzgibbons' lifeless body.

"That's three shots," Moore said nervously from their hiding spot in a building two doors down from the gas station.

"Not good," Blago said.

"I hear engines starting," Tatiana said excitedly. "Maybe they're leaving."

"Maybe. Let me check," Blago said as he worked his way through the debris in the building to an opening. It had once been a front window. Blago leaned out the window and saw the Vuk's Jeep and the truck with soldiers drive away.

"They're leaving," Blago said as he returned to his two friends at the rear of the building. "You stay here. I'll go and check to be sure it's safe to return."

As Blago started to leave the building, Moore cautioned him. "Be careful."

"You forget. I'm Blago. I'm indestructible," he said as he gave Moore a cocky grin and scurried to the gas station.

He slowly opened the rear door to the living quarters and listened. When he heard no noises, he walked inside. He quickly glanced around the room and then walked to the doorway to the garage bays.

Cautiously, he eased his head around the doorway so he could look into the garage bays. He again listened for any noises before proceeding. Not hearing anything, he walked into the bay and discovered Fitzgibbons' body. Even though he saw a massive loss of blood, he knelt next to the body and placed his hand on Fitzgibbons' neck. There was no pulse.

Saddened by the death of his friend, he stood and looked at the wise-cracking Brit's body for a few minutes. It was as if his feet were frozen in place and he couldn't walk away. Breaking out of the shock, he returned to the kitchen and walked to the shed to make sure his motorcycle was still safely hidden.

As he entered he looked at the ground to see if there were any footprints left in the dirt and there were none. Each time he took the motorcycle out or parked it in the shed, he would rake the dry dirt to cover his tire marks. He looked to the right and the rake was in its usual position.

He made his way to a pile of lumber at the rear of the shed. It was stacked eight feet high and almost touched the bare rafters overhead. Blago walked behind the lumber and pulled the tarp off his motorcycle. He smiled to himself, confident that no one had found it.

"That's a Honda XR600, isn't it?" a voice asked ominously from the rafters.

Blago spun around and found himself staring into the business end of a .45. Holding the weapon and smiling at his craftiness was the Vuk. Blago was stunned.

"Very clever of you to cover your tracks," the Vuk said as he dropped to the dirt floor. "Not so clever of you to allow me to trap you."

Blago wasn't going to let the Vuk see him sweat. He allowed his cocky smile to spread across his face.

Still pointing his .45 at Blago, the Vuk said in a threatening tone, "Let's get down to business. Were you at the farm today?"

Blago realized there was no use in denying it. "Yes," he replied.

"I give you credit. You are much more forthcoming than your dead reporter friend."

Blago reached to his shirt pocket and stopped. "May I have a smoke?"

"Certainly. Go ahead," the Vuk said as he watched Blago extract a pack of cigarettes from his pocket. "I'll take one, too."

Blago held the pack toward the Vuk and the Vuk took one of the protruding cigarettes. Blago extracted a cigarette and placed the pack in his shirt pocket. He reached into his pocket for his lighter and looked at the Vuk before pulling it out. "It's my lighter."

"Pull it out slowly," the Vuk said as he watched Blago's hand reappear. It was holding a lighter.

Blago flicked it and a bluish-yellow flame appeared. "Light?" he asked the Vuk.

"Yes, but very carefully. Don't get any ideas about trying to burn my face or my eyes," the Vuk warned.

"I wouldn't think of such a thing," Blago smiled as he leaned forward and lit the Vuk's cigarette. When he leaned toward the Vuk, he felt the Vuk thrust the .45 into his belly as a reminder not to try anything. Blago heeded the warning, but he was trying to figure how he was going to use one of the grenades attached to his belt. The tail of his shirt hid them.

The Vuk inhaled as he watched Blago light his cigarette and return the lighter to his pocket. Blago took a long drag on his cigarette and exhaled at the same time.

"So, what's next?" Blago asked.

"I think you know," the Vuk said as his finger tightened on the trigger, firing the .45. Blago fell to the side and onto his beloved motorcycle. His cigarette dropped from his mouth into the dirt as his life ended.

The Vuk saw the hand grenades when Blago's shirttail twisted. He took two more puffs on his cigarette and put it out. He walked to the motorcycle and unscrewed the gas cap. Taking one of the grenades from Blago's belt, he pulled the pin and held the grenade's lever down. He then carefully placed the grenade between Blago's upper arm and his chest so that anyone moving Blago would dislodge the grenade and allow it to explode.

The Vuk walked out of the shed and then cut through the back yard to the next block where his Jeep and the truck were waiting for him. It had been an eventful day. He planned to return the next day to survey the successful results of his trap.

From their hiding place, Moore turned to Tatiana. "I don't like this," he said when he heard the gunshot from the direction of the gas station. "I better go and check it out."

"No, please, don't leave me here by myself," she pleaded.

"It would be safer for you to stay here," Moore said as he tried to reassure her.

"I'm not staying here," she said defiantly.

Moore realized nothing would change if he pressed the matter. "Okay, okay. You can come with me," Moore said with exasperation. "But be careful."

"I will," she acknowledged.

The two left the relative safety of the debris-filled building and moved carefully down the back yards to the gas station. Moore led the way through the rear of the station and into the bay where he froze.

"You had better stay here," he said as he held up his hand to Tatiana.

"What's wrong?"

"Just wait here," he said as he walked over to Fitz's body. He looked at it in stunned silence for several moments. Then, he grabbed a nearby blanket and covered the body.

"Who is it? Blago?" she asked. She realized whoever it was had died.

"Fitz," Moore replied somberly.

Tatiana began to sob at the death of another one of her friends.

Moore approached Tatiana and placed his arm around her to comfort her. She gripped him tightly. She was feeling very vulnerable.

"We need to find Blago," Moore said. With an arm around Tatiana, he headed back into the living quarters and out the back. He looked toward the shed and started to walk toward it to see if Blago's motorcycle was still there.

Inside the shed, gravity caused Blago's body to slide off the bike, allowing the grenade to drop to the floor and the lever to be released. Before Moore and Tatiana entered the shed, the shed exploded in front of them.

The force of the explosion knocked the two to the ground as the shed turned into a fireball. Moore tried to maneuver so his body covered Tatiana to protect her from the flying debris.

"Get off me," she said as she pushed at his body.

Moore rolled off of her. "I was just trying to protect you," he explained.

She seemed miffed by his action, even though it was innocent. "I guess we won't know if Blago was in there," she said.

Moore looked at the blaze. "I'll check for his motorcycle after the flames die down." Moore thought it would be wise not to add he'd also look through the ashes for skeletal remains. "We're making good targets out of ourselves by being in the firelight," he said as they stood to their feet and he looked around. "We'd better get away from here."

"Do you think it's safe to stay at Pajo's?" she asked, looking back to what had been her home.

"Yeah. I don't think anyone will be back tonight other than Buck. It'll be easier for us to reconnect with him if we stay here." He looked at her in the burning light of the fire. "Do you think you can sleep there with Fitz lying in the bay?"

"Yes, I can do it. I slept in my own home for two nights after they killed my parents," she said somberly.

They returned to the living quarters and Tatiana dropped into a chair. She pulled her knees up and held them tight with her arms as she lost herself in her memories.

Moore moved into the garage bay and found a spot where he could watch the street and the occasional drunk Serbian soldier stumbling down the street.

An hour later, Andrea entered the living area and walked into the bay. "What happed to the shed?"

Moore jumped. He hadn't heard Andrea enter. "Explosion."

"No doubt. What caused it? Incoming rounds? Although it seems that the shelling has stopped."

"Don't know. It may have been a parting gift from our visitors." Andrea stopped in his tracks when he saw the covered body and blood on the garage floor.

"Is that Fitz?"

"Yes."

"Poor bugger." Andrea stared at the covered body. "You better tell me what happened," he said as he wiped away a tear. He walked to where Moore was seated and joined him in staring into the street.

Moore recounted what he and Blago witnessed at the farm and everything else he knew including the disappearance of Blago and his growing concern that Blago may have run into the Vuk and his men.

"That's good work. Not only did you get pictures of the Vuk, but you were a witness to his massacre of those poor people."

"It was awful," Moore said. "They beat them as they ran through the gauntlet, even the kids. Then, they shot them all before burying them in a mass grave."

"You just make sure you remember how to get to that farm. You'll need to provide that information for any war crimes tribunal. And protect that camera. By the way, where is it?"

"Gone."

Andrea's face fell. "Gone?"

"Fitz had it in his hand when he walked out to see the Vuk."

"Stupid Brit. He wasn't thinking. See what I said about thinking!"

Moore reached into his pocket and pulled out a roll of film. "This is the roll. I'd put a fresh roll in before Blago and I returned. I expected we might have to go through some checkpoints and thought it would be wiser to change it while I could."

"Well, what do you know about that! The kid was thinking. Good on you! What you have there is your ticket to punishing the Vuk. He can't get away from that evidence."

Moore nodded his head. But he thought to himself he'd trade the roll for the lives of Fitz and Blago, if Blago was dead.

"We can go through the ashes in the morning. Like you said, we'll see if the motorcycle is there and if Blago's remains are there."

Moore nodded his head again.

"And, we'll bury Fitz in the morning," Andrea added.

The Next Morning
Pajo's Gas Station

There was uneasiness in the air the next morning. Andrea and Moore searched through the smoldering ruins of the shed and found the remains of the motorcycle. They also found the skeletal remains of what they guessed was Blago.

Without saying anything they dug a small grave and placed Blago's remains and Fitzgibbons' body in the grave. After Andrea mumbled a few words in a quasi-prayer, they filled the grave and hurried into the gas station.

The streets of Vukovar were alive that morning. The survivors of the siege of Vukovar were making their way through the streets, which were littered from the debris of war. More than 30,000 Croatians headed for the riverfront. Word had spread through the town the blue-helmeted United Nations peacekeeping team had worked with the Serbian commanders to arrange a flotilla of ships to evacuate the survivors. Even the Vuk had donated a ship to the flotilla.

It was named *Zenobia*.

In the gas station, Andrea was helping Moore disguise Tatiana. They had her dress in a loose fitting shirt and worn pants. On her head, she wore a dark blue watch cap that hid her long hair. She had one of Pajo's old jackets on top of everything else.

The two men had smudged her face with dirt to help camouflage her beauty. Moore stepped back and looked at what they had accomplished.

"We need one more thing," he said as he walked to his gear and rummaged through it. "Here we go." When he turned around, he was holding a pair of dark sunglasses. He walked to Tatiana and said, "Try these on."

She placed the glasses on her face and looked at the two men.

"Much better," Andrea said.

Moore looked at his watch. "We should leave so we can get to the ships in time."

"Grab your gear," Andrea said as he walked toward the open garage door.

"What about your gear?"

"I'm staying," he said.

"But Buck, I thought we were all leaving," Moore said, agitated at this last minute change in plans by Andrea.

"Someone has to cover the so-called victory, but especially the continued ethnic cleansing."

Dropping his gear, Moore said with a defiant tone, "I'm staying, too."

"Not so fast, kid. I need you to go. You're a witness to what has taken place. What if something happens to me, who's going to write the story? Some Serbian PR firm? I don't think so. You need to write about your observations and the atrocity you witnessed at the farm yesterday."

Moore shook his head from side to side.

"Don't give me that," Andrea said firmly. "You've got to make sure that Tatiana gets out of here, too. Who's left to take care of her? Pajo's dead. Fitz is gone and so is Blago. You want her to fall into the Vuk's hands and what he has planned for her?"

"No."

"Then, do as I say."

"But…"

Andrea interrupted Moore. "No buts about it. Besides, I need you to do one other thing for me."

"What's that?"

Andrea pressed a computer disk into Moore's hand. "Get this published. It's full of reports of the atrocities and photos. It has to be published."

Moore looked down at the disk he was holding.

"Look kid. When this is all over, we'll meet in Georgetown for a drink. We'll celebrate our friends – Pajo, Fitz and Blago. We'll talk about our close brushes with the Vuk and how we survived. We'll reminisce, although not fondly, about our time here.

"But more importantly, we'll talk about the maturing of a snot-nosed kid." Andrea placed an arm on Moore's shoulder. "You grew up while you were here, Emerson. I've seen a change in you. And it's for the good."

Moore looked up at the tall reporter. "Thanks, Buck. This has been my personal odyssey. I've learned a lot from you and the guys, especially about keeping my head down."

"There you go," Andrea said as he patted Moore on the shoulder. "Keep your head down so you can report the next day. But, there's also a time to jump up and make a stand. I always hope I make the right decisions trying to differ between the two. I know I've made my share of mistakes."

"Don't we all?" Moore questioned philosophically.

"And at your age, think about all of the years ahead of you to make more mistakes!"

"Yeah." Moore rolled his eyes,

"Now, hide that disk on you somewhere where you won't lose it."

Moore unbuttoned a couple of buttons on his shirt and reached in. He brought out a plastic pouch which had been hanging from a leather thong around his neck. Inside the pouch was his passport. He slipped the disk into the pouch and inside of his shirt. "This is perfect," he said as he rebuttoned his shirt.

"Good, I'll walk with you two to the riverfront," Andrea said.

"Tatiana, we need to go," Moore called.

Tatiana was clutching a bag as she stood in the doorway, looking into the living area which had been her home. She didn't want to leave, but knew she had no choice if she wanted to escape the Vuk. She walked over to join Andrea and Moore.

The three made their way into the exodus, the throngs of people crowding the littered streets. Some were pushing aged parents in wheelbarrows or pulling them in small wagons. Others had horse-drawn carts. Anything to get them to safety onboard one of the waiting vessels.

Within the hour, the three were approaching the riverfront. Several ships were tied to the docks and had their anchors deployed in the current of the Danube River to help maintain their position at the dock. Their bows were pointed up river.

Lines of refugees were in front of the freighters, waiting their turn to board and travel up river to one of the refugee camps in Budapest. Unarmed members of the U.N. peacekeeping team were seated at tables next to the boarding ramps and registering the names of the refugees before they boarded.

Herding the refugees into the lines and watching them were scores of heavily-armed Serbian soldiers. The three found themselves pushed into a boarding line for an old freighter.

Moore looked up at the bow and saw the freighter's name. It was named *Zenobia*. It looked like it had seen better days. Moore then looked at the fast moving current as the line of people moved closer to the ship. They hadn't reached the bow of the ship and they were standing along the edge of the dock with their backs to the river.

"I'll stay with you until you register and start boarding," Andrea said.

"Thanks, Buck," Moore said as the line edged forward.

Andrea's eyes narrowed. "What have we here?" he asked as he saw the Vuk walking along the line and peering at people. He was followed by several members of his wolf pack and a large truck that kept pace with them.

Every few steps, the Vuk would stop and point to an attractive Croatian female. One of his men would pull them from the line as they screamed and escort them to the truck.

"Looks like the Vuk is having easy pickings for his human trafficking," Andrea observed.

When the husband of one woman engaged in a tug of war with one of the Vuk's men, the Vuk produced a weapon and fired a shot, killing the husband. The sobbing woman was then pulled to the truck and thrown in the back.

One of the U.N. peacekeepers ran over to the Vuk, but hastily retreated when the Vuk's men pointed their weapons at him.

"You need to write about this," Andrea said. "This is not looking good," he said as the Vuk neared them.

"Think he'll spot Tatiana?" Moore asked as he looked at the Vuk.

"Maybe. He certainly is looking closely at every female." Andrea watched the Vuk for a moment, and then spoke to Moore. "You're a target, too. I'm sure he knows you were with Blago at the farm massacre and the film they took was unexposed. He's after you and the film."

Moore looked around for an escape route. There was none. "What should we do?"

Andrea thought quickly. "Listen! Do as I say! I'm going to create a diversion. When I do, you two step backwards and climb under the dock and on the supports. It'll be dark soon and you can board then. Good luck, Emerson."

Before Moore could say anything, Andrea walked boldly away from the line and began singing a few lines from the Croatian national anthem. That caught the Vuk's attention. He fired two shots in the air and everyone diverted their attention to the Vuk and Andrea, who continued to walk away from the line.

While this was happening, Moore and Tatiana turned and climbed down the side of the dock. They found a space underneath the wooden structure on the support beams where they would wait until nightfall.

"Stop this singing, Andrea. Why are you doing this?" the Vuk asked as his anger began rising. He was already fuming because they hadn't found Tatiana or Moore. He was in no mood for any shenanigans. "You're not Croatian!"

"I was just bidding my Croatian friends bon voyage in a manner which I thought they would enjoy," Andrea retorted.

"Is that so?" the Vuk asked in a menacing tone. "Where are Tatiana and Moore?"

"I don't know," Andrea responded.

The Vuk glared stonily at Andrea, then a cruel smile crept across his face. "Well, then, I'd suggest you turn and face your Croatian friends and wish them bon voyage," the Vuk stormed as he walked next to Andrea.

Andrea with a smile on his face turned to face the line. He noticed that Moore and Tatiana had disappeared. His smile widened as he yelled, "Bon Voyage!"

No sooner had Andrea shouted than his world went black. He hadn't seen the Vuk pull out his .45 and point it at the right side of Andrea's skull. The Vuk pulled the trigger, sending an unsuspecting journalist into eternity.

The hushed silence in the line was replaced by several and then almost all of those in line humming the Croatian national anthem.

Furious, the Vuk grabbed an AK-47 from one of his men and sprayed bullets over the heads of the refugees.

"Enough," he shouted as the humming ceased abruptly and he returned the weapon to his man. The Vuk looked at Andrea's body and ordered it dragged away. Then, he continued his trek of selecting females for his human trafficking operation and his search for Tatiana and Moore.

Below the dock, Moore was huddling with Tatiana on one of the dock supports. He wasn't aware of Andrea's death. "We'll wait here until nightfall, then board the ship."

"But there are guards at the entrance ramps," she worried.

"Yeah, I know. We'll figure something out," he said as he tried to make himself more comfortable. Unconsciously, his hand went inside his shirt and felt the pouch to make sure it was still securely attached.

Around 3:00 a.m., Moore announced, "We should go now. I'd think the guards would be drowsy and not so alert now."

"How are we going to board?" Tatiana asked.

Pointing to the anchor chain which was pulled taut as it helped hold the ship in the river's current, Moore explained his plan. "We'll work our way upriver along these beams and then drop into the river. We'll let the current do some of our work, but we'll have to angle our swim to that anchor chain."

A sudden thought crossed his mind and he turned to look at Tatiana. "You can swim, right?"

She nodded her head. "Yes."

Relieved, Moore continued, "When we reach the anchor chain,

we'll shimmy up the chain like a couple of monkeys and enter the freighter through the hawse hole."

"What's a hawse hole?"

"That's the hole cut in the side of the bow for the anchor chain to run through," he explained.

"Is it big enough for us?"

"The real question is whether we are small enough to squeeze through it."

Tatiana looked at Moore. She had a skeptical look on her face. "What about the guards?" she asked again.

"I'm counting on them having their backs to the water. They'll be more concerned with people trying to board on the ramps. I doubt they'll be thinking of someone doing what we're going to do."

"I hope so," she said.

"Time to go," Moore said as he started making his way upriver along the cross beams. Tatiana was close on his heels. Five minutes later, he stopped.

"I think this is far enough. We'll let the current help us."

He began lowering himself to the beams at water level. She quickly followed. Within a minute, they reached water level. Moore stopped and removed his belt from his slacks. "I'll need your belt, too," he said.

"Why?" she asked as she took off her belt and handed it to him.

Moore connected the two belts as he talked. "We're going to tie us together so we don't get separated. Just in case."

He tied one end of the belt through one of her belt loops and did the same with his belt loop on his pants. "Not much, but better than nothing."

The two slipped into the cold water and began swimming at an angle across the river. The current pushed them downriver but also aided their progress. Within minutes they had reached the anchor chain. They clutched the chain as Moore looked toward the dock and saw that his assumption had been correct. There were several guards on the dock, but their attention was focused on the town.

"Ladies first," he said as he untied the belts.

It was a good thing that Tatiana was strong. She reached up and began pulling herself along the stretched chain. Her long legs were wrapped around the chain as she moved herself upward.

Moore allowed her a head start of twenty feet and then duplicated her efforts as he inched himself along the chain. He was grateful for the chain's angle as it would have been more difficult to do a vertical ascent.

When Tatiana reached the hawse hole, she eased herself through the opening and onto the ship's deck. Moore appeared through the hawse hole and quickly joined her. He sat with his back against the windlass.

Catching their breath as they sat, they didn't hear approaching footsteps.

"And just where do you think you might be going?" a rich baritone voice with an Irish accent asked.

Moore's heart sunk. They had been discovered. He turned to look up and smiled when he saw the U.N. emblem on the man's shirt.

"Home," Moore responded.

"And where would that be?"

"The United States," Moore responded as he stood and helped Tatiana to her feet.

"And where would the young lady be heading?"

Without hesitation, Moore replied, "The United States."

Tatiana smiled at Moore.

"Since the two of you took the roundabout way of boarding, I'd think that someone is looking for you. Would that be a safe assumption on my part?" he asked.

"That would be."

"Just as I thought. Well then, let's get you into some dry clothes. We'll be shoving off at daybreak," he said as he escorted the two below deck.

Two hours later, Moore and Tatiana were standing in the crowded bow section of the freighter as the U.N. crew raised her anchor and cast off her bow and stern lines.

Moore looked toward shore and raised his cup of coffee. "To Vukovar and the telling of her story," he said as he toasted the beleaguered town.

Tatiana raised her cup in a toast and then sipped her hot brew as the ship moved away from the dock and began to travel upstream to Budapest. Most of the passengers above decks kept their eyes glued on their hometown, with smoke arising from burning buildings. Within minutes, the town faded out of sight.

"Hungry?" Moore asked.

"Yes."

"Let's go and see if we can find some food," Moore suggested.

"I'd prefer to stay here and enjoy the peace. It's been so long since I've been able to relax. I hope you understand," she said as she looked at the handsome reporter.

"Oh. Sure. Let me see what I can find," he smiled and left to make his way through the crowd.

Parked along the riverfront about ten minutes north of Vukovar, the Vuk was seated in the passenger seat of his Jeep. He was smoking a cigarette. Between his knees was an unopened bottle of slivovitz.

Next to him, his driver commented nervously, "I don't see the *Zenobia* yet."

"Patience. Life is about patience and planning," the Vuk said as he watched the Danube flow by in the early morning dawn.

A few minutes passed before the driver announced, "There's the *Zenobia*!"

The Vuk nodded his head and a malicious grin spread across his mouth.

As the *Zenobia* pulled parallel to where they were parked, a huge explosion filled the air as the ship's bow struck a mine in the river. Death engulfed the refugees on the bow as it became filled with twisted metal and flames. Water poured into the large hole in the bow section and the ship's pumps couldn't keep up with the inflow. The *Zenobia* was sinking. From the bridge, the captain sounded the abandon ship alarm and the newly recruited U.N. crew members, who were not familiar with the ship, struggled to man their stations.

When the explosion happened, Moore had just stepped through a passageway onto the deck. He and the other passengers were knocked down and Moore's two sandwiches went flying. He jumped to his feet and began to race to the bow when a crew member stopped him.

"Help me with this lifeboat," he ordered Moore.

"I can't. I have a friend in the bow," Moore panicked. He was concerned about Tatiana.

"Well, you can kiss that friend goodbye. The blast killed everyone in the bow section. Poor sods. After everything they had to go through, they end up dead and just a few hours from a safe port. Now, help me."

Moore took two zombie-like steps toward the bow. He felt like he was in a daze.

"Forget it. They're gone. You've got to help me save the living." The crew member pointed to one of the davits. "Man that davit and help me swing this boat out."

Moore looked at the panic-stricken crowd of refugees pushing him and resigned himself to the task at hand. "What caused the explosion?"

"Heard we hit a mine. They've got rescue boats coming up river to us."

As Moore reached for one of the controls for lowering the lifeboat, he saw the Vuk's Jeep driving away in the early morning sunlight. He recognized it by the two flags on the front fenders. The Vuk had this planned the whole time, Moore thought to himself as he turned his attention to his work. He began formulating a story about the incident in his mind. He'd title it "Death on the Danube."

"Help my children. Take them." A woman held out two toddlers to Moore. He took the children and placed them in the lifeboat and then helped the woman into the craft. Moore was helping another woman into the lifeboat when another explosion rent the air. The ship had struck another mine. This one was fifty feet from where Moore was standing. The force of the explosion sent a number of bodies into the air and the water. Moore's was one of them.

Book Two
Despair
2001

Ten Years Later

Emerson Moore's Study
Alexandria, Virginia

Moore heard a noise in the doorway to his study. When he looked up, he saw a woman standing there. Her hip was tilted provocatively and she was studying Moore with a bold stare. She appeared to be in her early 30's, good-looking with blonde hair, a fine-boned face and piercing blue eyes. Aristocratic. Confident.

"I saw you with a blank look on your face. What were you thinking about, Honey? I know it wasn't me. Some redhead, no doubt."

A smile crossed Moore's face as he stood and walked around his desk. He placed his arms around the woman and gave her a playful pat on her butt. "You know there's no one but you in my life, Sweetie."

"Sure. Sure."

"You're the love of my life, baby. You and Matthew."

"And your work, especially your work. I think you're addicted to it," she teased as she pushed her body against his.

"There's only one addiction I have and I haven't found a cure for it," he said as she suddenly spun away from his embrace.

"And just what would that be, Mr. Big Time Reporter?" she asked seductively as she sat on the edge of his desk. Her skirt had ridden up, exposing her firm thighs.

Moore walked to the desk and held her tight. "My love for you, Julie." He held her tighter in his arms. "I just love holding you in my arms, Sweet Sugar."

"Just as long as I'm the only one you love holding in your arms!"

she teased as she hugged him back.

"I remember the first time you gave me a hug. It was just so different," Moore said as the two embraced.

"Oh?" she asked.

"Yes. It had two things hugs from other people didn't have."

"And just what would those be?"

He pulled back and looked into her blue eyes. He always loved the way she did her eye makeup, too. "It was full of affection and sincerity if you could say a hug had sincerity in it," he said as he allowed his gaze to drop to her full lips.

She noticed where his eyes were focusing. "Go on. Tell me about my lips."

"Very kissable. You give luscious kisses," he murmured. "I remember the first time I kissed you."

She half-rolled her eyes. "Go ahead. You've told me a thousand times."

"And I will tell you another thousand times. I said 'Wow! Man, can you ever kiss!'"

"Just make sure you don't experiment on any other women!" she teased. She saw how women looked at her handsome husband.

"Who, me?" he asked in mock surprise as he pulled back and looked into her magical eyes.

"I'm going to get a tee shirt especially made for you," she said as her eyes sparkled.

"You are? And just what will the shirt say?" he asked with a smile.

"He's mine."

"And I think I'll get one for you, too."

"And what will it say?"

"Taken!" he snickered, playfully.

She wiggled out of his arms and pushed him away. "You're incorrigible!" she teased again as she gave him a kiss.

Before they could continue, a small voice piped up, "I found you guys!"

"We weren't hiding, Matthew," Julie replied. "Daddy and I were just talking."

"You guys were kissing again, weren't you?" the five-year-old asked with glee at catching his parents in the act.

"Come here, buddy." Moore bent over and grabbed his son. He held him tight in his arms as he straightened. "I think someone needs a little attention."

The boy giggled. He knew what his father was going to do to him.

"I'm the kissing machine, the kissing machine," Moore said as he covered his son's cheeks with loud kisses.

"Daddy, stop!" he squealed as he wiggled to escape from his father's grip.

"I can't. The kissing machine is locked in the 'on' position," Moore teased as he continued to cover the boy's face with kisses.

"You'd better stop, Emerson. Matthew and I had better run. We'll be late for his doctor's appointment."

"Okay. I guess I'm going to have to stop." He gave his son one last and loud kiss, then set him on the floor.

"Go get your jacket," she said as the boy scampered out of the room. She turned and looked at her husband. He looked good. His dark hair had been moussed. He looked so suave in his white shirt with bold blue stripes and khaki trousers. He had a bright red tie which had been loosened around his neck. His red cufflinks matched his tie. A navy blue Ralph Lauren sport coat was hanging on the door knob. He could be on the cover of GQ, she thought to herself.

"You going to the office?" she asked although she had already made that assumption.

"Yes. I have a meeting to attend."

"Well," she said as she rubbed her body seductively against his and planted a moist kiss on his lips. "Maybe I can get on your schedule for a meeting tonight."

He knew what she had in mind and his big smile showed it. "Are you flirting with me?"

"No, I'm outright tempting you!"

With a growing twinkle in his eyes, he responded, "I'll clear my calendar for this evening. I'm all yours."

"You better be and only mine," she teased as she looked over her shoulder on her way out of his study.

Moore returned to his desk and sat in the swivel chair. He stared blankly at the laptop screen in front of him as he heard her leave the house and drive away with their son.

He allowed his mind to drift back to when he met her eight years ago. He had landed his dream job at *The Washington Post* and was on assignment to interview several of the leaders at NOW, the National Organization for Women, for a story he was writing about women's rights. Julie was one of the public relations managers and it was one of those "love-at-first-sight" things.

He asked her out for a drink and was impressed by her passion for women's rights. She was a strong advocate for women's equality and the elimination of workplace discrimination and harassment. When she began to talk about violence against women, Moore had shared his adventures in Vukovar several years earlier and what he had seen regarding human trafficking. They talked for hours and continued to meet as their mutual attraction for each other grew. They were married a year later and bought a home in Alexandria.

Moore's mind drifted to Vukovar. He recalled the incident on the *Zenobia*. He had recovered consciousness in a Hungarian hospital after being rescued by U.N. peacekeepers. They were onboard several ships that had been following the *Zenobia* upstream. He had been unconscious for a few days and he was fortunate that his wounds were minimal.

After his release from the hospital, he searched for Tatiana, but the search was complicated by the fact they hadn't registered to board the ship since they had sneaked up the anchor chain. After spending several days trying to locate her, he resigned himself to believing she had perished with others in the bow when the ship struck the first mine.

With the help of the *Washington Record*, Moore returned to the United States and wrote a series of articles about the atrocities committed in Vukovar and published the photos. He testified at The Hague as a witness to war crimes and crimes against humanity committed against the Croatians and other non-Serbs. His testimony and photographs supported the prosecution's case for murder, persecution, extermination, torture, inhumane acts, destruction, plunder and deportation.

Several Serb military and political officials, including the President of the Republic of Serbia, Slobodan Milosevic, had been indicted, found guilty and jailed for war crimes. Marko Marinkovic the Vuk was also indicted, but he had disappeared without a trace after the war. No one was able to find him.

The battle of Vukovar had exhausted the Serbian army and proved a turning point in the Croatian war much like the battle at the Alamo. A ceasefire was declared a few weeks after the fall of Vukovar, which remained under Serbian control until 1998. Then, it was peacefully reintegrated into Croatia.

A robin flew into his study's window with a thud and dropped to the ground from the impact. The noise brought Moore back to reality and he looked at his watch. Time to go, he saw. He shut down his laptop, grabbed his sport coat and headed for the garage and the short drive to *The Washington Post's* office.

Andrews Air Force Base
Washington, D.C.

Air Force One landed and taxied off the runway. It was returning United States President Jeffrey Koehler from his visit with the judges at The Hague where he had pushed for stiffer sentencing for the perpetrators of war crimes from the Serbo-Croatian war. He had been very vocal about the need to fully prosecute the war criminals, including Serbia's president Milosevic, for the atrocities committed against the Croatians and later in Bosnia. A worldwide manhunt for several of the generals and Marko Marinkovic the Vuk was underway to apprehend them and bring them to trial. Koehler was also behind the United States' efforts to place economic sanctions on any country which harbored the listed generals.

Koehler's head pivoted as he looked for Marine One, the presidential helicopter. "Where's the chopper?" Koehler asked as he deplaned and talked to his lead Secret Service agent, Kenfield Valero.

"We're just taking extra precaution today and motorcading you to the White House," the agent replied. He didn't want to tell the president NSA had picked up chatter leading them to believe an attack was being planned against Marine One. After two assassination attempts over the last two years, the agents were edgy about any possibilities of a third attempt against the popular president, who was restoring the U.S. as a top influence in international issues.

"Whatever you want to do," the lanky Koehler said. "You guys know what's best."

"Come this way, Mr. President," the agent said as he escorted the president past several vans. They were positioned to block the view from the road so no one would be able to observe as the president entered the presidential limousine.

A mile from the base, a 2001 Chevy van sat in a vacant parking lot. In the rear of the van were two men. They were focused on a monitor, which was showing live video of the president walking down the stairs. When he disappeared behind the line of vans, one of them spoke in Serbian. "Can you move in closer so we can see him get in the limo?"

"No," the operator replied. "I don't want to risk them seeing the helicopter," he said as he tried to zoom the camera lens in closer. The camera was mounted on a small, model helicopter which they controlled from the van. It was small enough to penetrate the tight security at Andrews Air Force base and bring the helicopter in close enough to see the president disembark.

"I can't get any closer," the operator said. "They're moving."

On the monitor, they saw the motorcade start its journey to The White House.

"Follow them," the first one said as he called a cell phone number. When the call was answered he spoke, "They are on their way."

There was no answer at the other end. All he heard was a click. He moved to the front of the van and sat in the driver's seat. He quickly started the van, and then began driving along a route parallel to that of the helicopter following the motorcade. If any deviation to the expected route occurred, he had strict instructions to communicate it.

As the presidential motorcade drove northeast to The White House, the trip was uneventful. That is, until the last few blocks when suddenly a semi-truck pulled crosswise in the street, blocking the motorcade's forward progress. Another semi-truck parked crosswise behind the motorcade, blocking its potential retreat.

The lead Suburban, containing armed Secret Service agents, suddenly exploded when two RPG rockets struck it simultaneously. Bullets from two AK-47's struck down the lead motorcyclists.

Seeing the ambush unfold in front of his eyes, the driver of the presidential limousine stomped on the accelerator and began to pull around the burning Suburban. As he did, the trailing Secret Service Suburban was also destroyed by two RPG rockets.

The limo didn't move quickly enough as RPG rockets were fired at it from both sides. Their targets were the limo's tires. All four tires were hit, bringing the limo to a standstill.

From the bushes in front of the buildings lining the street, thirteen ski-masked terrorists emerged. Four took positions in front of the first burning vehicle and four behind the last burning vehicle. Their job was to fight off arriving law enforcement support, which could be expected within minutes.

Two terrorists approached the heavily armored limo and attached plastique to its windows. After stepping back to join the other two, they leveled their AK-47's at the vehicle. The leader detonated the plastique, causing the side windows to shatter, exposing the occupants. Immediately, the terrorists riddled the interior with gunfire, killing the occupants.

As oncoming sirens filled the air, the terrorists withdrew into a nearby building and ran through it to its exit on the other side where two vans awaited them. They entered through the rear doors and sat on the floor where they took off their ski masks and opened waiting bottles of slivovitz to celebrate their completed mission.

In one of the vans, the leader looked at the members of his wolf pack. "Well done," Marinkovic the Vuk said as he took a swig from the bottle and passed it to his men. "Now, change clothes," he said as the men, between pulls at the bottle, discarded the dark green jackets and replaced them with regular street jackets. The men in the second van were repeating this exercise.

Shortly afterward, the two vehicles pulled into a warehouse where they parked. The men, except for the Vuk and Zarkov, jumped into four cars and drove out of the warehouse as they fled Washington.

Zarkov applied plastique to both vans and took the driver's seat in the remaining getaway car where the Vuk awaited him with a remote detonator in his hand. He started the car and they drove out of the warehouse. When they were half a block away, the Vuk depressed the detonator, sending the two vans up in flames.

A smile filled his face as the Vuk slipped on a pair of Ray-Ban sunglasses and the car headed across the bridge to Alexandria.

At The White House, an old, nondescript van pulled up to the entrance gate where it was stopped by heavily armed and edgy security guards. The faded lettering on the side of the van read "Ranney Plumbing."

One guard cautiously approached the van where the driver was opening the window.

"Tough day, isn't it?" the driver said.

The security officer's jaw dropped when he recognized the driver. "Valero, what are you doing in that van?"

The Secret Service agent responded, "Sometimes, you hate to be right, especially when it results in the death of friends." He motioned with his head toward the passenger. "We kept him alive."

The security guard looked at the passenger and recognized the president. "Mr. President, it sure is good knowing you made it."

"We lost some good people today just so I could be alive," Koehler said, somberly.

"Yes Sir. We did," the guard agreed as he stepped back and waved them through. "It's President Koehler. Call it in."

As the van drove through the gate, Koehler spoke. "Thanks, Kenfield. I appreciate everything you folks did today. Having me get into this van rather than the limo was brilliant."

"We weren't sure who might be watching. That's why we had those vans lined up so no one could see that you got inside one of them rather than the limo."

The Next Day
Alexandria, Virginia

Several early morning newspapers were strewn around the hotel room in Alexandria and the Vuk and his henchman fumed over their failed assassination attempt of the president. When they had checked into the hotel the previous day and turned on the TV in their room, they expected to enjoy watching the news reports about the death of the president. Instead, they heard about the trickery the Secret Service had used by delivering the president safely to The White House in a plumber's van.

The Vuk had exploded with rage. Only Zarkov's intervention prevented the storming Vuk from shooting up the room and giving themselves away. He had to take possession of the Vuk's .45 to prevent him from using it. Eventually, the amount of liquor which the Vuk had consumed caused him to fall into a drunken stupor for the night.

The next morning, Zarkov confirmed the Vuk was still sleeping soundly before he slipped out of the room and purchased a number of newspapers from a nearby drug store. He had been reading the stories when the Vuk awoke and walked into the bathroom to relieve himself.

"Anything about us?" he asked as he yawned.

"No. They said it was a group of unknown assailants. They are trying to trace the RPG launchers that were left at the scene."

"They won't find anything. All black market purchases," the Vuk said as he sat at the table and picked up one of the newspapers to read.

"Coffee?"

"Yes," the Vuk replied as he took the cup filled with dark roasted coffee, which Zarkov had made in the room.

Zarkov switched on the TV and they listened to the continuing news reports as they read through the newspapers.

"I see they found the vans," the Vuk said as he read.

"Yes. They're trying to trace them, too."

"Won't link them to us. Stolen," the Vuk said.

Nodding his head, Zarkov continued reading. "Hey, we know this guy!"

"Who?"

"That kid reporter in Vukovar!"

"What? Gimme that," the Vuk said as he grabbed the newspaper from Zarkov. His eyes virtually bored a hole through the photo of Moore. "Looks older," he snarled as he read the story Moore wrote about several Washingtonians' reaction to the attempted assassination.

"Our trip here may not have been in vain after all," he smiled coldly.

"What are you thinking?"

"I'm thinking we'll go after Moore. He did enough damage with his stories and testifying at The Hague. It's time to make him pay."

"What do you have in mind?" Zarkov asked.

"Let's see what we can find on him. Then, I'll decide."

"Where do we start?"

"We'll go to the library and search the Internet."

A few hours later, the two were sitting next to each other at the Alexandria Library on Duke Street. They were searching through information on Emerson Moore.

"I've got his address. He lives here in Alexandria."

"Good. And look what I've found." The Vuk sat back in his chair and pointed at the screen. "Here's a photo of him with his wife and son at some charity event," the Vuk said as a plan began to formulate in the back of his mind.

"Nice-looking wife," Zarkov said as he looked at the photo.

"I may have found a way to make Moore suffer. Killing him would be too easy. It's over in a second. Making him suffer lasts a long time," the Vuk grinned maliciously. "MapQuest his home and let's go for a drive."

Zarkov did as he was told and they left the library to return to their car. After studying MapQuest, they followed its directions to Moore's home. They parked close by so they could watch cars coming in and out of his driveway.

Three hours later, they spotted a bright red 2000 Nissan Altima pulling out of the driveway. There was a blonde woman at the wheel and they could see the head of a youngster in the back seat.

"His wife," Zarkov guessed.

"And kid," the Vuk added. "Follow them."

Zarkov started their car's engine and pulled it out of the parking spot. He kept the car at a discreet distance as they followed it. They drove across the Beltway bridge over the Potomac River and picked up 395 toward downtown D.C. Following the car to a small restaurant near the Navy Shipyard, they saw the woman park the car and unbuckle the boy's seatbelt.

They found a nearby spot to park and observed the blonde greeting another woman, then walking into the restaurant.

"Looks like they are having a late lunch," Zarkov said.

"Or a last supper," the Vuk joked morbidly. "You have your cell phone?"

"Yes."

"Keep it handy. I'm going for a walk. Call me when they come out of the restaurant," the Vuk said as he stepped out of the car.

"Will do."

The Vuk walked down a nearby street, shopping for the tool he was going to need for the next step in his plan.

Sixty minutes later, the Vuk's cell phone rang.

"Yes?"

"She just walked out of the restaurant. The other woman hugged her and is walking away. She's putting the kid in the back seat again. You better get back here."

"I'm almost there."

"She's in the front seat. Looks like she's started her car. You better hurry or we'll lose her."

"I'm here," the Vuk said.

Zarkov looked in his mirror and turned around. He couldn't see the Vuk. "Where are you? I don't see you," he said frantically as he worried about losing sight of their prey. He saw the Nissan pull out of its parking spot.

"I'm in the big, black box truck coming up to you. Go ahead and pull out so you're between me and her. We'll follow her back to her house."

Zarkov relaxed and did as he was instructed.

In the car and unaware she was being followed, Julie Moore picked up her cell phone and speed dialed as she drove.

"Hi, Sweet Sugar," Moore answered when he saw his wife's number appear on his cell phone.

"How's the day going for my good-looking man?" she asked as she visualized her clean-cut and dapperly-dressed husband at the office.

"Still hectic. I'm still running down leads on the assassination attempt," he said hurriedly.

"You sound rushed," she said

"I am. I'm sorry, Honey. I've got to focus."

"I understand." Then, switching to a seductive tone, she asked, "Think you'll be coming home early this evening?"

Moore recognized the meaning of the tone right away. "Oh, baby, you're making this difficult on me," he moaned.

"I meant to," she smiled. "Try to get home as early as you can. I'm putting Matthew to bed early." She cast a quick glance in the mirror and saw Matthew had fallen asleep.

"I'll do my best," Moore responded.

"You always do," she purred.

"Oh, man, you're killing me. I do have to go. See you soon, Sweetie."

"Love you," she said, but he didn't hear it as he had disconnected.

She sighed and turned her attention to her drive.

Julie was driving her vehicle on the Beltway beginning to cross the bridge over the Potomac when she noticed a black box truck pass the car behind her and move rapidly next to her. The truck was uncomfortably close to her side of the car when it abruptly veered into her car, causing it to scrape the side of the bridge. The car ricocheted off the wall and into the truck which now swerved into her vehicle.

When the truck struck her car, the car careened towards the side of the bridge. Striking the bridge, the car flipped over the guard rail. The last things Julie Moore heard were her son's screams mixed in with hers and the splash of the car hitting the water. Both she and her son drowned.

The truck continued across the bridge to the first exit where it pulled off into a parking lot. The Vuk quickly abandoned the vehicle and got into the waiting getaway car with Zarkov at the wheel.

The Vuk had a satisfied look on his face as he spoke, "Let's see how Mr. Emerson Moore enjoys suffering."

The vehicle drove back onto the Beltway and headed out of the area.

An hour later, the phone rang in the office of *The Washington Post* editor, John Sedler.

"Sedler here," his deep voice echoed as he spun around from his computer monitor to answer the phone. The look on his face changed to one of sorrow as the police captain, making the courtesy call, told Sedler about the horrific traffic accident.

The victims' bodies had been preliminarily identified as the wife and son of his ace investigative reporter, Emerson Moore. The captain was also a friend of Moore's and wanted to break the news carefully to Moore. Sedler agreed to inform Moore. Sedler had grown close to the young man whom he had recruited as an investigative reporter.

Hanging up his phone, Sedler stood. Before walking down the hall to Moore's office, he gathered his composure. Still shaken, he walked the few feet to Moore's office.

"Emerson?" he asked as he closed the door behind him.

Seeing the door close, Moore looked up at his mentor. "Oh, oh. Am I in trouble?" he asked, nervously.

"It's not you I'm here about." Sedler paused as he blankly looked out Moore's window before he continued.

"That look on your face tells me this is bad, really bad," Moore said with growing concern. "What is it?"

"Emerson, there's been an accident, a horrible accident."

Moore stood and went to Sedler's side. "What is it? What happened?"

"It's your family," Sedler said slowly. "They've been in a car accident and they – they've perished, Emerson."

"What?" Moore asked incredulously. "No, that's not possible!" Moore reacted as denial set in.

"I am so sorry," Sedler spoke softly as he put his left arm around Moore's shoulders.

Moore's shoulders slumped. There was a hollow look in his eyes as visions of his family flashed through his mind. "I can't believe this!"

"I'm sorry, Emerson, but it happened. We never know what fate has in store for us," Sedler responded philosophically.

"What happened?" Moore heard himself ask Sedler as he transitioned from denial to acceptance. It was as if he was in an unending tunnel. His vision became clouded.

"The police are still piecing it together. It appears they were involved in an accident on the Beltway bridge. According to witnesses, a large truck swerved into them and pushed them into the wall and then over the guard rail. The car flipped into the Potomac."

Moore was in a trance. "Did they die instantly or drown?"

"They haven't conducted autopsies yet. They want me to drive you to the morgue."

"I can drive myself," Moore said.

"I don't think so. I'll drive you there, then home. Or, you can stay at my house so you don't have to be alone."

"What about the truck driver? Did they get him?"

"Hit and run. The jerk didn't stop!"

Moore later wouldn't remember Sedler drove him to the morgue and helped him identify the bodies. The shock to Moore was overwhelming.

After driving Moore home, Sedler fixed Moore straight whiskey from Moore's liquor cabinet. Moore quickly downed it and asked for another. Sedler watched as Moore drank himself to sleep after sobbing for a long time.

The next few days flew by in a blur for Moore. He would have a vague recollection of making arrangements at a funeral home, attending the funeral and starting a leave of absence from his job.

His Uncle Frank and Aunt Anne had driven in from Lake Erie's

South Bass Island to console Moore, but Moore spurned their efforts. Their appearance triggered additional bad memories of the role he played in the death of his cousin when he spent summers with them as a teen in the island resort village of Put-in-Bay. Feeling rejected, they had returned to Ohio after the funeral service and talking with Sedler.

Moore's cheery and confident nature disappeared as he tumbled headlong into an inescapable oblivion. His attire and appearance took a 180-degree turn as he stopped shaving, allowed his beard to grow and schlepped around his house in a torn tee shirt and stained jogging pants. In his hand, he now carried a bottle of rum to help keep him in a drunken state and away from the reality of his loss. His laptop sat on his study desk, untouched for weeks.

Three times a week, Sedler would stop by to try to help Moore deal with his grief and drop off groceries. But Moore found solace in wallowing in his personal exile filled with self-pity. When Sedler surprised Moore by bringing along a grief counselor to assist Moore, Moore shocked both of them by chasing the counselor out of the house.

Moore was sinking further into an abyss full of self-loathing.

Between bouts of drinking, Moore found an interest in writing again. But it was a different style of writing. It was a suicide note. Sedler found it and several bottles of prescription drugs on Moore's desk during one of his visits three weeks after the funeral.

Sedler peeked in the living room and saw Moore sprawled on the floor. Quickly, he walked over to Moore and checked to make sure he was still alive. Satisfied, he returned to the study and began reading the note.

To Anybody Who Cares If Anybody Really Does,

I miss Julie and Matthew so much. I don't think I can take this pain much longer. I cry all the time. I feel bitter about them being snuffed out of my life like an ordinary candle. They weren't ordinary; they were both very extraordinary. Their time on this earth was so brief and my time with them was even briefer. I'm angry as hell our time together has ended.

I'll never hear the voice I loved so much or feel her special touch. She had a special way of always melting my heart. I'll never hear Matthew's laughter again or smother him with kisses. Now it's as if my heart is coming apart at the seams. I feel like my heart is bleeding my soul from the inside out.

It seems like God has turned his back to me. He no longer cares. Why would God allow them to be snatched from this planet so quickly? Julie was a good woman, wife and mother. Matthew was a bundle of joy and energy. He was so innocent and yet the fullness and potential of his life was stolen from him.

This is such a huge loss for me. I feel shattered. I'm filled with so much pain, stress, and disappointment. My life is nothing more than a continual nightmare. I'm trapped in it and there's no one to wake me up. I see no hope for things to get better. I can't stand living this life of torment and cold darkness. I'm overwhelmed and can't move forward. My tear ducts are dry.

Life without them is too hard. I've decided to end my gray days and sleepness nights and join them. Bury me with them.

Sedler finished reading the note. Then, he read it one more time. He sighed at the depth of despair that encompassed his friend. He realized he would need to recommit himself to guiding Moore back into the reality of the living. He placed the note in the study and went into the kitchen where he opened the blinds to let the sunlight in.

Opening every cupboard, Sedler took every bottle of liquor from the shelves and emptied them in the kitchen sink. Then, he went room-to-room, including the garage, in his quest to rid the house of liquor. He dumped the contents of each bottle down the kitchen sink's drain. He also opened the drapes and blinds in every room to allow the sunlight to fill the house.

When Sedler felt comfortable he had disposed all of the liquor, he began making a pot of coffee. While the coffee was brewing, he called his office and told them he'd be out for a couple of days, but would be available by cell phone and e-mail if there were any emergencies.

When the coffee was done, he poured two cups of it and carried them into the living room. He set one cup on the coffee table and sat on the sofa. He began drinking his coffee as he waited for Moore to awake.

An hour later, Moore moaned and stirred. His arm reached out for the bottle of rum that had been on the floor near him. Not feeling it, he moaned again. Slowly the bearded Moore rose up on his elbows to look through partially opened eyes for the missing bottle. His eyes squinted from the rays of the sun shining through the windows.

"You're not going to find it," Sedler's voice boomed.

Moore's body jerked in surprise. "I didn't know I had company." The words were garbled as he spoke. "Ugh, close the blinds."

"You don't know much of anything. But I will tell you something you should know," Sedler said firmly.

"What's that?" Moore mumbled from the floor.

"You're no longer going to find any booze in this house. Prohibition has been reinstated in your home," the wily editor said. "So has sunshine."

"What do you mean?"

"It's all gone. I poured it down the drain. You're on the wagon and back in the world of the living, effective immediately."

Moore moaned.

"Here, have some coffee." Sedler placed his coffee cup on the table and held out Moore's cup.

"I don't think so," Moore said as he smelled what Sedler was offering him and held up his hand in protest. "I don't do coffee anymore."

"I don't believe I made myself clear. You don't do liquor anymore. And you're going to drink this coffee if I have to sit on you and put a filler tube down your throat to get it in you." Sedler was an ex-Marine and in great physical shape for a fifty-five-year-old. He also knew how to take charge.

Moore reluctantly accepted the cup of coffee, and then let the cup fall from his hand. The cup broke and the rich brown liquid soaked into the beige carpeting. "Oops," he said as he dropped back to the floor.

Sedler didn't say anything. He stood and walked into the kitchen where he grabbed another cup and filled it with more coffee. He returned to the living room and stood on one of Moore's hands.

"Hey, what do you think you're doing?" Moore screamed as he pulled his throbbing hand from under Sedler's shoe.

"Drink this and don't try to be cute with me," Sedler said as he bent over and offered a second cup of coffee to Moore. Moore pulled himself up to a sitting position and accepted the coffee. He took one sip and spit it out.

"I wouldn't do that again," Sedler said as he gave Moore a kick in the right ankle. "I can make your life here very difficult," he warned.

"What life? I have no life," Moore said as he took another sip and rubbed his ankle with the other hand.

"It's time to move forward. Drink it up," Sedler ordered.

Tipping the cup to his lips, Moore downed the brew. "Okay, now are you happy?"

"Nope. Get on your feet." Sedler didn't wait for Moore to move. He reached down and grabbed him by the back of his shirt collar. Then, he jerked him to his feet.

"Aw, come on now," Moore protested.

Pulling one of Moore's arms, Sedler dragged Moore into the bathroom.

"What are you doing now?"

"Time to shave."

Moore found himself standing in front of the sink. His eyes were drawn to the mirror and he didn't recognize the hollow-eyed face staring back at him.

"What are you waiting for?" Sedler asked in a gruff tone. "You want me to take a straight razor to your face?"

Moore knew Sedler was serious. "No, I can do it." He turned on the faucet and wet his beard. Then he applied shaving cream to his face and began shaving off the three-week-old beard. When he was done, he washed off the foam residue and dried his face.

"Satisfied?" he asked.

"Not yet! Strip!" Sedler growled.

"What?"

"You smell. When was the last time you showered?"

"I don't remember," Moore responded.

"Strip and get in the shower or I'll throw you in," Sedler snarled.

"Okay, okay. Gee, can you give a guy some privacy?"

"You have five minutes," Sedler said as he stepped out of the bathroom, shutting the door behind him.

Moore showered and dried off. When he cautiously cracked the door open, he didn't see Sedler – but Sedler heard him open the door.

"Throw some clothes on. We're going for a ride," Sedler yelled from the kitchen.

Moore knew it would be wiser to do as he was told. Ten minutes later, he was in Sedler's car.

"Where are we going?"

"Not to any bar, I can guarantee you that. I heard you've been seen at several of them and stone drunk. Those days are over."

"Okay then. Where are we going?"

"I've got a friend who runs an alcohol abuse rehab center. We're going to see him. Then, we're running over to see another friend of mine who conducts grief counseling."

Moore turned sideways in his seat. "I appreciate what you're trying to do, but I'm not interested."

Sedler slammed on the brakes, throwing the unbelted Moore into the windshield. "Hope that knocked a little sense into you. Now, I want you to listen to me and listen to me good. We're going to have a little 'come to Jesus' talk. It's time for you to pull yourself out of the muck you're wallowing in and think about others. I went through some of the same feelings you're going through when cancer took my wife a few years ago. You remember when I missed some time at the office?"

Moore nodded his aching head.

"You've got to pull yourself up by your bootstraps and think about others and not yourself. These two people tonight are going to help you get refocused and deal with the tragedy of losing your family. It isn't easy. It wasn't easy for me, either."

Sedler stared through the windshield before continuing. He turned his head back to Moore. "You haven't called your aunt back either, have you?"

"No. I saw she called on my cell phone, but I didn't listen to the voicemail."

"That's a real shame you ignored that poor woman. She's going through her own personal tragedy and you don't give a crap!"

Moore's eyes widened. "What do you mean?"

"The woman had to call me and I spent time consoling her because you were so self-absorbed."

"What happened?"

"Your Uncle Frank passed away and she wanted you to come to

his funeral on South Bass Island. But you were too selfish. It's all about you now. Isn't that what you think?"

Moore sat back in shock. Since the tragic death of his cousin when they were teens together, Moore had stayed away from the island even though he loved his aunt and uncle dearly. He missed the tranquility of spending time in the islands. "How's she doing?"

"Better than you by a long shot," he said angrily as he began to accelerate.

Moore had flashbacks of the time he spent with them. They and his cousin, Jack, had always made him feel at home and showered him with love and kindness. His uncle would take his cousin and him boating and fishing. He'd also take them for rides in his 1929 Ford Model A truck. Moore remembered riding in the cream colored truck with green fenders during the Sunday parades and throwing candy to the bystanders.

"Here's what I'm prescribing for you and you better take it. If you don't, you're going to lose your dream job working at *The Post*. You'll also lose a chance at a good life which I'm sure that Julie and Matthew would want you to have."

Moore listened.

"You're going to see these two professionals tonight and work with them for the next week. It'll help get you started on the right path, but you have to do your part. Tomorrow, I want you in my office at 9:00 a.m. sharp. I'm putting you on unofficial probation. That will be between you and me. If you blow it, I'll fire you."

Moore nodded his understanding as Sedler turned his head briefly to look at him.

"I'm going to have you stop by human resources and get you set up on a leave of absence through FMLA. Then, you're going to return home and call your aunt. After you express your sympathy, you're going to tell her you're flying out to spend some time with her in Put-in-Bay. That way you both can help each other recover and deal with your grief. And you'll be away from the bars here in D.C."

"I can do that."

"You better because you have no choice in the matter," Sedler grumbled.

Moore thought it would be wise not to tell Sedler that Put-in-Bay had a reputation for being the "Key West of the Midwest" and had a bevy of bars. As they drove, he decided he would give it a try. He couldn't imagine a future without Julie and Matthew, but Sedler was right – they wouldn't want to see him throw his life away. He didn't want to lose his job and he loved Aunt Anne. Maybe it was time to return to South Bass Island, he thought.

Book Three
Dehumanization
2013

Ten Years Later

Aunt Anne's House
Put-in-Bay

The Jet Express slowed as it rounded Gibraltar Island and headed for its dock in Put-in-Bay, the idyllic island paradise set on South Bass Island in the western basin of Lake Erie. From his aunt's dock on East Point, Moore watched as the Jet Express moved gracefully through the calm waters of the bay. His eyes roved over the sailboats at their moorings and the docks filled with rowdy party animals and their watercraft. He looked at the Boardwalk and The Keys, two of his favorite restaurant/bar complexes on the island.

The Keys, located next to the Jet Express dock, was a complex of restaurants, brightly painted in Caribbean hues. Moore enjoyed the grounds which were a mixture of lush tropical plants, colorful umbrellas over outdoor tables and chairs painted in bright lime green, turquoise, tangerine and lemon yellow. On particularly hot days, he'd pull a chair close to one of the water misters to revel in its cooling relief.

As he surveyed the magical setting in front of him, Moore thought how glad he was Sedler suggested he visit his aunt as part of his grief recuperation process. It had been some time ago and he had made the permanent move to the island to live with his aunt. Sedler had been supportive, as it didn't matter where the forty-two-year-old investigative reporter resided.

High energy and 70ish, Aunt Anne had welcomed her nephew to her home. Between the two of them, they managed to overcome their losses of a husband, wife and son. Moore was also finally able to come to grips with the haunting role he had played in the death of his cousin during his final visit to the island as a teen.

Glancing at his watch, Moore stood and walked around the cozy two-story house and to the garage. He always smiled when he saw the 1929 Ford Model A truck parked inside. It had belonged to his uncle when he was alive. His aunt knew how much Moore loved the old vehicle and had assigned it to Moore's care. He didn't let her down. He maintained the vehicle and kept it spotless.

Today, he was driving out to the airport where he was going to spend some time with Ray Grissett, the owner of Miracle Airlines. Their motto was *If we land in one piece, it's a miracle.*

As he drove the Model A, he reminisced about meeting Grissett several months ago when he was in Egypt. Grissett had flown him to Bodrum, Turkey, in a twin engine plane with one unreliable engine. Grissett had constantly encouraged Moore to pray during the flight; something for which Moore needed no encouragement. Grissett's unnerving tactics had been a serious concern of Moore's – and it didn't help matters when Grissett joked incessantly about problems with his plane.

Grissett, who usually found himself in trouble with the Egyptian and Turkish authorities, had decided to return to the United States. Relying on Moore's comments about Put-in-Bay, Grissett relocated his operations to beautiful South Bass Island.

Moore had been surprised when village council member and *Put-in-Bay Gazette* publisher Barry Hayen had told Moore a few months earlier about the island's new air service provider. Parking the Model A next to the hangar that housed Grissett's plane, Moore started to walk toward it. He stopped when he heard hammering and loud voices coming from one of the apartments over the airport operations' office.

He climbed the stairs to the second floor and walked into the open door of the apartment as he recognized the two voices.

"I'm telling you it won't work that way. Here's what you have to do."

Moore grinned as he saw legendary island singer Mike "Mad

Dog" Adams holding a piece of copper pipe. Moore and the brawny Mad Dog had become close friends from their first encounter on the island even though their styles were different.

In contrast to Moore's tee shirt and khaki shorts attire, Adams wore black jean shorts and a black Harley Davidson tank top. The front of the shirt read "Wanna be my beer babe?" Adams also had an earring in one ear. Under his white ball cap, a ponytail hung from the back of his head.

The other occupant of the room was Ray Grissett, the quirky owner of Miracle Airlines. The slim man wore a soiled New York Yankees baseball cap, greasy tee shirt and worn khaki shorts.

"What are you two doing?" Moore asked as he looked at the two men standing in front of a small wooden kitchen table. On the table were a box fan, plastic tubing, a coil of copper pipe and an aquarium pump.

"Looky here. Iffen it ain't my favorite passenger," Grissett said as he straightened up and walked over to greet Moore. "It's about time you got your butt over here to welcome me. I'm here, you know, because of all the great stuff you told me about this oasis."

"I'm not sure about that. I'd say you're here because you smelled a business opportunity with the high tourist traffic we have here."

"Never entered my pea-sized mind," Grissett said as he snickered at being found out.

"Did you voluntarily leave Egypt?" Moore asked.

"You betcha. I left voluntarily before they involuntarily took my plane and locked me up."

"Drug running?" Moore asked.

"Nope, although I could've made a killing with my Turkish contacts. Probably should've."

"What was it then? I know there's more to it than your wanting to be near me," Moore teased.

"That's it. I wanted to be near a fun guy like you, Emerson. And that's all I'm going to say on this topic."

Moore shook his head from side to side as he realized that Grissett wasn't going to tell him the real reason why he left Egypt. "So, what are you two up to?"

Adams spoke first. "We're building him an air conditioner."

"Yep, the one in the winder is broke. Sort of like me," Grissett said as he took the coil and started to wrap it vertically around the box fan.

"I'm telling you it won't work that way, Ray," Adams said, exasperated.

Grissett stopped. "Why not?"

"How are you going to set the fan up when you've got the pipe lifting the fan's stand off the table? You have to wrap the copper pipe horizontally, Ray. Would you just listen to me?" Adams asked the quirky Grissett.

Grissett looked at the fan and saw what Adams was saying. "I knew that. I was just seeing iffen you'd catch it," Grissett said as he unwrapped the copper and then began rewrapping it horizontally in a spiral around the fan.

Adams threw Moore an all-knowing look. Moore grinned and shrugged his shoulders in response.

"Let me read the instructions for building this contraption," Grissett said as he grabbed a nearby pair of glasses and placed them on his face. He then started reading the instructions that Adams had written.

"Oh, no!" Grissett said.

"What's wrong now?" Adams asked.

"Something's wrong. My vision's blurred. Everything's gone fuzzy on me." Grissett looked around the room with a panicked look on his face.

Adams snatched the glasses off Grissett's face. "Give me those. You put on my reading glasses. Here's your glasses," Adams said as he picked up a pair from an end table.

"Thanks, Mike. I was worried. Real worried."

Moore chuckled. "Watching you two work is funnier than watching Laurel and Hardy," he quipped.

"Funny," Grissett said as he found what he was looking for in the instructions and took off his glasses.

Adams just smiled.

The three men then attached two pieces of plastic tubing to the ends of the copper pipe and connected the other ends of the tubing to an old fish tank pump that Grissett had found in the nearby hangar. Then, Grissett grabbed the power cord for the pump and started to plug it into an electrical outlet.

"Wait a second, Ray. You've got to put water in the line first!" Adams said. "How in the world do you maintain your airplane? You do put oil in the engine, don't you?"

"Yep. I was just testing you to see iffen you were paying attention," Grissett responded.

Moore saw a bucket on the floor and grabbed it. "I'll get some water." Moore saw the bucket wouldn't fit in the small kitchen sink and walked into the bathroom. It wouldn't fit there either. Moore cast a glance at the shower and shook his head.

"Got a problem there, don't ya?" Grissett grinned from behind Moore.

Moore turned around and saw Grissett holding a dust pan.

Perplexed, Moore asked, "And what am I supposed to do with that?"

"You'll see."

"This is going to be interesting," Adams said sardonically as he stood in the doorway and watched.

Grissett took the dust pan and stuck the wide part under the faucet. He allowed the trough-type handle to hang over the edge of the sink.

"Set the bucket here on the floor," he instructed Moore. After Moore did as he was told, Grissett turned on the water. The water flowed onto the dust pan, down the handle and streamed into the bucket on the floor. "See how easy that is!" Grissett said proudly.

"Clever," Moore agreed.

"If it was me, I'd just get a pan full of water at the kitchen sink," Adams offered.

"I guess that would have been easier," Moore concurred.

"I'm getting in a habit of bailing Ray out all of the time," Adams teased.

Grissett turned off the water and took the half-full bucket of water to the table where their cooling contraption waited. As he poured the water into the plastic tube which Adams was holding, Grissett said, "I've only been on this island a short time and I figured I should make Mad Dog feel wanted."

"Oh, Ray. You don't have to worry about Mad Dog being wanted. During his show at the Round House, all of the women want Mad Dog," Moore joked.

"Yeah," Adams agreed. "They want me to choose their friend and not themselves to join me on the stage for the blowing of the conch shell." With the lines full of water, Adams connected the tube to the fish tank pump. "You can plug in the pump and the fan now, Ray."

Grissett did as he was instructed and then turned on both devices.

"It'll take a few minutes, but then we should have a cool breeze blowing," Adams said.

Grissett reached for his nearby glass of beer and took a sip. Holding the glass, he started to walk across the room where he didn't see a foot stool on the floor. He tripped over the stool and fell.

"You okay, Ray?" Moore asked as he walked over to help Grissett to his feet.

"Forget Ray. More importantly, did you spill any beer?" Adams had a way of focusing on the real issues.

Moore shot Adams a surprised look as he helped Grissett stand.

"Not a drop," Grissett said as he took another sip.

Adams looked at his watch. "I'd better go, Ray. I've got a meeting."

"Okay, don't be late for your meeting."

"I'd better go, too," Moore said. "Welcome to the island, Ray. I'll be sure to stop back."

"Do that and be sure to tell people here to use my flight service."

"Will do," Moore responded as he and Adams walked out of the apartment and down the stairs.

"Need a ride, Mike?" Moore asked.

"Sure if you can drop me off at the art center."

"How did you meet Grissett?" Moore asked as the two sat in the antique truck and Moore started its engine before pulling onto Langram Road.

"I hired him to fly me to Algonac for a last-minute show."

"Did you fly in that four-seater? I think it was a Piper Twin Comanche."

"Yeah. Quite a flight."

"Yeah, any flight with him is quite a flight – and you never are quite sure when he's kidding you."

Adams smiled. "How do you know him?"

"I met him in Egypt and flew with him. Then, he helped get me out of a jam in Turkey."

"He puts jam on his turkey?" Adams teased.

"No, no," Moore started.

"I'm just teasing you, Emerson," Adams laughed. "You're way too serious all the time."

"Why are you going to the art center?"

"I've got my first art class to make. I'm taking up painting."

"You're taking up painting?" Moore asked incredulously as they drove past a golf cart filled with screaming island visitors.

"Yeah."

"I didn't know you like to paint."

"I've had enough experience painting garages; I figured I'll transition to the fancy stuff."

"Oh. What's today's assignment – boats, Perry's Monument, seascapes?" Moore asked.

"Today's nude model day," Adams grinned. "Why do you think I signed up?"

"You're going to start doing nudes?"

"You want to rephrase that, Emerson?" Adams chuckled. "Oh, I could just have some fun now with some unbelievable comeback lines, but I'll do my best to hold off since it's you, Emerson."

Realizing what he had said, Moore grinned sheepishly and rephrased the question. "I mean, you're going to paint nudes?"

"It depends. I figure I'll take my time studying the model. Make sure I get the right angle if you know what I mean?"

"Yes."

"I don't expect I'll get my painting done on time. She'll probably have to stay after class for me," he snickered.

The truck stopped in front of the art center. Moore spoke as Adams stepped out of the truck, "Have fun!"

"Oh, you can count on that!" the affable Adams smiled as he walked toward the building's entrance.

As Moore drove along Bayview and enjoyed his life in the bucolic paradise, his attention was drawn across DeRivera Park to the flashing red lights of the EMS ambulance. It was parked next door to T&J's Smokehouse. Two Put-in-Bay police cars were parked next to it.

Moore turned right on Hartford Avenue and pulled into a vacant parking spot across from the Boathouse Bar and Restaurant. Exiting the truck, he walked down the street to the pavilion where several policemen and bystanders were clustered together. As he neared the pavilion, he saw the EMS crew kneeling on the ground. They were working on a woman.

Moore saw his friend Tim Niese, who with his sons owned T&J's Smokehouse and several other major island properties, in the crowd and walked over to him.

"What happened?"

"Not sure. A couple saw this teen on the ground and yelled for help. We all came running," Niese explained.

Moore looked at the young, brown-haired woman on the ground. She appeared to be in her late teens. He didn't recognize her.

Suddenly a tall, dark haired man in his twenties ran up to the group. He cried out, "Sneky, what have they done to you?"

It was then that Moore recognized the man. It was Angel Dudich, the wine steward at Port Clinton's Mon Ami Restaurant and Winery, another of Moore's favorite haunts.

Dropping to the ground next to her, Dudich moaned when he saw his sister was unresponsive.

"We've called life-flight and they are on their way," one of the EMS crew said.

"Is she going to be okay?" Dudich asked.

"We're doing everything we can," he responded as they lifted her onto a gurney, leaving a pool of blood on the ground. They wheeled her to the ambulance with Dudich following. Within minutes, the ambulance with its siren shrieking headed to the Put-in-Bay airport where she would be life-flighted to Magruder Hospital in Port Clinton.

The police officers began moving the crowd away as they cordoned off the area as a crime scene.

"You can put that away," one officer said to a rough-looking man, who had been taking photos of the victim.

"Be glad to, officer," the man responded with a hint of sarcasm in his voice. The man grabbed the arm of the equally rough-looking woman next to him and started to stride away. The woman had a long scar on the side of her face.

As Moore and Niese walked toward the entrance to T&J's Smokehouse, Moore asked Niese, "Aren't you friends with Angel?"

"Good memory," Niese said as they entered the Smokehouse, the island's only country western bar and smokehouse, and headed to the bar. "Angel used to work for me until he took the job on the mainland. It was better for him since it was year-round employment."

"He's a good guy. I love his Bulgarian accent," Moore commented.

"So do his female customers. Drink?" Niese asked as Moore sat on a bar stool and looked around the remodeled facility. The former Crescent Tavern had gone through a huge makeover when Niese and his sons took ownership a couple of years ago.

"Sure, Pepsi."

"You must be working."

"I just might be," Moore said as he took the cold drink that Niese handed him. "Any idea what happened out there?"

"Now that I know it was Angel's sister, I might. Angel had called to see if I was going to be around today. He wanted to bring his sister out to the island, show her around and stop by to say hello."

"So, they never made it in to see you?"

"No. You know the story about his sister?" Niese asked between sips of his drink.

"Not really. I didn't know he had a sister until today."

"She lived in Bulgaria with her roommate. Their parents had passed away, so she was pretty much on her own. She went out one night to a nightclub and that was the last her roommate heard about her. She disappeared."

Moore wrinkled his brow.

"Then, she reappeared in Toledo. From what Angel told me, she had been drugged at the Bulgarian nightclub and ended up in the sex slave industry. Apparently, her pimp brought her into the country to Toledo and sold her body until she escaped."

"That's terrible. How ironic she ended up in Toledo!"

"Yeah, one of the United States' major gateways to human trafficking," Niese said. "Lucky for her she had family here. She borrowed somebody's cell phone and called Angel and he drove the fifty minutes to get her. He brought her back to Port Clinton and was working on getting immigration papers filed so she could remain in the U.S."

"Did they ever get her pimp?" Moore knew Niese was well-connected with law enforcement officials since he had worked for the Sandusky Police Department before becoming one of the biggest entrepreneurs on the island.

"Don't know."

Moore had flashbacks to his days in Vukovar and the Vuk's involvement with human trafficking. He had been reading articles about it over the years, but now his interest was piqued.

"Tim, you know everybody. Can you hook me up with anyone in law enforcement in Toledo I can interview?"

"Thinking of writing about human trafficking?" Niese asked.

"Maybe. I need to clear it with my editor and I want to talk to Angel's sister," Moore responded as he finished his drink.

"Let me think about who would be best for you to call. I'll get back to you," Niese said as Emerson walked toward the doorway.

"Thanks, Tim," Emerson said as he left.

Leaving the restaurant, Moore drove back to his aunt's house and parked the truck in the garage. He walked around the house and took a seat in one of the lawn chairs overlooking the bay. Pulling out his cell phone, he speed-dialed John Sedler.

"Sedler here," he answered with a tone of annoyance. He didn't like being interrupted when he was reviewing stories for the next edition.

"John, it's Emerson."

The annoyance disappeared and was replaced by genuine interest. "Emerson! And how is life in your island paradise? I don't know why I agreed to let you work from there," he teased.

"Sunny skies, nice breeze and a beautiful view of the boats in the bay," he cheerfully responded.

"Methinks you mean boats, babes and booze although I trust you've got the booze still under control."

"Definitely," Moore responded.

Sedler was glad to hear the continued positive change in Moore as he continued to progress in his recovery. "What's up?"

"I may have a line on a story."

"Go on."

"I just learned Toledo, which is about fifty minutes from here, is one of the major human trafficking gateways to the U.S."

Sedler's fingers flew across his keyboard as he called up a map of Toledo. "Wouldn't surprise me with its proximity to Canada," he said as he reviewed the map. "Go ahead and check it out and let me know what you find."

"There's a local angle, too."

"What do you mean?"

"One of the locals here has a sister who escaped from the traffickers. I'm going to chase that down and see what I can learn. It may take me into the thick of it."

"Like I said, go ahead."

"Great. Thanks, John. I'll be in touch." Moore ended the call and walked into the house where his Aunt Anne greeted him.

"Emerson, did you hear about the excitement in town?"

"At the pavilion?"

"Yes."

"I should have known you would. You always seem to be in the right place at the right time."

"Not always," he said as he took the steps to his second floor bedroom. He planned on spending some time on his laptop, researching human trafficking.

The Next Morning
Topsy Turvey's Island Grill

Having parked his golf cart in one of the vacant spots in front of Wharfside on Bayview Avenue, Moore entered the marina store next to the Boardwalk. He walked to the rear of the store and into Topsy Turvey's Island Grill, overlooking the waterfront.

"Mad Dog," Moore said in surprise as he spied Adams seated at the bar.

"Morning," Adams said as he took a quick glance at his watch and saw it wasn't noon yet. "Join me for a Bloody Mary?" Before Moore could say anything, Adams turned to the bartender and said, "Gary, give my friend here a Bloody Mary."

The bartender, Gary Milson, nodded his head and reached for a glass.

"Whoa, Gary. Not this early for me. Just give me a Pepsi."

"Wimp!" Adams teased.

"I try to be very careful with my alcohol intake," Moore said. "Remember I had a drinking problem some time ago."

"Yeah. Yeah. But don't say I didn't tell you so, they have one of the best Bloody Marys on the island."

"That we do," a voice said behind Moore. "And I've seen Emerson drink one in the past."

Moore turned on his bar stool and saw the owner, David Hill, behind him. "Hi, David. I love them."

Hill grinned and moved on to check on a couple of customers.

Moore turned back as Milson placed his drink in front of him. "Emerson, would you like a menu?" he asked.

"No, I'll take one of your Cuban sandwiches."

"Can't go wrong there," Adams said between bites of his sandwich. "That's what I'm devouring."

"So tell me. How did your nude painting session go last night?"

Moore asked inquisitively.

"I really don't want to talk about it."

"What's wrong? Did you get into trouble?"

"Nah."

"Was she pretty?"

"She was a 'he.' I quit the class. I'll just stick with painting garages."

Moore roared with laughter.

A few minutes later, Milson returned with Moore's Cuban and set it in front of him. Moore picked it up and took a bite of the tasty sandwich.

Adams, who had finished his Cuban, turned around on his bar stool to look out over the waterfront as he drank his Bloody Mary. "I bumped into one of Put-in-Bay's finest this morning. An old buddy of mine," Adams said as he referred to Put-in-Bay's police force.

"He said yesterday was an extremely unusual day on the island for them."

"How's that?" Moore asked between bites.

"There was a stabbing over by the pavilion by T&J's Smokehouse." Before Moore could tell Adams he was there, Adams continued. "The young woman died."

"That was the sister of a friend of mine," Moore said. "I'm going to need to give him a call."

"Sorry to hear that," Adams said. "Then, two teens disappeared."

"Oh?"

"Yeah, they were up here with some high school friends for the day. Somehow they got separated and their friends couldn't find the two when they had to take the Miller Ferry back to the mainland."

"Did they file a missing persons report?"

"I asked the same question, but he said that you've got to wait a couple of days before you can make a filing. They did take the report and asked them to send them a picture of the two teens. Then, they're going to comb the island to see if they can find them."

"That's terrible."

"Yes, it is." Adams looked at his watch again. "Got to run. Got to meet with some folks."

Moore bid him good-bye, finished his sandwich, paid his bill and returned to his aunt's house. There, he called Tim Niese and obtained the phone number of an FBI agent, who was involved with the Human Trafficking Task Force in Toledo. He called the man and set up an appointment for that afternoon.

An hour later, Moore drove his Mustang convertible to catch the Miller Ferry to the mainland. As he approached the ticket booth, Dale McKee waved him down. McKee was the general manager for Island Transportation, the bus service from the Miller Ferry to downtown Put-in-Bay.

"Emerson!" he shouted as Moore started to ease his car to the ticket booth.

McKee raced across the drive to Moore. He had been a sprinter in high school and still was able to cover ground quickly. He was one of the island's many characters and hard to forget with his easy smile, cigar clenched permanently between his teeth, mirrored sunglasses and thick head of silver hair. Moore often wondered to himself if McKee wore those sunglasses to bed at night.

"What's up?"

"Did you hear what's going on at The Butterfly House?"

"No."

"DEA agents are there. Chip and Mike drove over to see what it was about," McKee said breathlessly. He was referring to the two co-owners of Island Transportation and The Butterfly House at Put-in-Bay – Chip Duggan and Mike Steidl.

"Thanks for the tip," Moore said as he pulled his car out of line. "I'll go check it out."

Moore turned onto Langram Road and drove to Meechen Road where he made a left turn. When he reached Catawba Avenue, he turned right and drove to The Butterfly House at Put-in-Bay located on the grounds of Perry's Cave Family Fun Center, a tree-shaded mecca for kids with its putt-putt course, cave tours, laser tag and maze.

He turned left into the first drive and found a parking spot. He then walked over to where a number of DEA Suburbans were parked next to the 5,000 square-foot wooden-sided building with a dark maroon steel roof.

As he neared the building, he could see a number of DEA agents carrying boxes from the second building attached to the rear of the main structure. They were loading them in the rear of a couple of their Suburbans.

"Is there something I can help you with?" an approaching agent asked Moore.

Producing his press card, Moore responded, "I'm with *The Washington Post.*"

With a surprised look, the agent said, "Didn't take you guys long to get here!"

Moore grinned. "I live here and I'm friends with the owners."

"I can't let you go back there." He pointed to the area where the boxes were being loaded in the SUV. "You can go inside the store, but the agents inside won't let you go out back."

"That's fine," Moore said.

Moore walked through the covered porch full of rocking chairs and entered the building. The gift shop in the front had the normal "touristy" souvenirs like key rings, mugs, pins, magnets, jewelry and tee shirts. It also had garden decorations, house flags and wind-socks, educational toys, books, stained glass pieces, Fenton glass and Irish Belleek china. One section of wall was filled completely with beautiful butterfly specimens framed under glass, including a couple of tarantulas.

He walked across the honey-blond, wide-planked hickory floor to where the two owners were standing. "Looks like you've had some excitement this afternoon."

The pony-tailed Steidl was the first to respond. "Yeah, they've been here for about four hours."

"Drugs?" Moore guessed.

"Cocaine," the lanky Duggan answered. "Tell him about it, Mike."

"I'll take you out back when these guys leave," Steidl said, motioning to a DEA agent, who was guarding the entrance and exit areas for the 4,000 square-foot glass greenhouse. It housed from 400 to 500 butterflies, comprised of about 50 different species imported from butterfly farms in Costa Rica and Malaysia.

"Looks like a guy we hired this spring had somebody working with him at the butterfly farm in Malaysia. They had built a false bottom in the shipping containers and filled it with cocaine."

"Really! How did you find the drugs?" Moore asked.

"The guy called off sick today and I went back there to cover," Steidl explained.

"Yeah, and it's a good thing he can be clumsy at times," Duggan commented, familiarly. Steidl was married to Duggan's sister, Dee Dee, the third co-owner of The Butterfly House.

Steidl smiled. "I accidently knocked over one of the empty containers. When I went to pick it up I noticed the bottom seemed to have been dislodged. So, I checked it out and found the false bottom. I pulled it up and found bags of cocaine. We called over to Toledo right away and these folks showed up within two hours."

"That's amazing," Moore said. "What happened to the guy?"

"They don't know. They went to his rental unit on the island, but he wasn't there."

"Was he a local?"

"Not with that accent!" Duggan laughed.

"He was from Toledo. That should have been my first reason not to hire him," Steidl joked.

One of the agents approached the two owners and spoke. "We're done for now. We completed our forensics and photos. We're heading back to Toledo."

"Thanks," Steidl said.

"We'll be in touch and let us know if Panich shows up," the agent said as he left.

"Will do," Steidl responded.

"Panich?" Moore asked.

"Yeah. That's the guy from Toledo we hired."

"Is he Serbian?" Moore asked.

"Something like that."

Moore felt a chill run up his spine. His gut was telling him there was more to this than met the eye.

"Want to see the containers?" Steidl asked.

"Sure," Moore said.

Looking at his watch, Duggan said, "I'm going to pass. I'd better get back to the tour train." He was referring to the tour trains that their family operated to give island visitors a guided tour of South Bass Island.

Duggan left them and the two walked to the rear of the gift shop and through the first door of a double-doored entry hallway. Moore saw a sign labeled Clean Room.

"We'll go in there, but I thought you might want to peek into the greenhouse first." He looked back to make sure that the first door had closed. "Can't open this door until that one closes. Don't want any fugitive butterflies to make a break for it," he explained.

Steidl opened the second door and they walked into the butterfly exhibit through an air curtain, designed to blow any would-be-escapees to the floor. Immediately, they were surrounded by fluttering butterflies

"Friendly little critters," Moore said as they fluttered around him.

"You'll have to be careful when you leave. They like to try to hitchhike a ride out of the greenhouse."

"Sure are a lot of them!" Moore said in amazement.

Moore smiled as he looked around the exhibit which had a number of walkways, trees, plants, grasses and a wooden pergola covered with dried palms for shade. A waterfall structure at the back of the space provided a beautiful backdrop as well as soothing background noise in the room maintained at about 80 degrees.

"The USDA regulates us and all the plants and flowers you see. Because we are an exhibitor and not a breeder, all our plants are only for feeding purposes. They're not host plants where the butterflies can lay their eggs. They only provide nectar for the butterflies."

Steidl pointed at several feeders. "Those feeders are filled with rotten bananas and oranges so the butterflies can get their sugar fix."

"I see."

"Follow me and make sure no one is hitching a ride on you. You can use the mirrors on the wall to check yourself," Steidl said as they headed for the exit door and through another air curtain. He opened the door to the Clean Room and they walked in, closing the door behind them.

"This is the room where we handle all incoming shipments."

"Why is it so stark white in here?" Moore asked.

"It's supposed to make it easier to see 'hitchhiking' pests or parasites which may find their way into the imported packages and maybe out into our clean room.

"We are required to have a freezer and an autoclave. The freezer holds deceased, partially emerged or deformed butterflies. The autoclave is for burning as an alternative to freezing the remains. We have to have sanitary sinks, hot water, of course, and plenty of bleach and sanitizer to help prevent the spread of any parasites or diseases.

"Our shipments come in every week. The butterflies are packaged as pupae in a chrysalis, sort of like a moth's cocoon. The Malaysian shipment comes packed in styrofoam trays. Each species are laid out and labeled appropriately. The packaging keeps them cool to prevent them from emerging while in transit. If they emerge while shipping, they will die because there will be no air for them to breathe or space to open their wings. Sometimes, parasites kill them in transit.

"Once we open the packages, we inspect, inventory and hang the chrysalises. Most species get attached to a strip of paper towel hanging across the mouth of a plastic cup, but some of the larger species get pinned to a board in the hatching cabinet so they have ample room to hang and spread the blood to their wings upon emerging."

Moore nodded his head as he listened.

"Once the butterflies emerge, they are taken to the greenhouse in their cups and released into the exhibit. Unfortunately, butterflies only live about 3-4 weeks, which is why we need weekly shipments to keep up the population."

Steidl looked at Moore. "I've probably told you more than you ever wanted to know about butterflies."

"No, it was interesting. Do you have any of the Malaysian containers?" Moore asked.

Steidl looked around the room. "Doesn't look like it. They must have taken them as evidence." He walked over to a bulletin board and pointed. "Here's a picture of one of the containers. You can see they are typically anywhere between the size of a 6-pack and a 12-pack. They are usually wrapped in clear packing tape over plain brown wrapping, with a variety of different labels indicating 'live species, keep from freezing,' stuff like that. They also have red and white import labels and stamps from the various government entities which had inspected the shipment."

"And they got though the inspections?" Moore wondered aloud.

"Yes, amazing isn't it?"

Moore looked at his watch. "Mike, I've got to get to Toledo for a meeting. Can you let me know if anything develops?"

"Sure, Emerson. I'd be happy to let you know," Steidl responded.

Escorted by Steidl, Moore left the Clean Room and exited the remaining double door. He then hurried to his car and caught the next ferry. When they arrived on the mainland, Moore drove quickly toward Route 2 for Toledo. As he drove, he called his contact at the Human Trafficking Task Force to let him know he might be late.

An hour and a half later, Moore was seated in the Human Trafficking Task Force's office on Summit Street, overlooking the Maumee River. Sitting at the desk in front of him was the team's second-in-command, Brad Mullen. He was in his forties with dark hair, brown eyes and a graying goatee. He was on loan to the Task Force from the FBI. He had also worked for the Toledo Police Department.

"Thank you for making time for me today," Moore started.

"It worked out. I had a meeting cancel and was available. Tim Niese also called me on your behalf. You know I just love what he has done with that swim-up bar at Splash."

"He sure does have a knack for being innovative," Moore agreed. Then, Moore focused on his reason for meeting with Mullen. "I'm researching human trafficking for a story for *The Washington Post* and Tim thought you might be able to give me some insight. I did a little research online, but I like to get my information first-hand."

"I understand."

"Frankly, I was shocked to see what a role Ohio plays in human trafficking. Why is that?" Moore asked as he pulled a pad of paper from his briefcase and prepared to take notes.

"There are several reasons why you see so much trafficking in Ohio and why Toledo has become one of the key gateway cities for trafficking. We're close to the Canadian border so victims can be brought in through Michigan or across Lake Erie."

"They're coming in by boat?" Moore asked as he took notes.

"You'll see some of them. Customs agents board each freighter coming in and check their paperwork. Some are drugged and are inside the shipping containers. Others are transferred to pleasure craft out in the lake and brought in less conspicuously."

"Then they're shipped around the United States?"

"Some are. Some stay in this area. Toledo is strategically located near the crossroads of two major highway systems. You've got the Ohio Turnpike, running east and west, and the I-75 corridor, running south through Florida."

"When I did some research on this, I was surprised by the cheap labor part of trafficking," Moore mentioned as he looked at his notes.

"A lot of people are. They think sex slaves and forget the other side. Ohio's strong agricultural market in corn and soybeans helps drive the need for cheap labor. That's why you'll see more than 130 migrant labor camps in the state. You'll see a lot of illegal immigrants trafficked into agriculture, the textile industry, landscaping and small factory jobs," Mullen explained.

"Some of these illegal immigrants pay to come into the country and then have to pay back the transportation costs to the trafficker. They become nothing more than indentured servants and they think they can't complain because they're here illegally. They're paid less than minimum wage, get no overtime, are forced to work long hours and get limited meal breaks. Then, their paychecks are reduced for amounts allegedly owed to their trafficker."

"And they get these people from all around the world," Moore said as he thought back to his research.

"The entire world is at their beck and call."

"So, the United States is the major delivery point for the traffickers?" Moore asked.

"No, we're second. Germany is first."

"I guess I missed that in my research," Moore said as he looked up from his note taking.

"Then there's the sexual market. It's prostitution, pornography, servile marriage and sexual servitude. Did you know Ohio is ranked fifth in the United States for the largest number of strip clubs?"

"I had no idea. And I didn't realize the women in those establishments were part of the trafficking. I thought you'd see single moms trying to earn money for their kids or girls trying to work their way through college."

"There's some of that. But, there's the trafficking side where the women are forced to be there. Then you've got the massage parlors that operate as fronts for prostitution. You can see a lot of illegal Asians and Eastern Europeans working in those places."

"I've seen several newspaper stories about that. It seems like you read about raids every few months," Moore said.

"I'd like to see the newspapers publish the picture of the johns they find in the parlors. And you get all kinds like businessmen, law enforcement officers, lawyers, teachers, clergy, politicians, government workers, military men, truck drivers and migrant workers. We've identified at least one massage parlor in every major city in Ohio and many in proximity to highways for easy access for its clientele."

"And you still have the streetwalkers," Moore added.

"Yes, the independents and those managed by their pimps or traffickers. One thing we do track is the backgrounds of the people we bust. For example, the primary users of prostitutes in Cleveland are businessmen and law enforcement officers."

"I didn't know that." Moore's face registered a look of surprise at hearing the comment about law enforcement officials.

"It's surprising. We track it by category throughout the state." Mullen took a sip of his coffee as he watched Moore scribbling in his notepad. "We also have a problem with domestic trafficking of teens."

Moore looked up from his notepad. "That's the part that really troubles me. Preying on kids."

"It bothers all of us. Girls between the ages of eleven and fifteen are the prime targets. Many of them come from dysfunctional families. They may have been sexually abused or lived in poverty or they're runaways, throwaways or homeless. In one Toledo study, 91% were victims of abuse. They suffered from neglect, physical abuse, and sexual abuse. Fifty-seven percent had been raped by someone outside of their family, 29% were raped by someone inside their family, and 14% were raped by both.

"Their stories are sad. Some kids started prostituting themselves at age 11 because the parents used all their money for drugs. There wasn't any food in the house, no lights or gas. In some cases, mothers permitted the fathers to abuse their children because they were afraid the husband would leave them.

"Traffickers often prey on troubled minors because of the ease of isolating them from family and friends. They could manipulate them and exploit their dependency on an adult. The women and children are dehumanized and turned into marketable commodities where they often feel that's their place in life. In Ohio, a child disappears every forty seconds."

"That's horrific," Moore said as he continued to take notes.

"And that's an understatement," Mullen said. "The traffickers are master manipulators and can easily spot potential victims. They manipulate young girls into selling sexual services and giving the money to the trafficker. A lot of times, the pimp finds a girl, who doesn't have any self esteem or money. He then tells her how beautiful she is. He'll buy her clothes and pay for makeover sessions. It makes the girls happy.

"Then, one day, they lower the boom and tell the girls they owe them money and they have to work it off. It's a 'bait and switch' technique. Get the girls' attention and trust by 'baiting' her with gifts and money, and then 'switching' the situation to get payback. It all works in the favor of the trafficker."

Moore nodded as he listened. "I've read about the use of threats or violence."

"That's called 'guerilla pimping.' The traffickers use a soft approach to recruit a girl. They promise the girls a slice of heaven, but end up giving them a dose of hell. Then when the girl is in a controlled environment like their basement, they force the girl to work by using threats, physical violence, and intimidation. They'll even threaten to go back to the girl's home and kill her parents or sister. Stuff like that," Mullen explained.

Mullen continued. "There was an Operation Precious Cargo in Harrisburg, Pennsylvania, a few years ago. The investigation resulted in identifying 151 victims of prostitution. Forty-five of them were children. Seventy-eight of the 151 identified victims were from Toledo. The youngest was a twelve-year-old."

"That's heartbreaking," Moore said, stunned.

"Of the eighteen traffickers indicted, only one was from outside of Toledo. Sixteen of the traffickers pleaded guilty and received sentences of up to twenty-five years in prison. Two traffickers were found guilty at their trials and were sentenced between thirty-five and forty-five years in prison. Trafficking is a felony in Ohio."

Mullen handed Moore a file from his desk. "Here's some more information I thought you'd like to review. There are a couple of studies the University of Toledo and The Lucas County Human Trafficking Coalition developed. I listed some websites you may want to check."

"Great. This is a good start. What about the girls who are rescued? What happens to them?" Moore asked.

"It depends. Some go to rescue homes like Second Chance. Group homes seem to work the best for helping them transition away from their ordeals. Placing them in a foster home can be difficult because many of these rescued girls were raised in a tough home environment. They have a hard time adjusting to life in an *Ozzie and Harriet*-type of home. It's too difficult. The group homes are the best."

"I guess that would be difficult for them," Moore agreed.

Mullen nodded his head, then asked, "So, what else can I do to help you?"

Moore glanced at the files. "First, I want to go through this material and then I'll know what my next steps should be." Moore stood. "Thanks for taking the time to help educate me."

"No problem. You're going to help us by creating more press on this. Helping you with a story to educate the public and create awareness helps us in our efforts to free the girls and prosecute the traffickers."

After shaking hands, Moore left and headed back to Port Clinton and Catawba to catch the return ferry. As he drove along Route 2, he made a few phone calls. One was to get the phone number and address for Angel Dudich. He wanted to see how Angel was handling his sister's death.

As he neared Port Clinton, he took the Route 163 exit and drove along West Lake Shore Drive so he could enjoy the views of Lake Erie. He crossed the drawbridge and followed the road to the intersection with Madison Avenue. Turning left, he found a parking spot and walked into Kokomo Bay restaurant.

This harbor town restaurant was located steps away from the Portage River and the Jet Express dock in downtown Port Clinton. It was part of owner Bill Juhasz's complex which included a nightclub named Mango Mamas and The Great Lakes Popcorn Company, known for its tasty gourmet popcorn. Moore made a mental note to himself to pick up a large bag of their red-white-blue nutty vanilla popcorn for his aunt.

The friendly Juhasz spotted Moore when he entered. "Emerson, it's been awhile," he said as he escorted Moore to a table near the window overlooking the fish market. "What have you been up to?"

After Moore told Juhasz about his research on human trafficking, he looked at the menu and ordered a perch basket. When Juhasz returned with the fish and his Pepsi, Moore asked, "Is The Island Doctor singing tonight?" Moore was referring to island singer Scott Alan, who sang Caribbean and island tunes.

"Not tonight. He was here last night and we were packed," Juhasz said.

"I bet you were. I love his singing. There's just something about him that makes me sit back and veg out," Moore said.

"And his female fans were out of control. It was Fans Gone Wild night!" Juhasz grinned.

Moore nodded. "I've never seen anyone with so many groupies!" Moore said. In the past, he had witnessed females throwing themselves at the singer known for his good looks and captivating charm.

The Island Doctor dressed the part with a straw beach hat, colorful aloha shirts and shorts. He had the knack for getting the audience out of their seats and participating in limbo contests and conga lines. It was pure island fun!

He also sold Shot Doctor glasses. It was a stethoscope with a shot glass affixed to the end.

Finishing his meal and looking at the clock on the wall, Moore said, "I've got to run to catch the last ferry."

"Hope you enjoyed the perch."

"Loved it. The perch was great!" he said as he stood and walked next door to buy his aunt the popcorn. Their popcorn was dangerously delicious. After making his purchase, he exited the building. Fifteen minutes later, his car was in line for the ferry.

The Next Morning
Aunt Anne's House

Seated at his desk in his bedroom, Moore had been reviewing the material that Mullen had provided him. He had also spent time on his laptop checking the links Mullen had suggested he review.

When his cell phone rang, he answered. "This is Emerson."

"Emerson, it's Mike Steidl."

"Hi, Mike. How are things going out there? Hear anything more about Panich?"

"Yeah, that's why I'm calling. One of the DEA agents called a little while ago to see if he showed up for work today. I told him he hadn't and I also stopped by Panich's apartment. That's where it got real interesting."

"How's that Mike?" Moore asked as he straightened in his chair.

"I saw Chet there."

Moore knew he was referring to Put-in-Bay police chief Chet Wilkens. "Yes?"

"Remember the two girls who disappeared from the island the other day?"

"Yes."

"Wilkens found one of the girl's drivers license. It had been hidden under the mattress. He doesn't think Panich would have hidden it, because they didn't find anything incriminating in the apartment. He thinks the girls may have been taken there before they were taken off the island.

"One of Panich's neighbors returned to the island today. When the chief showed her the pictures of the two girls, she recognized both of them."

"She did?"

"Yes, and she said there was a woman with them. You couldn't miss the woman. She had a big scar running down the side of her cheek."

Moore remembered vaguely seeing somebody like that in the crowd around Angel's sister.

"She remembered seeing the four of them go into his apartment, but that's all she knows. She was leaving then to catch the ferry," Steidl said.

"I wonder if they were tricked into going into the apartment?" Moore questioned.

"Maybe. I thought it was an interesting connection and wanted to let you know."

"Thanks, Mike."

"Any time. I hope they catch Panich," Steidl said before he ended the call.

Moore looked at his cell phone and then keyed in Angel's number.

The phone was answered on the third ring.

"Hello?" Angel answered.

"Angel, it's Emerson."

Angel seemed to perk up a bit. "Hello, Emerson. When are we going to get together for that drink you promised me?"

Emerson thought it was interesting that Angel started the conversation in that direction. "Any time you want."

"Today would be a good day to drink. You heard my sister died?"

"Yes, Angel, I am so sorry," Moore reacted. "I share in your pain."

"I've got to make the funeral arrangements."

"Need some company?" Moore offered.

"That would be nice, but not now. You call me in a couple of days and we'll get together."

"I'll do that," Moore said. "Angel, I am so sorry," Moore repeated.

"So am I," Angel said before hanging up.

Moore decided it was time for a change in scenery. He grabbed his cell phone and walked downstairs and into the kitchen. His vivacious aunt was sitting at the table. In her hand was a handful of the popcorn Moore had purchased for her.

"Good?" he asked as he opened the fridge and helped himself to a cold bottle of water.

"Beyond belief," she answered before throwing the handful in her mouth.

Moore grinned and walked through the house and the porch. Walking down the steps, he headed for the dock where he sat on the edge. He withdrew his cell phone from his pocket and keyed in the number for the Human Trafficking Task Force in Toledo. Within a minute, he was talking to Mullen about the two teens who had disappeared, Angel's sister, and Panich. He also asked Mullen about the woman with the scar on her face.

"Yes, I know the woman," Mullen confirmed. "Her name's Anna Stokich. Lives somewhere in East Toledo, but no permanent address. Spends a lot of time in Naples, Florida. She's been busted a few times for aiding and abetting prostitution. Don't think I know this Panich fellow. I'll check him out. I hadn't heard anything about the two teens. Thanks for the heads up. I'll get in touch with the Put-in-Bay police."

"Glad to help."

"Sometimes, the pimps work in teams when they're recruiting girls. Having a woman with them like Anna makes them more approachable," Mullen said. "The girls feel safer and are more likely to go with them and then realize too late they're trapped."

"You mentioned East Toledo. Is that the area where most of the girls are?"

"Not really. They can be all over the city." Mullen looked at his watch. "I have a meeting coming up. Is there anything else I can help you with?"

"You've helped a lot. Let me digest all of this and I may be calling you back. Thanks, Brad."

There was one other person Moore wanted to call. It was Arnie Sutter, the owner and publisher of *The Western Basin Magazine* in Toledo. The two had met at the Mon Ami Restaurant in Port Clinton when they were enjoying the Sunday afternoon outdoor concerts.

Sutter knew everyone in Toledo and would be helpful with his knowledge of the area since Moore hadn't spent much time in Toledo.

When Moore called him, Sutter agreed to meet him for lunch the next day.

Moore's head was spinning. He decided to drive over to the Keys complex on the waterfront for a quick lunch. Upon arriving, he heard one of his favorite songs, Paul Simon's "You Can Call Me Al," being played from the small stage. He thought he recognized the voice and he was right. When he walked around the corner, he saw Scott Alan, The Island Doctor, singing it.

Alan spotted Moore right away and nodded his head at him as he continued playing without missing a beat. There were several dancers in the dance area. Moore smiled when he realized he knew two of the dancers. One was pirate brigand Bob Kansa, the designer of the official Put-in-Bay burgee. The other dancer was Bob's voluptuous, red-haired wife, Mary. There was something about those redheads, Moore thought to himself. He then remembered the local island author had a hot redhead as a wife.

Moore couldn't help himself. The music was irresistible. He worked his way onto the dance floor and began dancing with the two of them.

Bob gave Moore a high-five as Moore danced within reach. "Bring it on!" Bob said as he twirled.

Moore worked his moves as he recalled sailing with the Kansas on their catamaran, *Southwind,* which they also raced.

Mary shimmied over to Moore and up against him in a seductive manner, then backed away. Moore shook his head from side to side as he leaned toward her.

"Light it up!" Mary said as she leaned in with one shoulder and suddenly bumped her butt into Moore's hip.

"Very cheeky," Bob teased as he watched Moore and his wife dance together.

Soon the song ended and Alan started to play Jimmy Buffet's "Margaritaville." Moore and the Kansa's stepped off the dance floor.

"Looks like you two were having fun," Moore said.

"Absolutely," Kansa said. "Mary and I always have fun!" he said with a large smile and one eyebrow raised.

Moore had met the couple two years earlier at Put-in-Bay's Pyrate Fest. The two of them were extremely creative in designing and making their pirate costumes. Bob also had a Lotus which he raced. Moore was confident the folks at Dos Equis would be after Bob to be the "next most interesting man in the world" for their beer commercials.

"Want to join me for lunch?" Moore asked.

"We'd love to, but we're meeting some friends here for dancing. Another time," Bob said.

"We'll plan on it," Moore said as he started to walk toward the bayfront seating, but found Mary blocking his path. She gave him a quick kiss on the cheek, giggled and rejoined her husband on the dance floor.

As Moore walked, he saw island tobacconist, Richard Warren. He had also met Warren several years ago during Pyrate Fest. Warren had several replica pirate costumes that Moore admired. He also liked Warren's 1929 Ford Huckster, a truck with a covered area over the bed that was set up for vegetable sales.

Warren hand rolled cigars from tobacco leaves from the Dominican Republic and Brazil. He also imported cigars and sold them at selected island outlets. He had been to cigar aficionado events in Cuba, Key West, Dominican Republic, Honduras and China.

Warren also had a large warehouse near the Put-in-Bay airport. It housed his cigar and tobacco collectibles and antique toys. It also contained a large walk-in humidor.

Warren was sitting comfortably in a chair, enjoying the view of the bay and one of his cigars. When he noticed Moore, he waved him over. "Have a seat, Emerson."

"What're you smoking today?" Moore asked as he sat.

"A Fuente Double Chateau," he said as he exhaled. "Would you like one?" he asked as he began to open a small carrying case full of cigars.

"Sure. But let me order my lunch first. Did you eat?"

"Just finished," Warren said as he placed the cigar case on the table.

A waiter appeared at Moore's side and he ordered a black and blue grouper sandwich and a Book's Bushwackers – a Wendy's Frosty for adults.

"Beautiful day on the bay," Warren observed as he looked across the bay's blue waters.

"Every day here is beautiful," Moore added.

"Working on any good stories?"

"Yes. I've just started researching human trafficking." He proceeded to bring Warren up to speed between bites of the sandwich the waiter had delivered. He knew that Warren had a vast network of contacts and he might know someone who could help.

"Sounds very interesting, Emerson," Warren said as he knocked ash off the end of his cigar. "I have a friend in Toledo you may want to talk to."

"Is he in law enforcement?"

"In a manner of speaking, he is. He's a customs agent and checks all the ships coming into the Port of Toledo. Name's Ernie Corpening and he loves Put-in-Bay. He loves hanging here at the Keys."

"I'd like to meet him."

"I'll give him a call and tell him a little about you to make sure he's open to talking with you. Then he can call you. I have your number," Warren said as he looked over Moore's shoulder.

"Everybody has your number!"

Moore turned around in his seat and saw the congenial Scott Alan with his signature smile and goatee. "I don't know about that. You on break?"

"Yeah. Good crowd today. They're enjoying themselves. You doing good?"

"Just chilling," Moore responded. "You know Richard?"

"Do I know Richard or what?" Alan grinned at Warren. "He's the man. Makes my favorite cigars. Got any on you?"

"Sure, Scott. I've got Fuente Double Chateaus with me today. Emerson, are you ready for yours?"

"Yes."

The two men took the cigars Warren offered them, clipped the end and lit up.

"You're the best," Alan said as he inhaled and exhaled slowly.

"Very good," Moore agreed as he enjoyed his cigar. "I'm a 'once in a long while' cigar smoker."

"Scott, I hope you enjoy this as much as we enjoy your singing," Warren commented.

"I'm not sure there's any comparison. These cigars are so good!" Alan's attention was distracted by two bikinied blondes, who were seated at the bar and calling his name. "I've got to run. I see two candidates for Shot Doctors." Alan excused himself and ran to the bar where the two women threw their arms around him and kissed him in a warm greeting.

"That guy is a chick magnet!" Warren said as he watched the three of them laughing and teasing each other at the bar.

"He told me he gets better results with those Shot Doctors than he does with a string of Mardi Gras beads," Moore added as he watched Alan give the women stethoscopes with shot glasses attached to the bottom. "That's our Island Doctor at work."

Warren turned his attention back to Moore. "I've got an idea for you if you want to hear it."

"I'm all ears."

"Ever think about going undercover on this one? I bet you could get the real scoop."

"You must be reading my mind." Moore ran his hand over the stubble on his face. "That's exactly what I'm going to do. Grow out a beard. I'm overdue for a haircut anyway, so I'm letting it go.

Going for the scruffy look."

"It could be dangerous, too." Warren cautioned.

Moore sat back as he watched the smoke from his cigar dissipate in the fresh island breeze. "Nothing new for me. It's my job." Moore looked at his watch as the waiter appeared with his bill. "I should be getting back to the house. More research this afternoon, then I'm off to the Beer Barrel tonight."

"Who's playing?"

"The Menus." Moore enjoyed the high energy rock and roll band from Cincinnati. The lead singer, Tim Goldrainer, and Moore had developed a friendship. They both enjoyed reading the novels written by the island author.

"Maybe I'll stop by. I like their music, too."

Moore paid his bill and stood from the table. "Thanks for the cigar."

"Any time."

Moore excused himself and headed to his golf cart. He had always liked the easy going, gentlemanly Warren. On the way to his cart, Moore bumped into Kelly and Marty Faris. Kelly was the retired long-time superintendent/principal of Put-in-Bay's school and an island photographer. Marty had retired from her job at the Put-in-Bay Post Office. Moore had become friends with the couple and admired Kelly's photography.

"How are things?" Moore asked.

"Going well," Kelly replied.

"I'm staying too busy keeping Kelly out of trouble," Marty replied.

"One of these days, I need to include you two in one of my stories."

"Because of the tee shirt we bought you?" Kelly asked with a grin.

"Exactly," Moore replied. He recalled the two had given him a tee shirt which was lettered "Careful or You'll End Up in My Novel." They had found it while on vacation and bought one for Moore and the island novelist. "I bet it won't be long until our mutual friend puts you two in one of his novels," Moore laughed as he walked away from the couple.

"Any day now," Kelly said as the two waved at Moore and continued their walk along the bayfront.

The Next Day
Toledo Waterfront

Moore parked in one of the spaces in International Park and walked to the Docks, a complex of restaurants and bars along the banks of the Maumee River. The area was a mini-version of Put-in-Bay for partying, good food and people watching. Boats would pull into the docks and their partying would go from the water to the shore.

Of their restaurant choices for lunch, Moore had elected to meet at the Real Seafood Restaurant. He walked into the restaurant and asked for an outdoor table so he could view the water traffic and downtown Toledo across the river.

He didn't have to wait long.

"Emerson, it's been awhile," a voice called.

Moore turned from viewing the river to locate the source of the voice. Seeing the tall, broad-shouldered Arnie Sutter approaching, Moore stood to greet him. They shook hands and sat down.

"I think the last time I saw you was at the Mon Ami Restaurant at the afternoon outdoor concert. Colin Dussault was playing," Moore said as he looked at his friend. Every time he saw the guy, Moore couldn't help thinking how much Sutter reminded him of Hulk Hogan, the famous wrestler. He often thought they could have been brothers.

"Great music. I love the blues he plays," Sutter said.

"Great voice and it's just unbelievable how he plays the harmonica. I can just sit back with a glass of moscato and enjoy it."

"Me, too, but I'll take a beer," Sutter grinned as he responded.

"And is that what you'll be ordering?" the waiter asked. The two hadn't noticed his arrival.

"That'll be fine with me."

"I'm working. Better give me a Pepsi," Moore said as he watched two bikini-clad women on their boat.

The waiter took their orders and walked away.

"So, what do you have going on here with the unshaven look and longer hair? You've always been such a clean-cut guy. Were you ever a Boy Scout?"

"Yes," Moore answered. "How did you know?"

"Sometimes, you seem too squeaky clean. You need to loosen up more."

"That just might be happening over the next few weeks."

"Oh?" Sutter had a puzzled look on his face.

"I'm thinking about going undercover on this assignment."

"Working with the task force?"

"No, on my own."

"I'd advise you to be very careful. These guys play for keeps."

"I can always bail out when I need to."

"Unless you're in a situation where you can't."

Moore allowed a smile to cross his face. "Been there. Done that. I've always landed on my feet," Moore said as he recalled serious brushes with danger in the past.

"Just be sure you don't land at the bottom of Lake Erie with concrete shoes on," Sutter warned.

The waiter appeared with their drink order and set the drinks on the table. "And what would you gentlemen be ordering today?"

"Guess we better look at the menu," Moore said as he picked it up.

"I already know what I'm having," Sutter said as he pushed aside his menu.

"What's that?

"Perch sandwich."

"I guess you just made my decision for me. It's hard for me to pass up a perch sandwich," Moore said as he set the menu on the table and nodded to the waiter. The waiter walked away and the two resumed their discussion.

"So, you're committed to a story on human trafficking?" Sutter started.

"Yes. I've met with one of the guys from the Task Force and he was very helpful. I'm just surprised by the amount of it here."

"Don't let it get blown out of proportion. It's going on all over the U.S. We just seem to get a lot of publicity and notoriety for it."

"I'm sure you're right."

"Toledo is a great place to live. Everything is relatively easy to get to. It's the fourth largest city in Ohio, but offers the convenience of smaller towns. We've got the Hollywood Casino, museums, the Mud Hens baseball team and the University of Toledo. Plus, we have the Maumee River for boating and fishing, and we're not that far from Put-in-Bay."

"You working for the Visitors Bureau now?" Moore teased.

Sutter laughed. "No. I just don't want you to focus on the negative side. There are a lot of pluses to living here."

"I know. That doesn't make front page news, though. You take the bad with the good."

"Right you are."

Moore thought back to his research. "One of the biggest surprises for me was the staffing of strip clubs with trafficking victims."

Sutter nodded his head. "Yes, that happens."

"Then I heard about the northwest side's strip clubs and the hotel rooms by the hour. I didn't know that still went on," Moore said.

"But nothing like it used to be. The Task Force has really been cleaning up that market."

The waiter returned with their food and the two began chowing down their sandwiches.

Between bites, Sutter spoke. "Human trafficking is not always about the sex trade."

"I know. It's low-paid workers, too."

"Right, and teens. You ever seen those teens who are part of traveling magazine crews?"

"Yes. We had some on the island last summer. Kids making money for college."

"Not really. It's a scam. They recruit teens by telling them they can make money and see the United States. When they have a crew of twenty teens, they start off. The kids are worked ten to fourteen hours a day, six days a week and sleep three to a room in a cheap motel as they travel around a particular region."

Moore stopped eating and grimaced as he listened.

"The kids are given ten dollars a day for food because their earnings are on the books. The kids are beaten and threatened by the manager. Some of them disappear, probably killed. Some of them run away, but they're penniless. They have to find a phone and call home, if they have a home, to have money sent to them so they can get back to their families."

"I had no idea," Moore said.

"There's all kinds of human trafficking around us. It's not just the women part."

"As I'm learning," Moore said.

The two conversed over the next hour when Moore excused himself. He had a meeting in the restaurant lobby with customs agent Ernie Corpening that had been set up the previous day.

Moore walked into the restaurant's lobby where he spotted a uniformed customs agent. "Hi! Are you Ernie?" Moore asked as he approached the burly agent.

"Yep. And you must be Emerson Moore."

"Correct," Moore said as they shook hands.

"I've got my truck in the parking lot if you want to go on the tour I promised you on the phone."

"Sure."

Moore followed Corpening to the parking lot and into his truck. Within a few minutes, they were cruising down Front Street.

"I'll show you some of the warehouses and a couple we've got our eye on. The Task Force is watching them, too," Corpening said. "There's the new National Museum of the Great Lakes and the home of the Great Lakes Historical Society," Corpening said as they drove by the new facility at 1701 Front Street.

"I'm a member," Moore said. "I attended their H2O fund raising event last December. I used to visit their former location in Vermilion, but this one gives them more space."

"I toured it. Loved the display on the Coast Guard and rescuing people on the lake," Corpening said as he continued driving.

"How familiar are you with human trafficking, Ernie?" Moore asked.

"I know a little. Every ten minutes a person is trafficked into the

United States. There are over one million children exploited in the global sex trade. Ohio is the fifth largest state for human trafficking and Toledo is a major gateway city for sex trafficking. How's that for starters?"

Moore smiled at Corpening. "Impressive."

"See over there?"

Moore looked at the little café that Corpening was pointing toward.

"That's Tony Packo's," Corpening said as they drove by the famous restaurant. "Ever eat there?"

"Not yet. I've heard about it." Moore's eyes were taking in the neighborhood as they drove.

"Absolutely great food. Hot dogs to Hungarian vegetable soup to chicken paprikash."

"I'll have to make a point to try it. Any apartments back there?" Moore asked as he looked down Consaul Street.

"Oh yeah. It's an old Hungarian neighborhood. They've got rentals down there. Why?"

"I may be going undercover and I'll need a place to stay."

"Shouldn't be any problem." He looked at Moore. "You be careful if you go undercover with these guys. They're bad news."

"I'm sure," Moore acknowledged.

"No, I'm serious. Playing with those guys is like juggling hand grenades with the pins out," Corpening warned.

"Won't be the first time I've placed myself in jeopardy," Moore retorted, stubbornly.

They drove by towering piles of taconite for the steel industry and stacks of aluminum ingots.

"Toledo's port is more of a bulk port than a container port," he explained as he saw Moore looking at the taconite. He pointed to two tall gantry cranes. "That's Big Lucas and Little Lucas. They're the two largest cranes on the Great Lakes. They offload the containers."

As Corpening drove along Tiffin Avenue, he commented, "Over here, we have the Midwest Terminals. And over there is one of the terminals we have our eye on."

"Why is that?"

"It's rumored to be one of the entry points for trafficking victims. We've made a couple of surprise visits and they were cooperative in showing us around. But we didn't turn up anything."

"Do you check every ship coming in?"

"Yes. We have a heat-sensing device to scan over the containers and it tells if there's anyone inside. But the problem is the traffickers are getting smarter and are lining the containers so our scanners don't detect people inside."

"That makes life difficult," Moore said as Corpening pulled into a large parking lot and turned around.

"It does, but we're working on new technology which will help us overcome that."

"What about passing the victims off as members of the crew?" Moore asked.

"We board each vessel and review the paperwork to make sure it's legit. So far, we haven't caught anyone trying to sneak trafficking victims in through that route. We do have a growing problem though."

"Oh?"

"It's when the ship is in the lake and meets up with other watercraft. They can drop the women or illegal immigrants over the side and onboard these craft. Then they go to a quiet marina and offload them at night. Hard to catch them although we're doing more aerial surveillance."

Corpening drove Moore along Front Street and continued to point out warehouses and marinas as well as the new Hollywood Casino. He then returned Moore to his car at the restaurant.

Thirty minutes later as Moore was driving back along Route 2 to catch the Miller Ferry to Put-in-Bay, his phone rang. It was Sutter.

"Hi, Arnie," Moore said as he answered the call.

"I've got somebody you need to meet so you can understand the I-75 corridor and how it's used for trafficking."

"Who's that?"

"I've got you set up to take a ride with a truck driver, Izzy Watkins. Izzy was the one who spotted some teens going truck to truck at a truck stop. Izzy called the police. They ended up arresting 21 pimps and freeing 45 teenage girls from their prostitution ring."

"What a hero!"

"Don't say that to Izzy. Izzy doesn't like any of that hero stuff, just plain down to earth people, that's what Izzy is."

"Not too many of those left," Moore said.

"No, there aren't."

"I'm curious. What's Izzy short for? Israel?"

"Nope. It's Isabella – and whatever you do, don't call her Isabella," he warned. "You can make that mistake only once because she'll castrate you!"

"Yikes!" Moore exclaimed.

"In fact, she's volunteered to personally castrate all the pimps, truckers and johns who take advantage of young girls. Keeps a pair of hedge shears in the cab in case she gets the opportunity," Sutter added.

Moore winced at the thought even though he liked the idea. The punishment fit the crime, he thought.

"It's like her personal vendetta," he said. "They just don't make them like her any more."

"At least not that we know of," Moore said weakly. He had mixed emotions about meeting this infamous trucker.

The Next Day at Noon
The Truck Stop at I-80 and I-75

Moore pulled into the truck stop and parked his car. He'd be riding with Watkins for the next fourteen hours and picking up a good education. Walking into the restaurant area of the truck stop, he looked around for the woman and couldn't spot her. He withdrew his cell phone from his pocket and speed-dialed the number he had entered for her.

A phone on the counter close to where he was standing started to ring. Moore saw a large hand reach for the phone and raise it to the owner's ear.

"Ya here yet, twinkle toes?" the deep voice asked.

Moore started to grin as the 250-pound woman turned around in front of him to look toward the restaurant entrance. Under a Toledo Mud Hens ball cap was short, black hair. Her dark brown eyes meant business. She wasn't wearing any makeup and was dressed in a flannel shirt with the sleeves missing. She had on worn Levis and driving boots. She looked like a woman that no one would want to mess with.

"I think I see you," Moore said as he looked in her direction.

"Sitting right here in front of ya, dumbass."

The only response Moore got was a view of her back as she swung back around in her swivel chair and hung up the cell phone. She resumed eating her breakfast.

This is going to be really interesting; Moore thought to himself as he walked over and sat on the empty stool next to her.

"Can I get you anything?" a waitress asked as she appeared out of nowhere.

Before Moore could respond, Watkins answered. "Ya can get him my check and he don't have time to eat anything. Just give him a cup of coffee. And make that to go!"

Moore looked at Watkins out of the corner of his eye. She's a piece of work, he thought to himself as he paid the check and picked up the cup of coffee. Watkins was already walking toward the exit door and Moore hurried to catch up.

"Come on, Honey. We're burning time," she said over her shoulder as she headed across the parking lot toward the rows of tractor-trailers.

Watkins walked over to a Kenworth. "This one be ours," she said as she unlocked the door and climbed into the cab. Moore climbed into the cab from the passenger side and settled into his seat.

"Ya can throw your makeup bag in the back," Watkins said as she looked at the small duffel bag Moore was carrying. Within minutes, Watkins had started the diesel engine and the semi began pulling out of the truck stop.

"I already got the motion lotion," she said as she turned on the CB radio.

"What's that?"

Watkins turned her head and stared with a look of disgust at Moore. "Hell's bells. They sure did set me up with a virgin! It's fuel. Ya know what fuel is, don't ya?"

Moore nodded.

"Ya ever been in a semi before, buddy?"

"First time," Moore responded.

"Why do they always dump your kind on me?" she asked to no one in particular as she eased the rig onto I-75 and headed south. "If you don't show me any smarts, our time together is going to last as long as a carnival ride."

"I'll work on that," Moore responded.

"Ya do know where we're going, don't ya?"

"Atlanta."

"Good, you're not as dumb as I first thought," she said as she focused on traffic and occasionally spoke on the CB.

As they neared the Findlay exit, she took her eyes off the road and looked at Moore. "So, you're working on a story about human trafficking, huh?"

"Yes, I was told you could give me a trucker's perspective on the abuse of teens at truck stops."

"Well, from the get-go, I want ya to understand I don't have any personal experience with that. Ya understand me?"

"I didn't mean to insinuate…" Moore didn't get to finish as Watkins interrupted him.

"I have a real hard time with anybody abusing or taking advantage of any kids. I got a very short fuse on that topic," she said firmly.

"I heard you busted a prostitution ring at one of the truck stops."

"Somebody's been talking out of school. That's not up for print. Ya understand?"

"Sure. Can you tell me what happened?"

"It was about ten o'clock one night at a truck stop in Michigan. I was sitting in my cab painting my fingernails." She stopped talking and swung her head around to look at Moore. "You're too easy," she laughed. "Do I really look like someone who'd be painting her fingernails?"

Moore got it and pushed back. "No, you don't. You look like someone who'd have to be told to put the toilet seat down when you were finished peeing."

"Now, that's funny. I like that. I like that a lot."

For the first time Moore saw a hint of a smile cross Watkins' face. Maybe, there was hope, he thought.

"Anyways, I see this van driving through the truck parking area. It looks like they're trying to find someone or else to make sure they don't find any bears around. Ya do know what bears are?"

"Police," Moore answered proudly.

"Well, ain't you the smart one?" she asked. She wasn't going to cut Moore any slack.

She continued. "This van finally parks and its lights go out. It's just sitting there for about five minutes and the door opens. Two teenaged girls get out. They look like they're thirteen or fourteen. And ya can tell right away from their sexy attire they're working girls. They start going from truck to truck."

"They didn't advertise themselves on the CB?" Moore asked.

"Not all of them do that. They know the bears got their ears on. So, they walk up to the trucks and solicit the drivers. Cute girls, too, if they'd wash that makeup off their faces. It just irritates me to no end that someone is pimping out these kids.

"So, I got on my cell and called 911. I reported the girls and sat back to watch the fireworks. I knew I was in for a good show. I even started humming 'bad boys, bad boys, whatcha going do when they come for ya'."

"What happened?" Moore asked.

"It seemed like five minutes went by and I see three black-and-whites surround the van. The van driver tries to escape and plows into one of the police cars."

All of a sudden Watkins swerved the truck and then pulled back into her lane. "There was an alligator in the road," she explained.

"There are no alligators running wild in Ohio."

Watkins sighed. "Ya showing your dumbness again! That's what we call the tred from a shredded truck tire. Just not something ya want to hit."

"Right," Moore agreed.

Watkins continued her story. "So, they grab the driver and the passenger. It looks like they're caretakers for the two girls. Then, they get the two girls and they start talking. Later, I heard the two adults in the van decided it was better to cooperate with the police. In exchange for immunity, they revealed their entire network, or at least as much of it they knew about. That's where they busted 21 pimps and freed 45 girls."

Moore said. "I'm glad things worked out in the end."

Watkins raised both of her eyebrows, shook her head and continued, "Don't be so quick to jump to conclusions. I thought ya were supposed to be a top notch reporter there, Tinkerbelle."

"That's what I've been told," Moore said.

"It didn't work out so good for the two adults in the van."

"How's that?"

"Well knucklehead, they were found murdered after the trial. Both were missing their tongues. They had been cut out while they were still alive."

"Did they find the murderers?"

"Not that I know of. So, ya better be careful when you're digging around for information. These boys play for keeps."

"I keep hearing that," Moore said.

"Want to know something else that's a bit gruesome?"

"What's that?"

"Sometimes, the pimps have the girls branded."

"Branded!" Moore said, shocked.

"Yeah, that's what I call it. They have the girls get tattoos on the neck with the pimp's name so other pimps know who the girl belongs to." She looked with disdain at Moore. "Sometimes, I don't think you're playing with a full deck, Moore."

Moore smiled weakly.

"One of the problems this country has is sexualizing kids at an early age. There's such a focus on outward beauty. Did you know they have pole dancing lessons for girls as young as three-years-old?"

"You're kidding me?"

"No kidding. Youngsters can get botox injections and they get bullied at school and on Bookface."

"You mean Facebook," Moore corrected her.

"Whatever the hell they call it. You get my point!" she grumbled. "Then they got games like Grand Theft Auto where you can sleep with a prostitute, then kill her. It's no wonder today's youth are getting so confused!"

The two chatted back and forth as they drove along I-75 through Ohio, Kentucky, Tennessee and into Georgia. About an hour away from Atlanta where Watkins was going to drop him at the airport for the flight back to Toledo, Watkins started talking about her sister, Linda, who was a detective in Atlanta.

"Most people have no clue about human trafficking. In Georgia, every two minutes a child is sold as a sex slave. My sister told me over 7,200 men pay to have sex with a child in Georgia every month. The kids can see between two to fifty johns a day. Multiply that by forty-nine other states. That's abusing lots of kids!"

"That's terrible!" Moore said, disgusted.

"It's a lot more than terrible, Angel Food. Kids are beaten unmercifully. More money is made from the exploitation of children in Atlanta alone than is made from all sporting events and concerts combined there."

"Horrific!" was the only response Moore could give.

Watkins looked at Moore and then back to the road. With traffic building as they began to enter the metro area, she focused on driving and delivering Moore to the airport.

Sweet Dreams
Toledo's Northside

The low building's purple and pink neon lights seductively enticed drivers to stop and pay a visit to its tantalizing entertainment. Its lights lured men like a bug zapper's light attracted flying insects. Once inside, both could be deadly. "Come inside," the lights whispered softly to men's non-thinking brains.

This evening, Sweet Dreams Gentlemen's Club had a lap dance

special, two for the price of one. Accordingly, the club was packed. Twelve gorgeous, bikinied women between the ages of twenty-one and thirty, or so they said, were working the crowd of men, and the four men who were there with their wives or girlfriends. The dancers, whose bosoms were barely concealed by their tiny tops, were giving twenty dollar lap dances at the tables. But the women were trying to convince the patrons to enter a special VIP room for a more private dance that cost fifty dollars.

There wasn't an empty seat at the bar as two scantily-attired female bartenders worked feverishly to fill drink orders. The men at the bar were turned around on their stools so they could watch dancers in the crowd and the featured dancer on a lighted stage with a stripper's pole. She was slowly losing articles of clothing down to her g-string to the beat of the song "Bad to the Bone."

From a rear office door, a stocky man in his fifties emerged. He had a receding hairline and a reddish face. He had been a strong drinker over the years. His name was Eddie O'Malley.

After surveying the crowd and smiling at how busy the club was, O'Malley walked over to the bar. He was about to order a drink when a man jumped off a bar stool four seats down and rushed at him with a knife.

O'Malley spotted the man and his eyes widened as the man quickly narrowed the distance between the two. Before the man reached O'Malley and before the two beefy bouncers at the door could react, a bearded man jumped off his bar stool next to O'Malley.

The bearded man grabbed the attacker's knife hand and spun the attacker toward the bar where he brought the attacker's hand down hard on the bar, causing the attacker to drop the knife as he cried out in pain. Next, the bearded man spun the attacker around and punched him in the stomach.

The two bouncers appeared and restrained the attacker.

"Thanks," O'Malley said to the stranger. "You saved my life." He then turned to the attacker. "I don't know you. What's this all about?"

Between wheezes as he struggled to catch his alcohol-reeking breath, the attacker answered, "I was here a couple of weeks ago and I didn't get the two dances I paid for."

"What? And for that, you come at me with a knife?" O'Malley's face reddened even more as his anger swelled. "What are you? Crazy?"

"It smells like he's drunk," the bearded stranger said.

"I don't care what he is, but he's in a world of hurt," O'Malley stormed. Looking at his bouncers, he said, "Take him out back and break one of his legs."

"Whoa, wait a minute," the bearded stranger intervened. "Do you really want to do something like that? It just brings the police around when you don't need them poking around."

O'Malley looked at the stranger. "You got a point."

"Let me take care of him. After all, I'm the one who stopped his attack. Let me finish what I started."

O'Malley eyed the stranger. He looked like someone who could take care of himself. "Okay, you go out back with the boys here. Finish what you started and come back and see me," O'Malley said as he sat at the bar and ordered a drink.

The four men walked out of the rear entrance of the strip club to a dimly lit area of the parking lot. While the two bouncers held the attacker, the stranger pummeled his body and face with blows.

After a few minutes, the stranger said, "I could kill him, but I think I've done enough damage. Just drop him."

The two bouncers let go of the attacker and he crumbled to the ground. The three men then returned to the club. As the two bouncers walked by O'Malley, they nodded their heads, signaling they were satisfied with the beating the stranger had given the assailant.

O'Malley motioned to the stranger to sit next to him at the bar. "Thanks again. Let me buy you a drink. Peggy," he called out to one of the bikinied barmaids. "Give him what he wants."

"And what would you like?" she asked as she looked up at the bearded man.

"VO and seven," he replied as she scurried over to make the drink.

"So, where did you learn to fight like that?" O'Malley asked.

"Seal training."

"That was pretty good. I'm Eddie O'Malley. I run this club."

"Hello, Eddie."

O'Malley was perplexed since the stranger didn't readily offer his name. "So, what's your name? Can't you be a little sociable, here?"

The stranger took a long drink of the VO that Peggy had set in front of him.

"Alvey. Ken Alvey."

"Well, that's more like it Ken Alvey. And what kind of work do you do?"

"I'm unemployed." Alvey turned and looked at O'Malley.

O'Malley was getting irritated. "What did you do? Police work?" He wanted to check on the guy's background.

"Nope. I stay as far away from them as possible. I've had enough trouble with them in the past," Alvey said. "I'll be upfront with you. I did some time."

"Yeah, we all make some mistakes. In getting caught, that is. How long were you in prison?" O'Malley asked.

"Two years. Got out for good behavior provided I didn't get into any more trouble in Detroit."

"So you come down the road to Toledo?"

"Yeah, close enough to Detroit in case I need to pay back anyone, if you know what I mean."

"I know exactly what you mean. You know, I might have a friend who could use somebody like you. I'll give him a call tomorrow. Here's my card." He handed one of his business cards to Alvey. "Call me in the afternoon."

"I'll do that," Alvey said as he put the card in his pocket. "I need to score a job."

O'Malley waved to two of his dancers and the two women walked over to O'Malley.

"Listen, I appreciate what you did for me tonight. I'm going to give you a special thank you. Or, maybe I should say Cinnamon and Jasmine here are going to express my gratitude."

Alvey looked at the two gorgeous, buxom women in front of him. They both had the bluest of eyes and wore pink lipstick, Alvey's favorite color. Cinnamon had red hair and Jasmine was a blonde.

"Thanks, but you don't have to do that."

The two ladies put their arms around Alvey.

"Don't you like us?" Cinnamon cooed.

"Aren't we pretty enough for you?" Jasmine asked as she looked at him seductively.

"I do and, yes, you are both very beautiful," Alvey responded as he eyed the two dancers.

"Go on. Enjoy yourself," O'Malley urged as Peggy placed another VO on the bar for Alvey.

Alvey saw the drink and broke one of his arms free from the dancers' clutches. He downed the drink in three large gulps and turned back to the girls.

"Can't let a drink go to waste. Let's go, ladies. I'm going to enjoy this," Alvey grinned salaciously.

O'Malley said, "Girls, take him out back for a VIP dance. Give him a half dozen dances."

"We'll be glad to, won't we, Jasmine?" Cinnamon said as she pulled Alvey off the bar stool.

"Hmmm," Jasmine replied as she snuggled up to Alvey. "This is going to be fun."

"I'm counting on it," Alvey said.

The three of them disappeared through the doorway to the private VIP room.

An hour later, a grinning Alvey walked to his car in the parking lot. As he pressed his key fob to unlock his car doors, he heard approaching footsteps. He spun around and found himself facing the attacker from the bar.

The attacker spoke first. "Emerson, did you have to hit me so hard?"

"Just be glad it was me doing the hitting. You heard what they said. They were going to break your leg," Moore said as he stepped out of the Alvey character, a role he was going to use for his undercover work.

"Yeah, that was too close."

Moore pulled a stack of bills from his pocket. "Here, take this for your trouble. I appreciate you helping me tonight. It looks like I'm in."

The attacker took the money. "I wasn't going to take any money for this until I got the beating. I just owed you a big favor for not revealing who I was to the guys in Detroit last year."

"Glad you survived that mess up there."

The attacker started walking away, then stopped and turned to face Moore. "Emerson, one last comment."

"Yes?"

"Next time you need a favor like this."

"Yes?"

"Call somebody else."

The attacker disappeared around the corner and Moore stepped into his car. As he pulled out of the parking lot, he felt quite pleased with his first steps in going undercover. He hoped his luck would hold.

As he drove to the small apartment he had rented behind Tony Packo's Cafe, his mind drifted back to Cinnamon and Jasmine and the time he spent with them. Mullen had told him to try to connect with them and it was easier than he had expected. They could be the source of information on O'Malley if he played them right.

Moore planned to contact Mullen and give him an update on what had transpired, including the encounter with the two women. Mullen had been reluctant to support him until Moore told him he was going undercover with or without his support. Mullen had caved in and helped Moore with the Alvey role. Mullen had also alerted Corpening in case Corpening stumbled across Moore while the reporter was in his role.

Moore also was looking forward to telling his editor, John Sedler, how his research had gone that evening. He'd be sure to embellish the description of the time he spent with Cinnamon and Jasmine. He chuckled to himself as he drove.

A Warehouse
East Toledo

Moore's car pulled off of Front Street as it drove parallel to the Maumee River. Moore had talked to O'Malley, who had set up a meeting for him in a warehouse on the banks of the Maumee.

Moore's GPS guided him down a number of side streets to the warehouse. As he pulled in, he saw several semi-trucks backed up and workers loading and unloading them. There were several large, white Ford 350 box trucks in the lot. Moore parked next to one of them and sauntered to the door marked "Office."

"I'm Ken Alvey," Moore said when a man with a clipboard asked if he could help. "I'm looking for Milo Pavkov."

"What for?"

"I've got an appointment with him."

"Milo's out back," the man said. "Follow me."

Moore followed the man into the main warehouse which was filled with boxes and shipping containers. "He's in the back side of the building, by those offices." He pointed to the rear of the warehouse.

"Thanks," Moore said and walked toward the offices.

Just before he reached the door, a man shouted down from a steel walkway overhead. "Stop where you are!"

Moore looked up and saw a rough-looking man cradling a semi-automatic weapon in his arms.

"What are you doing back here?"

"I've got an appointment with Milo."

"What's your name?"

"Ken Alvey."

"Hold on a minute."

Moore watched as the man spoke briefly into a radio. The man continued to maintain eye contact with Moore as he spoke. "Okay. Go through those doors."

Moore walked through the door and found himself in a large

room. It had several chairs and tables. There was a refrigerator in a corner and a microwave on a counter next to a sink. A shelving unit held cases of beer and several boxes of liquor.

Four Slavic-looking men were in the room. One stepped forward while the others watched closely. Two of them were holding shotguns.

"You armed?" the one asked.

"No," Moore replied. "Are you?" Moore pushed.

"Not funny." The man glared at Moore with a stern look. "Then you don't mind if I frisk you?"

"Go ahead, pretty boy." Moore taunted in his Alvey role.

The man grunted and proceeded to roughly pat down Moore. Then he surprised Moore when he produced an electronic wand and ran it over and around Moore.

"What's that for?"

"Bug detector," the man growled as he checked for transmitting devices. "We don't want to get infected here," he laughed.

"Yeah," one of the three men yelled. "Zivi is allergic to bugs."

"And you better watch yourself," one cautioned. "Zivi specializes in exterminations!"

The other three men in the room laughed at the crack.

"He's clean," Zivi said, harshly, as he placed the device on the table. "Go through that door. You'll find Milo there."

"Thanks," Moore said as he walked past the dangerous-looking men and into the office. Moore felt like none of them was a stranger to violence.

Behind a large cherry desk and in a black leather chair sat Milo Pavkov, the man in charge of the Toledo operations for the Boss in Naples, Florida. He was six-foot-three-inches with a square jaw, graying hair and dark brown eyes that were now boring a hole through Moore.

"You don't look like Ken Alvey," Pavkov said. He was showing Moore a picture, which he had printed off his computer. "It says here Ken Alvey is the executive director of the Lake Erie Marine Trades Association in Westlake, Ohio. Is that what you do, Mr. Ken Alvey?"

"That's not me."

"I know. So, who are you?"

Moore was looking into the open jaws of a tiger and he knew this was not going to be easy. "I'm just a guy looking for work."

"So, you want to work for me?"

"I really don't know. Your buddy at Sweet Dreams suggested we meet."

"Well, I don't know you and he doesn't either." Pavkov said as he looked back at his monitor. "You a cop?"

"Not me. Wouldn't have anything to do with them."

"I heard that you know how to handle yourself."

"A little bit."

"So, if I was to have two of my bulls outside of my office come in here, you could put them on the ground like that?" Pavkov snapped his fingers.

Moore was hoping his bluff was working. He didn't want to have to put on a show as he knew he'd get the short end of the stick. He decided to tough it out. "Faster than that," he said nonchalantly.

Pavkov laughed. "I like that. Confidence. And you've got some smarts about you, too. I can tell that." He stared at Moore. "Okay, tell you what I'm going to do. You can work for me. I'll see how you do with some of the small stuff for starters."

"Thanks," Moore said.

"Zivi," Pavkov called and Zivi appeared at the doorway.

"We'll give Alvey here a try. Start him on the basics."

Zivi nodded his head and motioned for Moore to follow him. As he did, Pavkov called one of the other men into his office. "When that Alvey leaves today, follow him. Find out where he lives and see if you can break in. Go through his stuff and plant this in his apartment." Pavkov held up a miniature bug. "We'll see if this guy is everything he says he is."

The man nodded and left Pavkov's office. Pavkov was a fan of technology. He knew law enforcement was using it. So was he. That's how he was able to stay out of prison.

Moore's day was filled with moving shipments around the ware-house. He found himself driving a tow motor and unloading and loading skids of various goods from the semi-trailers. As much as he looked around, Moore didn't observe anything suspicious. At the end of the day, he drove to his apartment behind Tony Packo's Café and relaxed for the evening.

The Next Morning
Moore's Apartment

Leaving his apartment, Moore began driving to the warehouse. He had driven two miles when an alarm sounded on his cell phone. Recognizing the alarm, he pulled his car to the side of the road and picked up his cell phone. He quickly accessed the app that was the source of the alarm. It was the hidden surveillance micro-camera at his apartment.

Moore tapped the screen to see the image of his apartment from the micro-camera. It was hidden above the door sill and showed an intruder in his apartment.

Moore recognized the intruder as one of the men from Pavkov's office. Moore watched as the man went through the studio apartment. He didn't find anything incriminating other than a handgun, which Moore had hidden under his mattress. The man then pulled a small device from his pocket and hid it under the lamp shade. Moore made a mental note to check the device when he returned home that night.

Once the man finished and walked out of the apartment, Moore smiled as he closed out the app and pulled his car back on the road. It looked like they were checking him out. That may be taking him another step closer to his goal. When he reached the warehouse and reported to Zivi, he had another uneventful day.

Twenty minutes after Moore started work, Pavkov was in his office, listening to the report from the man who broke into Moore's apartment.

"Nothing other than a handgun. The guy doesn't own much as far as I could tell," he reported.

"We'll listen over the next few days and see what we hear,"

Pavkov said.

When Moore returned home that evening, he walked right over to the lamp and looked underneath. He saw that a small listening device had been planted and grinned to himself. Now was the time to take the next step.

Moore went into the kitchen area and prepared a bologna sandwich on rye bread. He grabbed a Pepsi out of the fridge and sat in a chair near the lamp. After devouring his sandwich and taking several sips of his drink, Moore picked up his cell phone and punched in a number. He put the cell phone in speaker mode and waited patiently for the call to be answered.

"This is O'Malley," the voice on the other end said.

"Eddie, it's Ken Alvey."

"Alvey, how're things going?" O'Malley asked. "Did you get a chance to meet my friend?"

"Yes, I did. I'm working for him now."

"Good, I'm glad to hear that."

"Eddie, I have a favor to ask you."

"Sure. Sure. Ask away."

"Those two girls you introduced me to?"

O'Malley thought a minute. "You mean Cinnamon and Jasmine?"

"Yes. They were two very special ladies."

"Beautiful, aren't they?" O'Malley replied.

"I was wondering if they would consider a private dance?" Moore asked.

"I don't know. They're rather new here. I haven't broken them in yet if you catch my drift," O'Malley chuckled softly.

"Could you see if they would like to come over to my place for a very private dance?"

"Sure, I can check. No guarantees. I'll call you back." O'Malley hung up.

Ten minutes later, Moore's cell phone rang. He answered it and once again put it on speakerphone. "Alvey here."

"This is going to be your lucky day," O'Malley chortled. "In fact, you're going to be doubly lucky. They're both willing to come over. I don't know what happened during that VIP lap dance session, but they sure are interested in you."

Moore smiled. "What can I say, Eddie? When you got it, you got it."

"Gimme your address and they should be over within the hour."

Moore gave him his address.

"And one more thing. This one is on the house. I remember who takes care of me and I take care of them," O'Malley said.

"Thanks, Eddie."

"No, it's me who should be thanking you," O'Malley said as he ended the call.

Moore set his cell phone on an end table and threw a glance at the lamp. He grinned as he was sure the listeners had heard everything that was said. They were certainly going to get an earful when the two girls arrived.

Within the hour, a car pulled into the apartment's parking lot. Moore looked out the window and recognized the two dancers. He walked out of the apartment and down the stairs to meet them.

The two women had exited the car and were walking toward the apartment when Moore greeted them. He hugged the redheaded Cinnamon first and whispered in her ear. She giggled. Next, he hugged the blonde Jasmine and whispered in her ear. Both girls giggled as they threw their arms around Moore and started walking toward the steps to his second floor apartment. Cinnamon dropped her right hand to Moore's butt cheek and squeezed it affectionately.

From their listening post in Pavkov's office, Pavkov and Zivi broke open a bottle of slivovitz. They had decided they would also enjoy themselves a bit as they listened to Alvey's sexual adventure. They heard the apartment door open and Moore's voice.

"Would you two hot ladies like something to drink?"

"I'd love to drink you in," Cinnamon purred.

"Save some for me," Jasmine added.

"Whoa. Whoa, ladies. Let's go a little slower. I want to be sure we all enjoy this," Moore said. He walked over and poured three glasses of Long Island Iced Teas which he had mixed before the ladies arrived. "Here you go, ladies."

Pavkov and Zivi heard the ice clinking in the glasses, followed by the sounds of kissing and moans. Then, they heard the sounds of a squeaking bed. The next hour was filled with moans and endearments as the two eavesdropped on Alvey's escapade.

After an hour, they heard Alvey say, "Would you two ladies like a drink or coffee?"

A feminine voice responded, "Get that cute butt back in here. We're ready to go for more."

"The guy's an animal!" Zivi said as he wiped several beads of sweat from his brow.

"I don't know about that. He reminds me of me," Pavkov commented as the moaning and bed squeaking started again.

After two more hours, they heard the squeaking stop and the sound of people getting dressed and cleaning up.

"Did you have fun?" one of the women asked.

"Cinnamon, it was an around the world event!" Alvey teased.

"We both had fun. Didn't we, Jasmine?" Cinnamon asked.

"Hmmm. I'll say," Jasmine agreed.

"How do you ladies like working at Sweet Dreams?" Alvey asked.

"It's a job. Why do you ask?" Cinnamon queried.

"Would you ladies like to work for me?" Alvey asked.

"Doing what?" Cinnamon replied with a question.

"I used to have ladies working for me in Detroit and I'm thinking of starting my own side business here. I think you two could make a lot of money if you worked for me."

"He's an ass peddler like us!" Zivi burst out to Pavkov as they eavesdropped from Pavkov's office.

"Shhh. Listen," Pavkov said as he cocked his head.

"What about O'Malley?" Jasmine asked.

"Screw O'Malley," Alvey replied. "I'll make it worth your while."

Jasmine looked at the dark-haired Alvey and smiled. "I'll do it. How about you, Cinnamon?"

"Sure, why not. We're not making much with O'Malley."

"Good. I've got a few details to work out. Why don't you write your phone numbers here and I'll follow up when I'm ready."

"Let me go first," Jasmine said. "You can call me any time," she said seductively.

After a minute elapsed, Moore said, "I'll walk you ladies to your car."

As they heard the door shut, Zivi turned to Pavkov. "The guy's a gentlemen too. He's walking them to the car."

"He's stealing those women from right under O'Malley's nose. Setting up his own business! Alvey's got some big cajones! I like that!" Pavkov bellowed.

"I've heard enough for tonight. You can set that to record so we don't miss anything. Then check it in the morning. I'm heading home," Pavkov said as he stood.

"Okay," Zivi said as he made a couple of adjustments on their recording device.

Back at the apartment parking lot, Moore was leaning into the car through the car window. "Thank you, ladies."

"Just don't get any ideas about us doing the real thing, Emerson," Cinnamon said.

"Why not?" Jasmine said. "I bet it could be a lot of fun," she teased.

Moore had a wide grin as he spoke to the two undercover officers. "You ladies were so convincing, especially with the moans. You need to win an Oscar for acting the way you did."

"You can personally give me my Oscar," Jasmine said as she looked over at Moore.

Moore threw a wink.

"It was a good thing you whispered what was going on with the bug you found. We'd have blown your cover if we opened up in there," Cinnamon said.

"I needed to do something to reel these guys in and you two certainly have helped my efforts. I'll be sure to let Mullen know how you helped me."

"Glad to be of assistance," Jasmine smiled suggestively from the passenger seat.

"You two be careful when you get back there," Moore cautioned. "I'm afraid he's going to be looking for you two to turn tricks for other customers."

"We won't be around too much longer. We've just about completed everything we need on O'Malley, but we need to sweep in Pavkov and his boss."

"I'll see what I can do on my side," Moore said. "Drive safe," he said as he stood back and Cinnamon started her car. As she started to pull away, she yelled, "By the way, you do have a cute butt!"

Moore laughed and yelled back. "So do both of you!" He turned and walked back into the apartment building.

As time progressed, Moore's scrutiny by Pavkov and Zivi continued. They were growing more comfortable with him. They had started testing him by having him deliver small packages around town. Moore had assumed the packages were full of cocaine, but they were filled with sugar as they tested him for two days. Then, the sugar was replaced by cocaine.

On this day, Moore was talking to Zivi outside of Pavkov's office. Suddenly, Pavkov yelled, "We're going to get raided in a few minutes. Make sure we're clean."

Pavkov's men had been trained for these types of raids. They worked methodically to ensure any illegal activities ceased and all contraband was safely hidden.

Moore spoke to Zivi as Zivi made a quick inspection tour. "What's this all about? How does he know we're being raided?"

Zivi grinned. "Technology."

"Technology? Somebody call Pavkov and tip him off?"

"Better than that. You can get a breakdown in communications. We've got video cameras set up on buildings in the area. We're always watching. Apparently, he saw a bunch of Suburbans heading this way. Those dumb schmucks can be spotted a mile away in those Suburbans."

Zivi was right. Five Chevy Suburbans pulled into the parking lot and emptied out five armed U.S. Customs agents from each one. A number of them surrounded the warehouse while the others walked inside.

"Let's get back to the office."

The two hurried back to Pavkov's office and arrived just steps ahead of three agents, including Ernie Corpening.

"What can I do for you kind gentlemen?" Pavkov asked.

"We've got a warrant to search the premises," Corpening explained.

"Be my guest. I have nothing to hide," Pavkov said as he leaned against the door to his office. "What are you looking for?"

"Illegal immigrants and drugs. You want to fess up…?" Corpening didn't get to finish his question as his eyes focused on Moore.

"What's he doing here?"

"He works for me. Why?" Pavkov asked with interest. "You know this guy?"

Corpening smiled. "We busted him in Detroit a couple of years ago. He was involved with running a prostitution ring. Caught him bringing one in from Canada."

Moore didn't say anything. He just stared at Corpening.

Pavkov's eyes widened at hearing the information. "That's news to me." He looked from the agent to Moore. "So, why didn't you tell me about this?"

Moore copped a sullen look. "I needed a job and you didn't ask. I did my time and got off early for good conduct."

Pavkov swung back to look at Corpening. "You heard the man. He paid for his mistake. Looks to me like he's trying for a fresh start."

"Back to the business at hand. You don't mind if we look around, do you?" Corpening asked.

"No, no. Be my guest. I don't have anything to hide," Pavkov responded. He knew his drugs were carefully concealed in hiding places within the walls and in a truck that was driven off the premises a minute before the agents arrived.

Two of the agents began searching through the office area as Corpening walked out to watch his team search through the warehouse.

"Bears on the water," Zivi said as he looked through one of the open garage doors toward the river and saw two Customs Service boats idling their engines off the warehouse property.

"No one is going to find anything," Pavkov said proudly. He turned to Moore and asked, "So, Alvey, you ran girls?" Pavkov wanted to build upon what he had heard Alvey offer the ladies in his apartment.

Moore nodded his head. "I had a few peanut butter legs in my stable. Not a big operation."

"You surprised me on that one. I don't know why, but I didn't figure you for running girls," Pavkov lied.

"Life's full of surprises," Moore countered.

"And you did time?" Pavkov asked.

"Yeah, I took the rap."

Pavkov looked at Zivi and raised his eyebrows. "This could be very useful for us."

Zivi nodded his head several times in agreement.

When the agents finished their search and came up empty-handed, they left the building and returned to their vehicles. After they drove away, Moore returned to his work.

In his office, Pavkov spoke to Zivi. "Check Alvey out with folks we know in Detroit. See if it's true he ran a prostitution ring."

"I'm on it," Zivi said as he headed for his car to drive a short distance away to use a pay phone.

At the end of the day, Moore was preparing to leave. He headed for his car and started the engine as he saw a freighter making its way up the Maumee River toward the warehouse's dock. He had heard they were expecting a special shipment and assumed it was in the containers on her deck. As he began to drive out of the lot, he suddenly hit the brakes as he saw the name of the ship. It read *Zenobia*. A chill went up Moore's spine.

He knew the *Zenobia* had sunk years ago in the Danube River. He peered closely at the vessel and realized it wasn't the same freighter he had been aboard. It was eerily coincidental a ship with that name would be docking here. He released the brakes and drove to his apartment.

As he drove, Moore thought back to Mullen and how he had helped him choose his cover. Choosing Alvey was a perfect fit for the assignment. He knew he didn't have to worry about the real Alvey surfacing. The real Alvey had entered the federal witness protection program and was involved in providing insight into Detroit's prostitution rings.

Back at the warehouse, Zivi was briefing Pavkov. "Looks like he's the real deal. That's what the boys up there said."

"Good. Maybe we'll expand his delivery services."

"You thinking Naples? Have him meet the Boss?"

"That's exactly what I'm thinking," Pavkov replied.

The Next Morning
Pavkov's Warehouse

As Moore parked his car and walked toward the warehouse, he could see Big Lucas, the large crane overlooking the Maumee, unloading containers from the *Zenobia*. Moore was curious and wanted to ask questions about the ship, but entered the warehouse and applied himself to his work.

Midmorning, Zivi interrupted Moore's work.

"Come with me."

Moore followed Zivi, who led him to Pavkov's office. Pavkov was leaning back in his chair. An unfiltered cigarette dangled from a corner of his mouth.

"Alvey," he started. "I've been thinking."

"Yes?"

"With your background, you might be somebody who could help my business."

"I'm still learning about warehousing," Moore responded.

"Not that business!" Pavkov snarled. "I'm talking about my other business. It's much more profitable."

"I'm listening," Moore said.

"Check him," Pavkov said to Zivi. "You have a cell phone?"

"Yes."

"Give it to Zivi."

"Why?"

"You won't be needing it."

Moore reluctantly handed his cell phone to Zivi, who had picked up a wand and was running it over and around Moore as he checked for bugs.

"He's clean," Zivi said as he placed the cell phone on a table outside Pavkov's office and returned to stand next to Moore.

"Was that really necessary?" Moore asked.

"You'll understand as we talk. I am a very careful man. That's how I avoid doing time. Right, Zivi?" Pavkov looked at Zivi.

"Right," Zivi responded.

"My office is swept for bugs twice a day. I'm constantly changing cell phones so no one can track my numbers or calls."

"So, what's this all about?" Moore asked.

"I'm going to bring you in. You can start working for me in my distribution business."

"Distribution business?"

"Yeah. We do a little coke business and prostitution."

"And where does my distribution come in?" Moore asked.

"Alvey, you're going to make deliveries for us. I'll have you run coke to some of the major dealers and you take loads of women to drop-off points."

Moore had several questions, but thought he better stay in character as Alvey. "And what's it worth to me?"

"You'll get paid well. You'll see. You've got to trust me."

Zivi spoke. "He pays us well."

"Count me in," Moore said. "I've got nothing to lose."

"Good. Now there's one other thing I should mention to you." Pavkov stood and loomed over Moore. "Don't get any ideas about screwing with me. You do your job, I'll take care of you. You screw me and I'll screw you, too. I'll cut your intestines out while you're alive and stuff them down your throat for starters," he threatened.

Moore couldn't help but grimace at the thought. "No problem."

"Good. Now, go with Zivi. You've got your first delivery to get set up."

"I'm on it," Moore said as he followed Zivi out of the office door through the warehouse. As they exited the building along the riverfront, Moore asked. "Where are we going?"

Zivi continued walking toward the area next to the *Zenobia* where a number of shipping containers had been unloaded.

"Where are we going?" Moore asked again.

Zivi pointed to one forty-foot shipping container that had been unloaded onto a flatbed truck. "We're picking up that truck."

The two men climbed into the truck and drove it inside the warehouse to a secluded area. It had been completely portioned off from the rest of the warehouse. Zivi parked the truck next to a large box truck.

As the two climbed out of the flatbed, Zivi spoke. "This is a special cargo." He began unlocking the doors to the container. When he opened the doors, Moore was stunned by its contents.

Inside were eight women, huddled in a corner. Moore's eyes swept through the container. He saw sleeping bags on the floor, some bags of food, two lanterns and trash. Two buckets in the opposite corner served as toilets for the occupants.

Moore was aghast at the situation and Zivi could tell by the look on Moore's face. "Alvey, this was the worst part of their trip. This shipment is from Bulgaria. They're recruited there with an offer to become models in Toronto. The girls jump at the chance for a fresh start and take the tickets and assistance we give them with their forged documents.

"Once they land in Toronto, we meet them at the airport and take them to a safe house. There, we break them."

"Tell them they owe you the money for the airplane tickets and put them out to work?" Moore asked as if he were the savvy Alvey.

"Yeah. The stubborn ones we beat. Sometimes, we show them a picture of their family and tell them we will go to their homes and kill them unless they work for us."

"Do you run them from the safe house or put them on the street?"

"Too risky. We get a hotel room and advertise them on an

Internet site. Sometimes, we set up a massage parlor and run them through there. Then we bring them here."

"On the *Zenobia*?"

"Usually. It's the Boss's ship."

Moore's eyes widened. "Pavkov's?"

"No, the Boss. You'll meet him when we make our delivery." Zivi continued with his explanation. "We load the girls in the last container to be loaded so they're stacked at the highest level. We don't have to worry about the crew getting nosy because they all work for the Boss."

"Is the Boss here?" Moore asked.

"No, you'll see soon enough."

Moore moved the conversation back to the transporting of the women into Toledo. "What other ways do you ship them into Toledo?"

"There're several. Some are hidden in transport vehicles and come over Detroit's Ambassador Bridge or through the bridges in Buffalo. Sometimes, we have large cabin cruisers pick up the girls in Canada and run them here, although U.S. Customs seems to be pulling over more boats from Canada. That's making it riskier for us."

Zivi turned his head and looked at Moore. "You sure do ask a lot of questions."

"I'm just trying to understand the nuances if this is going to be part of my job."

Zivi gave Moore a long stare and then turned his attention back to the women. "Do you all speak English?"

All responded affirmatively with heavy accents.

"Good. We'll be taking you on a short trip to where you'll enjoy the ocean and sand."

"Short trip?" Moore asked quietly.

"Play along with me," Zivi said, pressing a .45 into Moore's hand as he held one in his own. "Now, I want you all to get out of there. We have food for you and showers so you can get cleaned up. Come on out," he said as he waved his weapon at them. "And don't get any ideas about trying to make a break for it."

Zivi spoke to Moore in a low tone. "We only shoot them as a last resort. We've got too much invested in them to kill any of them. Shoot to wound if you have to shoot at all."

"Got it," Moore acknowledged.

The women moved together as if in a herd and followed his directions as he pointed to a table where sandwiches and coffee were waiting. The women ate and drank quickly.

"Showers are over there." He pointed to a large shower room with sinks and toilets. "You've got ten minutes," he said as the women rushed to take showers.

Finished with their showers and dressing, the women walked out of the shower room and stood in a group in front of Zivi.

Gesturing toward the box truck, Zivi spoke to Moore. "Alvey, unlock and open up that truck."

Moore walked to the truck and unlocked the latch. As he rolled up the doors, he was surprised by the sight in front of him. Twelve hammocks were hanging from the truck's sidewalls. Two were occupied.

When Moore looked at the two, he recognized them from their photos in the *Toledo Blade.* They were the two missing teens from Put-in-Bay.

"Help us," they screamed as they tumbled out of their hammocks and started to rush toward the open door.

With the greatest amount of reluctance, Moore held up his hand. His face was chagrined. "Stop," he said. Moore was torn. Free the girls now or continue with his role-playing. He cast a look at Zivi, who was aiming his weapon at Moore.

"Something wrong, Alvey?" he asked suspiciously as he watched Moore. "You know these girls?"

Moore reacted quickly. "No. Just saw their pictures in the paper."

"Make sure they don't get out." Zivi looked at the other women and ordered them into the box truck. Quickly, each one climbed past Moore and entered the truck where they joined the sobbing teens.

"Lock it up," Zivi said as he headed for the truck's cab.

Moore did as he was instructed and walked around the truck where he climbed into the passenger seat.

"Zivi?"

"Yes," he responded as he backed the truck out of the warehouse.

"What's the fixture on top of the cab?"

"Tracking device. The Boss knows where we are the entire time," Zivi answered as he pulled the truck onto Tiffin Avenue. Within minutes, they had driven by Tony Packo's and were on I-75 South.

"Where are we headed?" Moore asked.

"Naples, Florida."

"Naples! I didn't pack!" Moore said, slightly irritated.

"We'll get what you need along the way. Sometimes, Pavkov and the Boss like to surprise us with unannounced trips. That way, it's less likely to leak to the police."

Moore didn't comment as they drove under the Navarre Road bridge.

"It's kept them clean," Zivi added.

After they passed the Ohio Turnpike, Moore turned to Zivi. "Zivi, how did you get in the business?"

Zivi eyed Alvey and wondered if he should give the new guy any information. He thought back and remembered they had cleared Alvey. He decided he'd open up. Alvey seemed like he was going to be a long-term fit.

"I've known Pavkov since I was a kid. We grew up in East To-ledo, over behind Tony Packo's Restaurant. Pavkov started a gang when some of the other gangs tried coming into our neighbor-hood."

"Did you guys start right away with prostitution and drugs?"

"Nah. We started a protection service for the businesses in the community. Nothing was going down without our say-so. When guys tried to do break-ins or robberies, we took care of them."

"What about the drugs and trafficking?" Moore asked.

"We fooled around a bit. Nothing major. Then, Pavkov met the Boss."

"Who's that? Somebody from Detroit?"

"The guy was from Canada. He had been doing the drug and human trafficking stuff for years and wanted to expand into the United States. He began making contacts with businessmen like Pavkov all along I-75 to Naples." Zivi paused and chuckled softly at his comment about calling Pavkov a businessman.

"How did he find Pavkov?"

"He wanted someone who had operations by the river. He asked around and heard about Pavkov. The rest is history." Zivi turned and looked at Moore. "Funny thing you didn't run into him in Detroit with the girls you were running."

"I was small time. It sounds like he was looking for the big time guys."

"How many women did you run?"

Moore thought quickly as he made up a response. "Five usually."

"Where did you get them?"

"Runaways and strip clubs," Moore responded. "I'd recruit the dancers by offering them more money than what they'd make in the clubs."

"You beat them?"

"Only when I had to," Moore responded in character. "Of course, I had to take each one of them for a test ride."

"Yeah, I bet you enjoyed that." Zivi snickered as he recalled listening through the bug as Alvey had his encounter with the two dancers from Sweet Dreams. "I'd be Pavkov's enforcer for him. I'd beat and threaten the girls. I always got my pick of the litter as a bonus."

"Were you his hit man, too?"

"When I had to be. Pavkov knew he could count on me. I usually used piano wire and strangled the girls we caught after they tried running away. It taught the others a lesson."

Moore turned his head to look out the window as revulsion filled him.

The two men chatted off and on as they drove through Cincinnati and up the hill in northern Kentucky to Florence where they were welcomed by the well-known water tower, lettered with the words "Florence Y'all."

"I'm getting off at the next exit. I need to pee," Zivi said as he steered the truck up the exit ramp past the Florence Mall. "You can gas her up and drive the next section."

"Sure. How far are we going to drive before we get a motel room?" Moore asked.

"Alvey, what are you made of? We're driving straight through to Naples. You and I are going to take turns," Zivi muttered as he pulled off the road and into a gas station. "Come on. I'll swipe my credit card."

Moore did as he was told and joined Zivi at the gas pump. Once the pump started, Zivi started to walk toward the building. "Need anything?"

"Sure. Coffee with cream."

Zivi disappeared inside.

Moore quickly looked around for a pay phone to call Mullen. He spotted one next to the entrance door through which Zivi had entered the gas station. Too dangerous for him to make a call without being spotted, Moore thought. He resigned himself to filling the tank and looking for another opportunity to alert Mullen.

Five minutes later, Zivi emerged from the building. He was carrying two coffees, a large overcooked hot dog and a big bag of chips.

"Thought I'd eat before I snooze," Zivi said. He looked toward the rear of the truck and asked, "Were they quiet?"

"Not a peep," Moore answered.

"Good."

The two returned to the cab and downed their food. Shortly afterwards as they neared Williamstown, Kentucky, Zivi began to snore. As they drove through Lexington, Moore heard a soft knocking on a closed window panel to the cargo area.

Moore looked at Zivi and saw he was in a deep sleep. Carefully, he reached around with one hand and slid open the panel. Holding a finger to his lips, he looked over his shoulder and saw one of the abducted teens from the island at the small window. Her face was filled with anguish.

"Can you help us?" she whispered.

Moore shook his head negatively.

"I want to go home," she pleaded in a normal voice.

That woke up Zivi.

"What's going on here?" Zivi grumbled angrily.

"The bitch is crying. She needs to take a pee," Moore replied.

"Pee in the bucket," Zivi said as he slammed the slider shut.

"Leave that closed!"

"I just wanted to be sure that we didn't have a problem back there," Moore said weakly.

"If there was a problem, we'd hear them all screaming. Leave it shut!"

An hour south of Lexington, Zivi's phone rang. He had a brief conversation with the caller. "We've got to make a stop at a truck stop south of Knoxville."

"Why?"

"Got a pick-up to make."

"How's that?"

"You'll see."

Once they drove through the sloping mountains north of Knoxville and passed through the city, Zivi watched for the exit. When he saw it, he directed Moore to drive down the ramp and make a right at the traffic light.

"Pull in over there." Zivi pointed to a self-service car wash next to a truck stop.

Moore parked the truck and the two men hopped out of the vehicle. They walked to the rear.

"We're here," he said after dialing a cell phone number. "White box truck. Just parked."

He paused. "Yes, I see you."

A black Cadillac pulled up near the rear of the truck and a tall black man stepped out. He moved quickly around the car and opened the door for the occupant in the passenger's seat.

The blonde twenty-six-year-old woman was wearing a striped dress that revealed her pregnant belly. She had a tattoo on the side of her neck that said "King Kole." It was the nickname for her pimp.

Moore remembered Izzy Watkins telling him tattoos were commonly seen among sex trafficking victims. "They're branding their women. They treat them like cattle," she had said.

"Open the door," Zivi said to Moore, "while I take care of business. And be sure none of them run away."

Zivi and the man spoke briefly and the man handed Zivi an envelope containing a large sum of money. The man returned to his car and drove away while Zivi escorted the woman to the back of the truck.

Zivi and the woman walked to the truck where Moore was standing guard at the open door.

"Get in there," Zivi commanded the woman as he looked at the women swaying in their hammocks. "Not too much farther, girls," Zivi lied.

The woman climbed in and Moore closed and relocked the door.

"I'll drive," Zivi said as he headed for the cab and Moore walked to the passenger side.

"What was that all about?"

"Damaged goods. The stupid whore got herself knocked up. We're going to take care of her and sell the baby when it arrives. There's a good market out there for people who want to adopt a baby," Zivi explained.

"A little more cash on the side," Moore agreed. "I've thought about getting in the baby market," Moore added as he spoke in the Alvey role.

South of Macon, Zivi exited I-75 at the first exit in Tifton. He drove to a nearby gas station where he refilled the truck and bought a dozen submarine sandwiches and water bottles. Then, he drove several miles into the country. Finding an isolated road, he pulled over and parked the truck.

"We'll let them get some fresh air," he said.

The two men walked to the rear of the truck where Moore unlocked the door and opened it. The bright light poured into the vehicle's interior, causing the girls to cover their eyes.

"Everybody out. Stretch your legs and don't try to run away," Zivi bellowed as he waved his .45 at the girls. As the girls began exiting the vehicle, he pointed to one of them and shouted, "Empty that bucket." Zivi was referring to the bucket the girls had been using as a toilet.

The girl carried the bucket to the rear and handed it to another one who emptied it in the nearby ditch.

Taking a sandwich and water bottle for himself, Zivi threw the bag to the ground. "Help yourselves," he said.

Moore threw him a sidelong glance as he moved in to take a sandwich. Before he could get one, the island teen with whom he had talked through the sliding window handed Moore a sandwich and water bottle. She whispered as she placed them in his hands, "Please help my friend and me."

Moore looked more closely at the girl and was crestfallen when he saw she had a blackened eye. "Who gave you the black eye?" She motioned her head toward Zivi. "He did before he raped me."

"Hey. No talking over there!" Zivi called.

Moore took his food and walked to the other side of the girls so he could deter any runaways from that side. He sat on the ground and unwrapped his sandwich. There was no taste to it. The stress about delivering the girls was stealing away any appetite he thought he might have had. He pitched his barely eaten sandwich to the pregnant girl. "You're eating for two. Might as well have my sandwich."

Moore opened his water bottle and sipped from it as he looked over his group of captives. Delivering them to the Boss was going to be very difficult for him.

Zivi's cell phone rang. "Yes?" he said. He talked for a few minutes, hung up and motioned for Moore to join him.

"That was Pavkov. He saw we're stopped and wants to know what we're doing."

"How does he know we're stopped?"

"Did you forget what I told you?" Zivi pointed to the fixture on top of the truck's cab. "It's a GPS tracking device. He's watching us! And he can send a signal that shuts down the truck if he thinks I'm running off with the girls to sell them to somebody. Like I'd do that!"

"You tell him we're taking a food break?"

"Hell, no. I told him you were itching to test drive one of the girls." Zivi laughed crudely after he said it. "I told him we pulled over so you can get that itch scratched."

Moore glared at Zivi. He started to make a remark, then thought better of it.

"Pavkov told me something else that you might find interesting."

"Oh?"

"Yeah, he got a call from O'Malley. You remember him? The guy who runs Sweet Dreams."

"Yes," Moore responded.

"Apparently your two girlfriends have disappeared."

Moore hoped it was on their own volition and that nothing had happened to them. "Is that so?"

"You know anything about it?"

"Nope."

"Didn't you have them over to your apartment?" Zivi slipped.

Moore knew it was confirmation they had been listening. "Yes, I did. How did you know?" He played dumb.

"O'Malley told us," Zivi lied. A movement out of the corner of his eye caught Zivi's attention and he looked toward the girls.

"Runaway!" Zivi yelled suddenly as he stood and aimed his weapon. "Stop! You little bitch!" he screamed.

Moore looked to his right and saw the girl to whom he had given his sandwich was running down the road.

"I said stop!"

The girl ignored him and kept running. Without hesitation, Zivi fired. The bullet caught her in the back of the head and she tumbled headfirst into the road.

"We're out of here!" Zivi said angrily at having to kill one of their income-producers. "Back into the truck. All of you. Back into the truck," he screamed.

"What about her?" Moore asked. He was visibly shaken.

"She's road kill! You want to hang around in case the police show up? You want your fingerprints on her? We're leaving now!" Zivi bellowed as the last girl scampered into the truck and Zivi shut the door.

"You drive!" he snapped at Moore as he locked the door and headed for the passenger side of the cab.

Moore returned to the truck and started the engine. He retraced the route they had driven and returned to I-75 South.

The entire time, Zivi was cursing quietly under his breath about killing the woman and how he was going to explain it to Pavkov and the Boss. Moore drove silently and began to formulate a plan to free the women without jeopardizing his undercover role.

Several hours later, the vehicle was passing through an undeveloped stretch of Charlotte County between Punta Gorda and Ft. Myers. The sides of the road were filled with thick vegetation. Zivi was snoring and Moore was driving. When Moore saw a Florida State trooper running a speed trap, Moore accelerated the truck and drove fifteen miles an hour over the speed limit as he zoomed by the trooper.

Within moments, Moore heard a siren and saw the trooper's flashing lights closing in on the vehicle. Moore slowed down and the siren woke up Zivi.

"What's going on?" Zivi asked as he looked through the outside mirror at the approaching police car.

"Don't know. I was going the speed limit," Moore lied.

"When we stop, you walk back to his car. I'm going to open the sliding window and make sure the girls stay quiet. We don't need them yelling because they realize the police pulled us over."

"Right," Moore answered as he pulled the truck to the side of the road and parked. Shutting off the ignition, he walked to where the trooper had parked his car on the berm.

"Afternoon, officer," Moore started.

"Going a little fast there weren't you?" the officer asked as he walked toward Moore.

Moore stopped and spoke in a low voice. "Sir, I'm working undercover and am going to need your help. Don't look, but there's an armed man in the cab of the truck and the truck is full of women who are being trafficked. You're going to need to call for back up."

The trooper threw a quick glance at the truck and began to reach for the radio on his shoulder. Before he could depress the key, Zivi stepped out from around the right side of the truck. "I wouldn't do that," he warned. He was holding his .45 in his hand and it was leveled at the officer.

"Drop your weapon and walk toward me," he said.

The trooper looked at Moore and Moore shrugged his shoulders. "What are you doing?" Moore asked as he turned to follow the trooper.

Before Zivi could respond, the women in the truck started banging on the sides of the truck and screaming for help.

"Watch," Zivi said as he motioned for the trooper to walk into the brush next to the road.

Moore followed Zivi and the trooper ten feet into the brush where Zivi ordered the trooper to drop to his knees. He began to place his .45 against the back of the trooper's neck when Moore interrupted Zivi.

"Zivi, you better drop your weapon."

Zivi turned and looked at Moore. Moore had pulled out his .45 from the back waistband of his pants and was pointing it at Zivi.

"What the hell are you doing?" Zivi stormed.

"Let him go."

"What are you? Crazy?" Zivi had a look of surprise on his face.

"Drop it," Moore ordered again.

Zivi swung his weapon around and began to point it at Moore. "Why you little piece of…"

Moore's gun fired before Zivi could pull the trigger on his weapon. Moore caught Zivi squarely in the chest and Zivi dropped his weapon as he fell to the ground. Moore ran over and kicked the weapon away as the trooper radioed for back up.

When he finished, the trooper looked at Moore. "Thanks."

Moore stared at Zivi as he twitched. "I couldn't let him take you out," Moore said. Moore dropped the gun to the ground and sat down next to it. Funny, he thought to himself, but he didn't feel very remorseful about shooting Zivi. In fact, Moore thought Zivi looked like road kill now.

Within minutes, five state trooper vehicles converged on the scene along with an ambulance. Moore unlocked the truck and slid open the overhead door. The girls were helped from the truck and into a waiting police van. The two teens from the island abduction walked over to Moore before they entered the van.

"Thank you," the one said. "I knew you'd find a way to help us."

"You've been through enough already. I couldn't deliver you girls to the guy who runs this operation," Moore explained. He wished he could have helped them sooner.

She and her friend hugged Moore before turning and climbing into the van.

As the ambulance pulled away, the first trooper walked up to Moore. "I don't think he's going to make it."

"I was afraid that was going to happen," Moore said.

"You mentioned you're undercover. For which agency?"

"None. I'm an investigative reporter. My real name is Emerson Moore," Moore said. He quickly provided the trooper with a re-cap of what had transpired and his work with the Human Trafficking Task Force in Toledo. He also mentioned he had witnessed the murder of the pregnant woman in Tifton, Georgia, and provided him with the details.

"I'd like to finish my assignment and I'm going to need the help of my SWAT team friends in Naples."

"We'll see what we can do," the trooper said.

"I'll need to use your cell phone to call them."

"Sure," the trooper said as he handed Moore his cell phone.

Moore keyed in the number for the unit captain, Bob Siwel. Moore had met Siwel a couple of years earlier when he was writing a story on drug running into Naples. Siwel had helped him with information for the story and allowed Moore to go through abbreviated SWAT training. He was now involved with the Southwest Florida Regional Human Trafficking Task Force.

When Siwel answered the phone, Moore briefly explained what had transpired and he expected Pavkov to be calling shortly, knowing the truck had been parked. Then, he outlined his plan for penetrating the Boss's operations.

"Sounds good to me, Emerson," Siwel said. "We've been trying to get in there, but he's using technology against us."

"I'll hit the road and should be there in a few hours."

"Is there a tracking pod on the truck?" Siwel asked.

"Yes."

"Be sure to cover the tracking device. Wrap it in aluminum foil and secure it with duct tape. That way the satellite beam can't get through the foil and track you or turn off the engine."

Moore thought for a moment. "I saw some foil from the sandwich wrappers in the back of the truck I can use and I believe there's a roll of duct tape in the cab."

"Good. Let me talk to the trooper and tell him what we're doing. I'm going to see if he won't escort you the rest of the way to our facility."

"Thanks, Bob," Moore said. "The Captain wants to talk to you," Moore said as he handed the phone to the trooper.

After the two men talked and ended the call, the trooper said, "I need to clear this with my superiors." He walked back to his car to talk privately and place his call.

Moore walked to the open back of the truck and climbed inside. He found scraps of aluminum foil and exited the vehicle. He found the duct tape and climbed onto the top of the cab where he placed the pieces of aluminum foil around the twelve-by-twelve-inch fixture to block the signal. He then secured the pieces in place with the duct tape.

Almost immediately, Zivi's cell phone, which had been left in the cab, began to ring. Moore scrambled down from the cab's roof and swung into the cab. He reached for the cell and answered. "Alvey."

"Alvey, what in the hell is going on? You guys have been parked for an hour. And now, the tracking signal has been lost."

Moore started to relay a story which he had concocted as he drove. "There's been a problem."

Pavkov impatiently interrupted, "Put Zivi on the phone!"

"I can't. That's part of the problem."

"What do you mean Zivi is part of the problem."

"I don't know, man. He just sort of wigged out on me. He went off on me in the truck and then we parked. He got in my face and threw a few punches. Then he took off in the truck without me," Moore explained.

Pavkov was suspicious. He knew Zivi could have a temper and explode, but wasn't sure he was buying Moore's explanation. "Alvey, how did you end up with the cell phone?"

"I grabbed it when I got out of the truck. I thought I'd have to call you and let you know he weirded out. Lucky for me I had it." Pavkov wasn't sold. "And why did the truck tracker fail just now?"

"Don't know. Maybe it's coincidental. The satellite system could be down or the tracker failed."

Pavkov looked at several other monitors and saw the other vehicles he was tracking were still receiving and sending signals. "The satellite system is working fine."

"I can't explain it," Moore said.

Moore received an earful as Pavkov unleashed a series of expletives. He finished his tirade by saying, "That S.O.B. better check in with me and deliver the merchandise. I want you to rent a car and get your butt down to the Boss's place. I'll call him and let him know what happened and that you're driving in. He won't be happy if this whole thing falls apart. Zivi better show up there. I don't know what happened between you two, but we'll get to the bottom of it."

"Like I said, he just went off on me. Is he on some medication?"

Pavkov began cursing again and gave Moore the address to the Boss's place. Then, he furiously hung up.

"Somebody isn't happy," the trooper said. He had been listening to the conversation from next to the truck's cab.

"Not a happy camper!" Moore said.

"I got the okay. I can escort you to the Task Force's compound."

"Great," Moore said as he scooted across the seat and behind the steering wheel. The trooper returned to his car and the two vehicles headed for Naples.

A Few Hours Later
Naples, Florida

The two vehicles exited I-75 in Naples at the Golden Gate Parkway. Moore followed the trooper west to Airport Road. After making a couple of turns, they turned onto The Patriot Way and to the Southwest Florida Regional Human Trafficking Task Force's facility. The two vehicles drove up to the building and parked in front.

The trooper and Moore entered the building and were ushered into Siwel's office.

"You look beat, Emerson," Siwel said as he greeted Moore. Siwel had the powerful build of a weight lifter, with close cropped hair. He was wearing a tan polo shirt with a badge and desert-style camouflage pants.

"It's been a long drive," Moore responded as he shook hands with Siwel and plopped into a chair.

Seeing Moore was who he said he was, the trooper excused himself and returned to his vehicle, then headed back to Punta Gorda.

"Tell me what you've been up to," Siwel said as he settled back in his chair.

Before he could begin, a man walked into the office and gave Moore a cup of coffee.

Moore recognized him as the head of the aviation and water units, Mark Chertney. The guys had given him the nickname of

Chutney. He was taller than Siwel and similarly attired.

"Thanks, Chutney," Moore said appreciatively. He then began telling them what transpired since his initial involvement with the murder of Angel Dudich's sister in Put-in-Bay.

"And it all leads you here," Siwel said.

Moore nodded his head.

"Sure sounds like our boy in Immokalee," Chutney suggested.

"It does." Siwel turned his head toward Moore. "This guy, the Boss, shows up a few years ago and sets up shop in Immokalee with military-style precision. He's very careful and it's hard to pin anything on him. We're suspicious he's running prostitutes and drugs."

"It's more profitable to run the women than drugs," Chutney volunteered.

"How's that?" Moore asked with a perplexed look.

"Drugs are consumed once you use them and you have to smuggle more in. Once the prostitutes are smuggled in, they produce a steady income stream because they can be used over and over."

"He's right," Siwel said.

"We had a problem with what we called the Cuban landings. Mule ships would anchor offshore where they were met by go-fast boats with fake bottoms. The Cuban women would be transferred from the mule ships to the go-fast boats and brought here. We cracked down on them and targeted boat ramps. That type of importing of females has been virtually eliminated in this county," Chutney explained.

"So, they've resorted to trucking in females from illegal crossings from Mexico or, as you've discovered, through Canada and down the I-75 corridor," Siwel said.

"I don't understand. If you think the Boss is running the drugs and prostitution, why don't you bust him?"

"Can't do anything unless we have a witness or probable cause. Then, we can get a search warrant and raid his facility. So far, we haven't been able to do anything. It's frustrating."

"No witnesses?"

"Like Bob said, the guy is smart and careful. For example, five women were set up in a migrant worker camp on the day the migrants were paid and had been drinking for an hour. The women were in a mobile home that had been modified inside with five doors and five individual bedrooms. Each door was painted a different color.

"Three heavily armed guys worked a table where the pictures and corresponding door color for each girl was displayed. The migrant workers paid fifty dollars to spend thirty minutes. When they paid, they were given a poker chip, matching the color of the door they wanted to enter. Then, they waited in lines outside of the doors where two more armed men took their chips and allowed them to enter the rooms," Chutney explained.

"Could you sweep in and bust them?" Moore asked.

"We do when we learn about it," Siwel said. "The problem is the armed men won't talk. They serve their time and return to their jobs when they're freed."

"It's a rare event when you get one of them to talk. And even then, they won't talk about the Boss," Chutney added.

"What about the women?" Moore asked. "Don't they talk?"

"Too scared. They've been terrorized and have succumbed to being victims. They know they are here illegally and can be deported. They don't talk," Siwel said.

"Can't you trace the trailer's ownership?" Moore asked.

"Difficult. They pay cash. A lot of times they buy them through Craigslist," Siwel said. "There's no paper trail to track."

"I see," Moore said. "Maybe I can help."

"How?" Siwel asked.

"Pavkov gave me directions to the Boss's place in Immokalee. I'll rent a car and drive over there. Since I'm on the inside with them, I bet I can pick up the evidence you need."

Siwel looked at Chutney. "That's pretty dangerous with this guy."

"Rumor has it he's an animal," Chutney said.

"Too risky for you, my friend." Siwel said as he looked back at Moore.

"My mind is made up. I'm going in," Moore replied with a tone of determination.

"Listen, you're not trained in this stuff. You need to have had tactical training to be able to protect yourself," Siwel said, concerned for Moore.

"And the fact that I don't could work to my advantage. If this guy is as savvy as you say he is, don't you think he'd spot me right away?"

"He's got a point," Chutney reflected. "You could end up in a gator hole," he warned.

"I don't know," Siwel said. He wasn't convinced that it would be wise to allow Moore to follow through with his plan.

"Like I said, I'm going forward with it. There's nothing you can do to stop me. You don't have any grounds," Moore said, firmly.

Siwel looked at Moore. He realized trying to discourage him would be fruitless. "Okay, it's your funeral," he said reluctantly.

"But wear a wire so you at least have backup listening."

"Can't do it. In Toledo, they ran a wand over me to make sure I was bug free. I'm sure this guy would do the same."

"He's right," Chutney agreed.

"All right. But I sure hope you keep your wits about you," Siwel said.

"I will. I hope my wits are on full and not half-full," Moore joked weakly.

"One thing I can do is to take you on a flight over his compound," Chutney suggested. "That will give you some insight."

"Or, we can send a drone over and you can watch from here," Siwel offered.

"I'd prefer the flight. It will give me a better perspective."

"You've got it," Siwel said. He turned to Chutney. "You want to take him up?"

"Sure. We can go now if you'd like."

Moore stood. "Perfect." He followed Chutney out of the office and to the rear of the building and through the hangar, which held a Cessna 182 Skylane and two Bell-OH 57 helicopters.

"Climb aboard," Chutney said as he stepped up and into the plane. "You'll want to put this headset on after you fasten your seatbelt."

Moore did as he was instructed and soon heard the chatter from the Naples Municipal Airport's control tower as Chutney started the plane and taxied out of the hangar. He requested and received clearance to take off and the plane rolled down the runway. Within moments, they were airborne.

Chutney banked the plane and pointed it toward Immokalee. "You hear me okay?"

"Roger that," Moore grinned.

"Sounds like I've got a regular aviator next to me," Chutney smiled back. "These traffickers are pretty slick in the way they entice females to work for them."

"That's what I understand."

"There was one case where a pretty twenty-year-old girl was working at a taco stand in Guatemala. One of her regular customers started to date her, said he loved her and begged her to move in with him, which she did.

"As soon as she did, his entire demeanor changed. He became a control freak and beat her. She wasn't allowed to leave the apartment or talk to anyone else. After a week, he started taking her to back alleys and selling her for money. That went on for four years."

"That's terrible. Did she escape?" Moore asked.

"Nope. The guy decided he could make more money off of her in the United States. So he drove her and two other women to Mexico City where he made arrangements to sneak them across the border into the U.S.

"A van was waiting for them and took them to New Orleans, Biloxi, Panama City, Tampa, and Naples to be hookers. Their traffickers would keep the money and tell them it was to cover their housing, food and other expenses. When the three women didn't do as they were told, they were threatened and beaten."

Moore spoke again into the mic on the headset. "Did they ever get away?"

"Yes. Lucky for them one of their customers in Naples felt sorry for them and gave us a tip. We busted them and placed the women in a safe house. The traffickers are singing like canaries. That'll help us break the rest of that ring."

After a quick 20-minute flight to the east, Chutney paused as he looked out the window. "There's the compound." He banked the plane and they flew over the three acre compound. It had ten-foot high walls surrounding it on its perimeter. There was a guarded front gate with a guard shack. Several box trucks and vehicles were parked on the grounds. A two-story office fronted a large warehouse.

"Pretty big," Moore said as they circled.

"It is. Take a good look because we don't want to spend time circling. Not a good thing for them to see the Sheriff's plane overhead," he said as he straightened the plane and pointed it toward the Naples Airport.

"So, have you seen any women being delivered to his compound?" Moore asked.

"Nope. We use a drone for surveillance and have watched. Haven't seen anything. No women in the compound yard. The one problem for us is those box trucks, like the one you were driving, pull inside the warehouse and the warehouse doors are shut. There's no off-loading in the open. He's pretty crafty."

"I'm not sure the word should be crafty," Moore said. "I'd say he's cunning or devious, just based on what I've been able to ascertain."

"Yeah, I could go along with that."

The Boss's Compound
Immokalee

"Out of the car!" the guard ordered as Moore stopped in front of the gate to the compound.

Carefully, Moore stepped out of the vehicle and found it surrounded by four armed men. Their weapons were pointed at Moore as one of the men began to search the car.

"Name?" one demanded.

"Alvey," Moore responded.

"Yeah, we were expecting you." He approached Moore and patted him down. Then he took a hand-held scanner and ran it over Moore. "He's clean," he said after searching him for a wire.

The man, searching the car, pulled it into a parking space outside of the gate and parked it. Next, he popped the trunk lid and searched the trunk. "We're good," he called.

"You can go in. First door on the right," the first guard said as the gate opened wide enough for Moore to walk through. It closed behind him when he entered the compound.

Siwel was right. These guys were very careful with their security, Moore thought to himself. Moore noticed several wireless security cameras and motion sensors mounted around the compound. There were numerous vehicles, including two large box trucks, parked in the yard.

When Moore entered the small office, he panicked. Seated at a desk was a familiar looking man. Moore realized he had seen the man working at The Butterfly House at Put-in-Bay. He must be the missing Panich. Moore hoped his long hair and beard would be enough to hide his identity since Panich and he hadn't conversed when he had visited The Butterfly House.

"You're Alvey, right?" Panich asked.

"Right."

"Where's Zivi?" Panich asked.

"You've got me!" Moore replied.

Panich's only response was an icy stare.

"Pavkov told me to rent a car and drive here," Moore continued.

"Yeah, the Boss wants to talk to you." Panich motioned with his head toward a stairwell. "Upstairs."

Moore walked to the stairs and followed them to the second floor. When he walked onto the next level, he saw an open door. He looked into the room. Inside were several cabinets and tables. One table had a large aquarium and Moore could see it contained a small python. He shuddered. He didn't like snakes.

A man, smoking a cigarette, was standing with his back to the doorway.

On a table in front of him was another man. He was strapped naked to the table. A towel had been stuffed into his mouth so that his screams couldn't be heard.

"I'm looking for the Boss," Moore said as he poked his head inside the doorway.

"Well, you've found me. Come in," the man with his back to Moore said.

Moore began walking toward him. As he walked, he said, "I'm Alvey."

"I know."

Just before Alvey reached the Boss, the Boss spun around. Moore stopped in his tracks. He was shocked by what he saw. His face went white as he recognized who was standing in front of him. He had aged, but Moore wouldn't have forgotten him.

"What's wrong? I scare you, Alvey?" the Boss smirked.

Standing in front of Moore was the Vuk. It had been years since he had seen him, but Moore recognized him. Memories of his days in Vukovar flooded Moore's mind.

"Answer me, Alvey. What's wrong? I'm not used to asking questions twice," the Vuk said angrily as he turned back to the man on the table.

Moore exhaled as he realized the Vuk hadn't recognized him. He wrestled with how to respond when he saw the cigarette burns on the man's body. He decided to use that as an excuse. "I guess I'm just in shock at seeing those burns on his body."

"Ya like that? I don't put up with any garbage from anybody. This one here thought he could get away with skimming some of the profits from running some of the girls. Now, he's paying the price."

The man on the table was in extreme pain. He turned his head toward Moore. His eyes pleaded for help. Moore knew there was nothing he could do without breaking his cover.

"I've burned him about 50 times," the Vuk said as he took his cigarette and touched it to the man's skin. The man's body jerked and twitched in pain. He moaned through the gag. The Vuk wanted Alvey to see this as a deterrent to lying or stealing from him.

"I think that's enough burning." The Vuk put out his cigarette and picked up a sharp knife.

"What are you doing?" Moore asked.

"Ever fillet a fish?"

"No," Moore replied as he began to realize what the Vuk was going to do to the nude man.

"Then you probably haven't filleted the skin off a man, have you?"

"No," Moore answered with a shudder.

"It's relatively easy to do. You cut the skin in a horizontal slit and into the subcutaneous tissue," he said as he expertly wielded the knife in a feathering motion as the victim moaned with extreme pain and tried to twist away. "The blade cuts through the collagen which binds the epidermis and dermis to the subcutaneous fat."

The Vuk looked up from the cuts he had made. "I impressed you with my knowledge of medical terms, didn't I?"

Moore felt like he was ready to vomit. "Yes," he said weakly.

"Learned it from one of my clients. He loved to visit my girls. I grilled that doctor about torturing people. You see, I like to make them pay dearly for being disloyal to me." He placed the knife on the table and walked over to the doorway. "Panich?"

"Yes," the voice downstairs replied.

"Come up here and finish what I started."

Within a minute, Panich had run up the stairs and picked up the knife to continue slicing the man.

"Have you been disloyal to me, Alvey?" the Vuk asked as he peered intently at Alvey.

"No," Moore replied as he looked at the victim, who had passed out from the pain.

"Where's Zivi?"

"I don't know."

The Vuk walked over to Moore and then began to walk around him. He stopped behind Moore and Moore heard a click, then he felt something sharp against the back of his neck.

"Are you sure you don't know where Zivi is?"

"Positive," Moore replied.

The Vuk pulled back the knife that he had held against Moore's neck and folded it. He then placed it in his pocket. "You see what happens to people who lie or try to take advantage of me, don't you?"

"Yes."

"Don't let me catch you doing that, then." The Vuk joined Panich at the table and continued his discussion of filleting. "Now, we grasp the edges of his outer skin and tug it." The Vuk and Panich began pulling off the man's skin.

"I'll be back," Moore said as he ran out of the room and found a bathroom down the hall where he began to vomit. When he composed himself, he reluctantly returned to the room where the Vuk and Panich were beating the skinned man with ball bats. Within minutes, the man died of cardiovascular shock.

"Clean up the blood," the Vuk ordered Panich as he walked toward Moore. "Come with me, Alvey."

The two walked down another set of stairs into a secluded area at the rear of the complex.

"I want to show you where you and Zivi were going to deliver your shipment of girls." He produced a key and unlocked a door.

"I've got one of the best bottom bitches in the world working for me. You do know what a bottom bitch is, don't you?"

"Yes. It's a girl who's worked herself up and helps manage the girls and recruit others," Moore said. "I had one when I ran pro skirts a couple of years ago."

"Right," the Vuk said as he opened another door and they walked into a room with two guards. The guards followed the two into the room full of bunk beds. Each bed was occupied by a woman.

"Anna," the Vuk called to a woman, who was seated on a bed and talking with one of the girls. "Come here."

The woman arose and walked toward them. She had long brown

hair and a large, disfiguring scar on her cheek. Moore thought she fit the description of the woman, who had been seen with Panich when Angel's sister was killed and the two teens were abducted.

As the woman neared Moore, she blurted out in surprise, "Emerson!"

Moore then recognized her as Tatiana.

Before Moore could say anything, he heard the Vuk yell, "Grab him."

Moore found himself restrained by the two guards as the Vuk walked in front of him. "I thought there was something vaguely familiar about you. Emerson Moore, the one who got away from me in Vukovar. You were the only one to survive."

"This is awkward," Moore said, knowing his cover was blown and dropping all pretense of acting as Alvey.

The Vuk laughed at Moore's predicament. "Gotcha!" the Vuk roared as his eyes bulged with glee. He nodded his head to Anna. "Even Tatiana ended up with me despite your and your friends' attempts to keep her away from me."

Tatiana's face was crestfallen as she realized she had blown Moore's cover.

"When the *Zenobia* blew up, my men found Tatiana on the riverbank. Pity that her beauty was ruined by the explosion," the Vuk growled.

"I thought you were in the bow!" Moore said as he looked at Tatiana.

"I was, but I went to search for you. Lucky for me, otherwise I would have died. I was blown overboard and the Vuk's men found me. The rest is history," she said.

"She had no choice but to work for me. With that scar, no man but me wanted her." He smirked at his comment. "Lock him up!" the Vuk ordered. The Vuk turned on his heels and walked away.

The two guards forced Moore to walk with them to another part of the building. There, Moore was thrown into one of a number of barren, cell-like rooms. The door's lock clicked as it closed.

Moore looked around his cell. It had no furniture, no windows and a cold concrete floor. The ceiling was ten feet high and a bare light bulb was in the middle. In the corner was a bucket for a toilet. Moore sat down with his back against the wall and faced the door, which had a small window in it.

Two hours later, Moore saw a face at the window and heard the door being unlocked. He remained seated as it opened and Tatiana walked into the room. She sat on the floor next to Moore and placed her head on his shoulders.

"I am so sorry, Emerson," she sobbed at her accidental betrayal of her old friend.

"No problem," Moore said, as he reached up to stroke her head.

"They were bound to find me out. It was just a matter of time."

"It's been so long since we've seen each other."

"It has," Moore agreed. "I thought of you from time to time," he said as he continued to stroke her head.

"I have, too."

"Why didn't you try to contact me?"

She looked into Moore's eyes. "I couldn't remember your last name or what newspaper you worked for. I think the explosion on the ship caused me to lose part of my memory."

"So, how did this all happen? How did you get mixed up in this mess with the Vuk?"

"When the ship blew up, I was blown overboard. I swam to the riverbank and one of his patrols found me. They didn't know who I was at first because of the bleeding." She unconsciously ran her fingers along the scar on her face. "After they cleaned me up, one of his men recognized me and contacted the Vuk. He had me sent to his headquarters where he raped me continuously for several days."

"Tatiana, I'm sorry," Moore said as he tried to imagine the trauma she had endured. "Why didn't you try to escape?"

"Where was I to go? I had no one. My family was killed. The only person I knew was you and I didn't know where you were!" She paused a moment and took a deep sigh before continuing. "He told me no one would want me because of my scar and I was better off with him. What could I do? I was sixteen-years-old and with nothing."

"I understand," Moore said as he recognized the control the Vuk had exercised over her. It was typical of what he had learned about pimps controlling their victims. "How did you end up in Florida?"

"After the war, we moved to Germany. The war crimes people were trying to find the Vuk and he felt safer there. Some of his closest men went with us. They got involved even more with prostitution. And he made me help him recruit and manage the girls."

Moore nodded as he listened.

"One day, he got a tip there was going to be a raid on us. So, we left Germany and went to London. He used his connections and started bringing in women and girls from Eastern Europe for another prostitution ring. He left one of his men to run it and we went to Toronto where he set up another ring.

"We were living there when he got mad at the President of the United States for helping convict Milosevic. That's when he set up the attack on the President."

Moore interrupted. "I didn't know he was behind that. I was working in Washington when that happened and I don't think his name surfaced at all."

"He was mad, really mad he didn't kill the president," she recalled. "He came back to Toronto and drank for days. He beat me several times. I still have some of the scars on my back."

Moore placed his arm around her and pulled her tight. After a minute, he asked, "What's he going to do with me?" He had already guessed the answer.

"He'll kill you," she said. "Torture you like he's done with the others."

"You've seen this?"

"Several times, he made me watch. He said this is what would happen to me if I ever tried to leave him."

Moore turned so he could look at her. "If I could get you out of here, would you be willing to testify against him?"

"No one gets away from him," she responded, knowing her fate was sealed.

"I got away from him once. I think I can do it again," Moore said. "I can take you with me."

"Really?" she asked incredulously. "You think you can get away from him when you're locked away here? Look around you.

There's no escaping him. The only escape is death."

"No, I think I could come up with something," Moore said, optimistically.

Tatiana pulled away from him. "You're dreaming. No one gets away from the Vuk." Tatiana stood. "I better go before I'm missed." She walked out of the room and closed the door.

Moore heard it lock and sat back. He began devising a plan for their escape.

The Next Day
The Boss's Compound

"Strap him there," the Vuk ordered the two guards who had escorted Moore from his locked room to the room where the Vuk had filleted the man the previous day.

Moore twisted as he tried to free himself from the grip of the two guards, but it was to no avail. They were joined by Panich who affixed the straps to Moore's arms and legs, securing him to the tabletop.

Moore's plans to escape just fizzled. He didn't have a chance to break away from the two escorts when they took him out of his locked room. Now, he found himself strapped to a table.

He saw another table in the room close to his table. There was also a man strapped to it. He was naked. The man's head was also strapped down. His mouth had an apparatus that kept it wide open.

"Mr. Emerson Moore," the Vuk started. "I want you to see what happens when someone betrays me."

Moore turned his head so he could see the Vuk. Curled around his arms was a baby python.

"This is my baby. His name is Crusher."

The Vuk walked to the end of the table where the man's feet were and unwrapped the young python from his arms. He set it on the man's feet and the man started jerking as the python began snaking its way up the man's legs.

"Crusher hasn't been fed in a number of days. I'm sure he is very hungry," the Vuk said as the snake made its way to the man's groin. The man's eyes widened in fear and he screamed.

The Vuk turned to a nearby container and opened it. He reached in and withdrew something. When he turned around, Moore could see he was dangling a mouse by its tail. The mouse saw the snake right away and twisted as it tried to escape from the Vuk's grasp. The snake raised its head and locked its eyes on the live meal in front of it.

"Down the hatch," the Vuk bellowed sinisterly as he dropped the mouse into the man's open mouth.

The man tried to scream and then began choking as the mouse made its way down the man's throat. The mouse was followed quickly by the python.

The man's body convulsed as he tried to fight, but it was hope-less as the six-foot python blocked all air to the man's system. The man's body relaxed as death took control. The room was quiet as the occupants watched the snake beginning to inch backward.

Within a minute, the eight-inches of snake, which had entered the man's throat, had retracted itself. The snake turned its head and looked at the Vuk.

The Vuk was holding another mouse in his hands. He looked at Moore. "Are you ready?"

Moore's eyes widened in terror as the Vuk walked towards him. "Remove the brace from his throat and bring it here, Panich."

Panich jumped to the task and quickly removed the brace and handed it to the Vuk. "Set Crusher on Moore's feet."

Panich returned to the table and picked up the snake. He walked to the foot of Moore's table and gently placed the snake on Moore's feet. Moore began twisting to free himself, but the straps were too tight.

The Vuk dangled the mouse over Moore's tightly closed mouth. "Ready?"

Moore clamped his jaws together in anticipation of the guards trying to wedge it open. He could feel the python working its way up his body.

"Not today, Moore," the Vuk said as he dropped the mouse into the python's open mouth. "Maybe tomorrow, or the next day. I'll let you worry about the end of your life. You now know it will be brutal."

The Vuk laughed as he picked up the python and returned it to its tank. "Take him back to his room."

When they released the straps and allowed Moore to stand, they had to support him. Moore's body was shaking. He was emotionally drained by what he had witnessed and what was in store for him. Supporting him, the two guards began walking Moore out of the room.

"Hold on," the Vuk said. "There's one more thing I should tell you."

Moore looked up at the Vuk.

"Your wife and child. I believe their names were Julie and Matthew?" the Vuk asked with a cruel smile.

The adrenaline began to rush through Moore's body when he heard the Vuk mention their names. "What about them?"

"I believe they died in an automobile accident."

"Yes. What about it?"

"Do you know what really happened?" the Vuk asked.

Moore had a perplexed look on his face. "What do you mean?"

"I was driving the truck which forced them to crash into the side of the bridge and into the river. Pity they drowned." The Vuk began to laugh uncontrollably.

"You killed them!" Moore screamed. He tore away from the grip of his captors and charged at the Vuk. All of the emotions he had held within since their deaths unleashed and powered his action.

Before he could reach the Vuk, Panich tackled him, knocking Moore to the ground. As Moore and Panich rolled about the floor, Moore grabbed one of Panich's fingers and pulled it back, dislocating it and causing Panich to scream.

As Moore tried to free himself, the two guards pounced on Moore and restrained him. When they had him under control, they stood him back up.

"I could have just as easily taken you out, but I wanted you to suffer. Your reporting on Vukovar hindered my efforts to remain in Serbia after the war and I had to leave. I owed you!" The Vuk laughed again.

"I'll make you pay," Moore screamed as he tried to break away from his captors.

The Vuk looked at his watch and back to Moore. "I don't think you have the time you need to pay me back. It's running out." The Vuk looked at the two guards. "Take him away and make sure he doesn't escape."

The two guards, tightly gripping Moore, marched him out of the room and back to his holding room. They shoved him through the door and slammed it shut. Then they locked it.

Moore's chest was heaving as he caught his breath. He began to sob as he realized he was responsible for the death of his wife and son.

Later That Day
The Boss's Compound

The sound of his cell door being unlocked caught Moore's attention. Moore stood and watched as the door opened and Panich entered. He was carrying an electric cattle prod in his hand.

Moore noticed the finger on his other hand had been taped and bandaged. He grinned to himself as he realized the pain he had caused Panich.

"It wasn't a good idea for you to embarrass me in front of the Boss," Panich said as he approached Moore with the prod extended and pointing at Moore. "Now, it's my turn to give you a taste of pain."

Moore eyed the distance between him and the partially open door.

"Don't even think about it. The guards are down the hallway.

You wouldn't get very far," Panich warned.

Moore thought to himself, where was a light saber when you needed one? He squatted and lowered his center of gravity.

Panich lunged forward and Moore dodged to his left, but Panich swung the prod in an arc and caught Moore in the back, sending an electrical charge of 5,000 volts into Moore's body. Moore contorted with the pain.

Panich chuckled at Moore's discomfort. He stepped back to position himself between the partially open door and Moore. "Why don't you try to run past me?" he asked between slitted eyes.

Moore feigned to his right, causing Panich to move in that direction. Then, Moore juked to his left and charged Panich from the side. When Panich belatedly tried to swing the prod back to Moore, Moore had Panich in his grip. He knocked Panich to the floor and the prod fell out of Panich's grasp. As Moore began pummeling Panich, the door to the cell opened and the two guards entered.

Out of the corner of his eye, Panich saw the two guards and screamed, "Get him off me. I'm going to burn his eyes out!"

"I don't think so," a feminine voice said as the two guards were pushed into the room and the doorway showed Tatiana standing in it. She held a .45 in her hand and it was now pointed at Panich.

"What in the hell do you think you are doing?" Panich roared as he and Moore separated and got to their feet.

As Panich focused on Tatiana, Moore picked up the cattle prod. He touched it lightly to Panich's butt. Panich jerked as the volts surged through him and he found himself on the floor. He twisted around and gave Moore a deadly glare.

Moore looked at Tatiana. "Thank you, Tatiana."

Tatiana just smiled. She didn't say anything in response to Moore's gratitude.

"What are you doing?" Moore asked.

"I heard what the Vuk has in store for you and I couldn't let that happen."

"You know you can't stay here, now?"

Tatiana sighed. "It's time I change my lifestyle. But I'll need your help," she said.

"You got it!" Moore smiled. He looked back at his three captors and said, "We better get moving." Moore joined Tatiana and they stepped into the hallway.

Closing the door and locking it, Moore asked, "Now, how do we get out of here? We can't go through the front gate."

"Come with me. We may be able to scale the wall near the back," Tatiana said as they began to race through the building.

Back in the cell, Panich reached into his pocket and extracted his cell phone. "Amateurs!" he said to his two cellmates as he keyed in the number to the guardhouse. When the phone was answered, Panich yelled, "Moore and Tatiana are escaping. Get men to the back wall and alert the Boss. And get somebody to Moore's cell to free us!"

As guards ran toward the rear of the courtyard, Moore and Tatiana exited the rear of the building. They spotted a large box truck parked next to the wall.

"Quick," Moore yelled. "We'll climb up on the hood and the cab. Then we can climb over the wall."

They raced to the truck. As they neared it, three armed guards rounded the corner of the warehouse and saw Moore and Tatiana. They opened fire as Moore and Tatiana ducked behind the rear of the truck.

"Now what do we do?"

Moore looked at the two weapons. He and Tatiana had a .45 with only one clip and a cattle prod.

"I don't know." Moore's mind raced as he looked around the courtyard for a way to escape.

Sticking her head around the truck, Tatiana fired two shots, sending the advancing guards lunging for cover.

"That slowed them down," she said proudly.

Before Moore could comment, an explosion rocked the wall twenty feet behind him. After the smoke cleared, they saw a gaping break in the wall. It was eleven feet wide.

"What happened?" Tatiana asked.

"I have no idea, but that's our exit."

Tatiana shot off two more rounds before Moore grabbed her hand and the two ran towards the destroyed section of wall. As they ran, the guards opened fire again. Three feet before they ran through the wall, Tatiana screamed as two bullets tore through her back. They entered her body below the shoulder blade.

Tatiana dropped to the ground. "Run," she yelled to Moore when he bent down.

"Not without you," he said. He picked her up in his arms and carried her through the opening as bullets continued to fly.

"Here! Over here!" a voice bellowed.

Moore saw the open sliding door of an old, white van. Standing next to it and dressed in a black tee shirt and jeans was Siwel. He ran to the van and Siwel helped him place Tatiana inside. The two men jumped in and Siwel slammed the door shut.

"Get us out of here!" Siwel yelled to his deputy, Jill Tracy, at the wheel.

"Going to warp speed," Tracy said as she slammed her foot down hard on the gas pedal.

The van accelerated quickly and went around the corner before the Vuk's guards emerged from the opening in the wall. They had no chance to fire on the escaping van.

"What are you doing here?" Moore asked as he held Tatiana's head in his lap and Siwel broke open a medical kit and applied a compress to the wounds.

"Chutney had a rocket-armed drone overhead so we could watch what was going on," Siwel answered.

"That's how we knew where to position our van," Tracy called from the front of the van.

"I thought you might need some back up. The only thing we could do was put you under surveillance. When Chutney saw you two trying to escape, I gave him permission to punch a hole in the wall for you. Armed drones come in handy for that type of stuff."

Moore turned to look at the wounded woman in his lap. "Hang in there, Tatiana, We're heading for the hospital."

Tatiana looked up at Moore. She wanted to speak, but when she opened her mouth, blood gurgled out.

Moore looked at Siwel. Siwel shook his head negatively. Moore turned his attention back to Tatiana as the van turned another corner.

"Thank you, Tatiana. I couldn't have done it without you," Moore said as he gently stroked her head.

She gurgled blood again.

Moore ran his hand down the scar on her face. "You've always looked so beautiful to me."

A slight smile crossed her face and then her eyes stared lifelessly at Moore. Her body went limp.

Siwel reached over and closed her eyes. "I'm sorry, Emerson."

"Me, too." Emerson said sadly as he stared at Tatiana. "It took a lot of guts for her to do what she did today. She risked everything to free me and she paid the price for it."

Five minutes later, Tracy pulled the van up to the hospital's emergency room entrance and Tatiana's body was taken into the emergency room even though it was too late.

"Come with me!" Siwel grabbed Moore's arm and they rushed to a waiting helicopter for the brief flight back to the Task Force's headquarters at the Naples Airport on The Patriot Way.

During the flight, Moore related what had transpired during his captivity and that the Boss was really the Vuk, who was wanted for war crimes. He also included the revelation that the Vuk had killed his wife and son.

"We've got more than probable cause now," Siwel said as he radioed the Task Force's headquarters and gave instructions to quickly get a search warrant and prepare for a raid.

When they landed, Chutney greeted Moore and Siwel. He had the search warrant in his hand. "We're ready to go. Good thing we had the most recent architectural drawings of the building. We've studied them to familiarize ourselves with the layout."

They rounded the building and saw the SWAT team loading into the Bearcat armored vehicle and the armored van. In front of the two vehicles was the box truck that Moore had driven to Naples.

"We're going to have to move quickly. They're probably destroying files and laptops before they leave the building."

Before Siwel could speak, Moore stated firmly, "I'm coming with you!"

"Not sure that's a good idea," Siwel said.

"I'm covering the story. You've got to let me go," Moore said as he thought of another reason why he should be allowed to accompany the SWAT team. "Besides, if I drive the truck they think it's Zivi showing up. I can crash the gate and everybody follows me in."

Siwel looked at Moore for a moment. "Okay, you can go. Chutney, hook him up with some body armor."

Chutney handed him the gear and Moore quickly slipped it on.

"Not a bad idea, although I'm riding with you," Siwel said as he followed Moore to the truck and Chutney returned to the building to run the drone operations.

Moore reached the truck first and climbed into the cab. He reached under the seat where he had hidden his .45 after killing Zivi. He stuck it in the waistband of his pants just before Siwel opened the passenger door.

"Let's roll," Siwel said.

The three vehicles led by a police car with flashing lights and a siren raced out of the parking lot for the drive to the Immokalee warehouse.

"I don't think I told you, but Toledo SWAT is moving in on Pavkov's warehouse and Sweet Dreams. They should have O'Malley and Pavkov in custody shortly."

"That's good news!" Moore said as he followed the lead police car.

"When we get closer, the lead car will drop to the back of the line. We'll jump to the front and take the gate."

"What about their counter-surveillance measures?" Moore asked as he drove.

"We can jam the wireless cameras you told me about. Chutney will do that with his drones."

Siwel's cell phone buzzed and Siwel answered. "Siwel here." After a brief conversation, he disconnected. "More good news."

"What's that?" Moore asked as he kept his eyes on the road.

"That was Chutney. One of his drones observed three box trucks leaving the warehouse and heading for I-75. A drone followed them while he radioed state troopers to pull them over."

"Did they get the Vuk?" Moore asked excitedly.

"Nope. They were full of women. They were running them to a safe place. We got the drivers and will be able to take the trafficking victims to a safe house."

The police car in front of them shut off its lights and siren as they neared the Vuk's warehouse. It then pulled over, as did the others.

Moore climbed out of the cab and on top of it where he removed the aluminum foil covering the tracking device. He climbed back into the cab and threw the aluminum foil on the floor. "They should see us coming now and think it's Zivi finally showing up."

"And hopefully drop their guard a bit," Siwel added.

Moore drove around the waiting police car and continued driving to the warehouse. The Bearcat and armored van followed immediately behind the box truck. The police car took its new position at the end of the line of vehicles.

In the Vuk's office, Panich saw the tracking light for Zivi's truck appear. "Looks like Zivi's on his way here," he yelled to the Vuk who was walking down the hall.

"What?" the Vuk asked as he entered the office.

"See there," Panich pointed to the screen. "He's close."

The Vuk had a puzzled look on his face as he stared at the screen. "How do we know it's Zivi?"

"Who else would be driving his truck? He must have taken some side trip for whatever reason. Maybe one of the girls escaped and he didn't want to show up until he recovered her," Panich guessed. He and Zivi were close friends and he wanted to do anything he could to curb the Vuk's wrath.

"Call the gate and alert the guards Zivi is coming. But tell them to be careful and open the back of the truck to be sure we don't have any surprises." The Vuk was suspicious.

"Okay," Panich said as he reached for the radio and alerted the gate guards. After he completed his task, he walked down the steps to the first floor lobby so that he could greet Zivi when he walked in. He wanted to warn him to be careful when he met with the Vuk.

As the parade of vehicles drove within a block of the warehouse, Chutney activated the drone's jamming device, effectively neutralizing the compound's wireless cameras.

When the guards saw the approaching truck, they held their weapons in the ready position. They were taken by surprise when the truck didn't slow, but sped up as it closed the distance to the gate.

"Here we go," Moore said as he slammed the truck through the compound's gate and drove straight to the entrance door.

His truck was followed by the Bearcat. The guards at the gate began firing their weapons, but their resistance was short-lived. The armored van had stopped at the gate and its SWAT team emptied out. They shouted to the guards to drop their weapons. When the guards turned and started to fire on them, the SWAT unit cut them down.

Upon exiting the armored vehicles, the SWAT element split into perimeter and entry teams. The perimeter team took cover as they were taking fire from the Vuk's outside guards. They engaged the Vuk's men and quickly eliminated the threats with lethal fire from their M-4's. The entry team was ready to breach the doors and enter the warehouse.

At the front of the warehouse, Moore recklessly ran past the SWAT team and through the lobby door. His adrenaline had taken over his brain. As he entered the lobby with the .45 he had pulled from his waistband, a bullet struck the door frame. Moore whipped around and saw Panich holding a pistol.

Without hesitation, Moore fired, dropping Panich to the ground. Suddenly, Moore felt a firm grip on his shoulder and he was spun around. He found himself staring into the angry eyes of Siwel.

"What in the hell do you think you're doing? You're out of here!" Siwel roared as he pulled Moore out of the building. "Have you lost your frigging mind?" Siwel asked as his SWAT team tossed flash grenades into the lobby and entered to clear the front part of the building.

"I'm going to kill the Vuk. He killed my family," Moore said with a wild look in his eyes.

"That's exactly why you're not going in there. You're not rational. You're not thinking. You're not trained. You're not in law enforcement. And we want the Vuk alive," Siwel snapped at Moore.

"But..."

"No buts about it. You're done. You're staying here."

The two listened to the radio chatter and heard the explosions and gunfire as the SWAT team cleared the first floor and advanced to the second floor. The entire exchange was over in five minutes. Two SWAT team members had been wounded and all of the warehouses defenders had been killed.

When the shooting stopped and the warehouse was secure, Siwel said, "Okay, we can go in. I want you to identify which one is the Vuk."

"He'd be upstairs," Moore said as he walked in and climbed the stairs to the second floor. He led Siwel into the room where he had been tortured and saw two bodies on the floor. Neither was the Vuk. As he turned to leave, he saw the Vuk's python wasn't in its tank.

"The Vuk's pet python is gone," Moore observed.

"That's interesting," Siwel said as he looked toward the empty tank.

As they left the room, several SWAT team officers entered to remove the two bodies.

Moore led Siwel down the hall to the Vuk's office, but it was empty. They walked through the entire second floor, but none of the bodies belonged to the Vuk. Descending the rear stairs to the first floor, Moore and Siwel inspected the first floor area, including the warehouse and rooms where Moore and the women had been held.

Next, they exited the building and reviewed all of the bodies that had been removed from the building. The bodies were lined up in a row in the compound's parking lot. None of them belonged to the Vuk.

"He must have escaped," Moore said as he and Siwel returned to the vehicles where the SWAT team had congregated.

Siwel radioed Chutney and verified the drone surveillance had shown only the three trucks leaving the compound.

"The only vehicles that left the compound were the three trucks and they were under drone surveillance the entire time. The troopers were confident there were no hidden compartments in them."

"What about the hole in the wall I escaped through? Could the Vuk have used it?"

"No, we've had everything under surveillance since you escaped," Siwel responded.

"What about the women? Could the Vuk have disguised himself?" Moore asked with deep frustration in his voice.

"The Vuk doesn't strike me as someone who'd try to escape like that. Besides, the women would have told us when we rescued them."

"I guess so," Moore said as he looked back at the building. Something was bugging him, but he couldn't put a finger on it.

"The troopers are checking out the women to be sure," Siwel added.

"Mind if I take a last walk through the building?" Moore asked.

"No can do. You can't go back in there unescorted."

"What's next?" Moore asked.

"We'll do a thorough sweep of the building to see if there are any hidden rooms. Some place where the Vuk may have escaped detection from us during our initial sweep," Siwel said.

He studied the building for a moment and then added, "I think he's still inside." Siwel turned to address his team, who were waiting for his go-ahead for the operation's next phase.

When Siwel was distracted, Moore started to walk toward the lobby door. He didn't take more than two steps when suddenly a series of explosions began rippling through the building. Moore and the SWAT team members in the compound dropped to the ground as the building began imploding. Debris filled the air as fires started throughout the structure.

"He must have had it wired," Siwel said. He turned to Moore as they both stood to their feet. "I'd guess your buddy just committed suicide."

"Why would the Vuk do that?" Moore asked as he watched the flames.

"He was cornered in the building somewhere. Probably realized we'd find him. He knows the drill from his years in the military," Siwel answered.

"Yeah, and probably didn't want to stand trial," Moore surmised.

"Maybe," Siwel said. He looked at the burning building as sirens in the background signaled the approaching fire trucks. "Once they get this fire out, they'll search for his remains."

Moore's shoulders seemed to relax as the tension left him. He felt a sense of relief and retribution at seeing the Vuk's end. Moore's short journey for vengeance was now over. He could relax. Moore took a deep cleansing breath as he began walking away from the remains of the burning building and the Vuk's ashes.

Kingfisher Station
Punta Gorda, Florida

After completing paperwork and interviews for the Human Trafficking Task Force, Moore filed two stories with *The Washington Post* on his undercover work in human trafficking. He was told the Task Force in Toledo had conducted a raid on Pavkov's warehouse and had captured Pavkov and most of Pavkov's men. They also had O'Malley in custody.

Moore needed to step away from all of the activity and work on completing his exposé on human trafficking. He called Gary Mazey, an eccentric friend of his in Punta Gorda to see if he could hang with him a few days and finish writing his exposé. Then he talked with Siwel who asked that he stay in touch since he was a witness to everything which had occurred.

It was less than a two-hour drive from Naples to Punta Gorda. Moore was driving on the southwest side of Punta Gorda on Deltona Drive to Kingfisher Station. It was Mazey's ecolodge in the former studios of the KIX Country radio station on the banks of Alligator Creek, close to Port Charlotte Harbor. Moore had met Mazey when he was covering the damages from Hurricane Charley.

Moore turned left off Deltona Drive and into the lodge's parking lot where he pulled into one of the vacant spots. Moore grabbed his newly acquired gear and walked up the ramp to the lobby and bar area of the building. The building was set on stilts in a mangrove swamp.

As he walked into the lobby with its rich Brazilian hardwood floor, a voice shouted, "Well, it's about time you made it here to check out my new place."

Moore turned and saw the gray-haired and bearded Mazey standing behind the counter. The lanky fifty-year-old was in great shape for his age, partly due to his active lifestyle. Between building docks, remodeling homes and buying rental property, the high-energy Mazey had little time to sit back and be lazy. Lazy Mazey was not a term that would fit him. Sometimes, Crazy Mazey was a better moniker.

Moore shook hands. "Looks great!"

"This is nothing. Wait until you see the rooms. I've got seven rooms here and out by the creek we've got two beaches, kayak rental, Boy Scout camping grounds and dockage for larger watercraft."

Mazey shoved a registration book in front of Moore. "Just sign in here and I'll show you your room, then we can take a tour of the place."

"No computer registration?"

"Nah. I don't need that fancy stuff."

Moore signed in and Mazey wrote in the room number. "Follow me."

Mazey walked Moore down to his room where Moore deposited his bag. Then, they returned to the lobby and Moore grabbed a cold

Pepsi before following Mazey outside and down the path to the dock.

"Yeah, I promised a couple of folks we'd go out sailing together. They're at the dock getting their boat ready," Mazey explained.

After two hundred yards, they emerged from the mangroves and they walked onto the dock.

"That looks bigger than a creek to me. Sure that's not a river?" Moore asked as he saw Alligator Creek for the first time.

"Yeah, I know. It's a lot bigger than a creek," Mazey responded.

"You've got a lot of kayaks," Moore said as he saw the kayaks stored upside down.

"Those are my rentals for the mangrove swamps. It's so thick in there, boaters have to have a GPS so they can find their way out."

"Why do you store them upside down?"

"Water moccasins."

"What do you mean?" Moore asked.

"Water moccasins will slither in and curl up in the bow. Then, you get bit when you stick your feet in the kayak."

"I wouldn't like that."

"And you have to be careful when you're in the mangrove swamps. The water moccasins climb up in the trees and will drop down on you as you kayak."

Moore shuddered at the thought.

"There's Larry and Sandie. Come on. I'll introduce you," Mazey said.

A man in his forties with a crew cut and a long-haired, slender woman with a killer smile, who was in her late thirties, jumped off their thirty-foot Irwin.

"I'm Larry," the man said as he shook hands. "This is my sister, Sandie."

"Nice to meet you," Moore said to Larry before he turned to the saucy-looking Sandie. "And it's really nice to meet you." Moore's eyes sparkled when he greeted her. He thought about switching boats to sail with Sandie, but knew it wouldn't be fair to Mazey.

"It's nice to meet you, too," Sandie replied with a deep southern accent. Her green eyes glowed as she smiled at Moore.

"Whoa, that's quite an accent!" Moore said. "Where are you two from?"

"Dickson, Tennessee," Sandie replied. "My friends call me Grits," she said in a self-deprecating manner.

"I'm not too sure I could call you Grits. You're much too attractive for a name like that," Moore teased.

Sandie's face blushed as she smiled demurely.

"We need to get moving," Larry urged, anxious to get under way.

"You're right," Mazey said as he walked toward his forty-eight-foot Soverel.

Moore walked over and joined Mazey on the Soverel as the other two boarded their Irwin.

"They're real nice people. The two of them are divorced and they spend time down here when they can. They love to sail," Mazey said as he readied the boat.

"What can I do to help?"

"Stay out of my way," Mazey cracked. "Nah, you just sit back and relax. From what you told me about your undercover stuff on the phone, you need to get some of that stress out of your life."

"Thanks, Gary," Moore said as his eyes turned back to the Irwin where he caught Sandie staring at him. He waved and she waved, then turned to readying the boat.

Within minutes, the two sailboats had cast off their lines and were moving down Alligator Creek and entering Port Charlotte Bay.

"Nice boat you have here," Moore marveled.

"Yeah, I bought it at a bank auction. Got it for next to nothing, then restored her. It was custom built for the owner of Soverel boats. That's why she's laid out so nice. When you go below, be sure to check out the berth in the aft cabin. It's king-size."

"I'll do that."

Moore freed his mind and took in the fresh wind and the azure water of the bay as Mazey shut off the engine and began running up the main sail.

"Take the helm and hold her into the wind," Mazey said.

Moore jumped to the wheel and complied with Mazey's request.

On board the Irwin, they were also preparing to raise their main sail. Below deck, danger lurked. The gas line for the Atomic 4 auxilary gas engine had a small leak and fumes were building in the bilge. When the bilge pump started pumping, it sparked and caused an explosion. The force of the explosion blew Larry and Sandie into the water.

"That's not good!" Mazey said as he dropped the sail. "Start the engine and head us over to them," Mazey said as he began to return to the helm.

Moore's previous sailing experience came into play as he started the engine and pointed the Soverel toward the flaming Irwin. When Mazey replaced Moore at the helm, he pointed to the life ring. "Get that ring and throw it to them when we get closer!"

Moore moved quickly and grabbed the life ring and a couple of flotation devices as the Soverel closed the distance between them and the burning boat. Mazey was on the radio, calling in the fire to the Coast Guard.

As they neared the two in the water, it appeared Sandie was floating unconsciously and Larry was struggling to keep her afloat. Moore threw the life ring at Larry and then jumped into the water with the two flotation devices.

"I've got her," Moore said to Larry when he surfaced. Larry grabbed hold of the life ring and watched as Moore held up Sandie.

In the meantime, Mazey had edged the Soverel up to the three in the water. He used his boat hook to pull Larry closer and then pulled him onto the dive platform.

"Tie this under her arms," Mazey yelled as he threw the end of a line to Moore.

Moore secured the line around her and then helped lift Sandie out of the water as the other two pulled in the line. Once Sandie was on the deck, Mazey and Larry helped Moore reboard.

The three knelt around Sandie, who was beginning to regain consciousness.

"Are you okay?" Larry asked as the sirens of an approaching Coast Guard cutter echoed in the background.

"Yes, just a little woozy," Sandie answered. She tried to sit, but dropped back to the deck.

"Take it easy. Not too fast," Moore said.

"Looks like your boat's a goner," Mazey said as he looked at the burning hull.

"Better the boat than us. We've got insurance," Larry said as he also looked at the craft awash in flames.

"What happened?" Sandie asked from her prone position.

"Don't know. She just exploded. All I remember is I heard the bilge pump kick in," Larry said.

"You probably had a gas leak," Mazey surmised. "I've seen that happen with other fires."

"How do you feel?" Moore asked.

"Better," Sandie said as she made it up to a sitting position.

"You better thank Emerson for rescuing us. He jumped in and helped us both," Larry said.

"Awe, you're so sweet," Sandie said as she kissed Moore on the cheek. "Thank you."

"Hey, what am I, a carp?" Mazey asked. "I helped, too. Don't I get a kiss?"

"I was just getting warmed up for you," Sandie teased as she leaned over and gave Mazey's bearded cheek a light kiss.

"That's more like it," Mazey grinned through his beard. Then he looked at Larry. "Don't even think about giving me a kiss," he teased.

Larry puckered his lips and then said, "I'm much better than my sister."

"And I'm not going to find out," Mazey replied quickly.

"You don't know what you're missing!" Larry joked.

"What I want to know is how do you know whose kiss is better?" Moore asked.

"Well, we are from Tennessee. You mean it's not normal to kiss your sister?" Larry continued to joke.

"Only in Tennessee," Mazey said. "Uh-oh? We've got company."

Everyone turned their heads to look at Mazey and then in the direction he was looking. Approaching them was a police boat and a TV news boat. Overhead, a TV helicopter appeared and began filming the burning boat.

"Looks like we'll be on TV and in the papers," Mazey said.

Mazey was right. The four of them were flooded with reporters and TV crews as they interviewed them and heard about Moore's rescue of Larry and Sandie. The story appeared on the evening news and websites as well as the next day's newspapers.

The next morning found Moore, Sandie and Larry seated on one of the outside decks at the Kingfisher Station, enjoying cups of coffee and a light breakfast of fresh fruit.

The door opened and Mazey walked onto the deck. "Look here. They've got pictures of your boat burning in the *Herald-Tribune*."

"Let me see, Gary," Larry said as he took the newspaper and shared it with Sandie. "Now, that's a fire!"

"Read the article. It's all about our hero, Emerson," Mazey said. "Larry, you can read, can't you?" Mazey teased.

"Stop it!" Larry responded with mock disgust.

"I'm no hero," Moore retorted, modestly. "I just jumped in. Anyone would have done that."

"Too bad she didn't need mouth-to-mouth. I would have been happy to give it to her," Mazey teased.

"So, would I!" Larry joked.

"You're a hero to me," Sandie said with a coy smile to Moore as she ignored the mouth-to-mouth chatter.

Moore noticed her smile and returned it.

"You're a hero to me," Larry repeated in a mocking tone. "Better be careful with her, Emerson. She totes a concealed weapon."

Moore had a puzzled look on his face as he looked at Sandie. She was wearing a white bikini as she sat in the morning sun.

"What's wrong, Emerson?" Sandie asked.

"I'm just trying to figure out how you can conceal a weapon when you're wearing something as little as that bikini," he teased.

"Silly man, it's in my room."

"I swear, she only takes the gun off when she's in the shower, swimming or in that bikini," Larry added.

"Only someone from Tennessee would know that information about his sister showering!" Mazey teased. "You sure you don't kiss your sister?" he asked as he rubbed Larry's crew cut.

"Hey, watch what you're doing!" Larry said as he shrank from Mazey's touch.

"Better be careful, Gary. That's something only our mama is allowed to do to Larry," Sandie kidded.

Changing the subject, Moore asked, "What's on the agenda for today?"

"You guys want to go sailing on my boat since we didn't get to take our sail yesterday?" Mazey asked.

"Sure," Larry replied.

"Sounds good to me. Emerson, are you going to join us?" Sandie asked.

"I will if you can first give me an hour. I need to return a few phone calls and e-mails." Moore knew he should be working on his exposé, but he was enjoying the laid back company of his friends, especially Sandie.

"That will work," Mazey said as he stood. "I've got a couple of chores to complete before we go."

"I'm going to stay here and soak up some rays," Sandie said as she reached for a bottle of Australian Gold suntan lotion and began to squirt it on her body.

"See you in a bit," Larry said as he sat back to read the story about their boat.

An hour later, the four of them were walking along the path to Mazey's sailboat where they spent the next six hours sailing. When they returned to Kingfisher Station, Mazey made drinks and grilled fresh vegetables and fish on his outside grill.

As Moore stifled a yawn, he looked at his watch. "You all have been great company, but I think I'll crash for the night."

"Party pooper!" Sandie teased.

"If you guys knew what he's been through the last few weeks, you'd understand," Mazey said.

"What happened?" Sandie asked.

"I'll tell you a little bit about it in the morning," Moore said as he raised his arms and stretched. The combination of a fresh breeze and being in the sun for most of the day on the sailboat had taken its toll. The three Seagram VOs and Seven Ups also contributed.

"I'll give you a hint," Mazey said. "He was undercover and almost got himself killed."

"Oh, my!" Sandie said.

"A real hero!" Larry said as he sat up from his slouching position in the deck chair.

"Don't get overly excited. It's not that big of a deal. I'll tell you more in the morning."

"I want to hear it now," Larry pushed.

"Shush. You do like he said and wait," Sandie said to her brother. "Sometimes, I want to trade my brother for a new dog," Sandie teased.

"Yeah, and I hope it's a mad dog!" Larry joked.

"You sure can tell you two are brother and sister. But I'm crashing," Moore said as he reached into his pocket to check his cell phone. "Shoot. I left my cell phone on your boat, Gary."

"You can get it now or in the morning. No one messes with the boat."

Moore looked toward the path leading to the dock and decided to wait until morning. He wouldn't be able to check his voicemail messages until then. He didn't know he missed hearing an important message that came in two hours earlier.

Within an hour, everyone returned to their rooms and peace settled on Kingfisher Station. It wouldn't last for long.

The clock in the lobby at Kingfisher Station showed 2:25 a.m. Outside, a slight breeze rustled the leaves of the mangrove trees. The water in Alligator Creek was smooth and reflected the moonlight. Kingfisher Station's dock stood quietly in the muted light from a solitary security lamp.

Into the light, a go-fast boat glided quietly with muffled motors. Once it reached the dock, its motor was cut and two armed passengers furtively jumped off. They secured its bow and stern lines to the dock.

Next, they made their way up the path to Kingfisher Station. Keeping to the shadows and close to the building, they walked past the rear entrance to the lodge and walked up the ramp to the main entrance.

The leader gripped the doorknob and found it unlocked. He twisted it and opened the door. The two men held their automatics at hip level as they entered. After closing the door quietly behind them, they stood still and listened to the sounds in the lodge. Not hearing any movement, the leader walked to the registration desk where he flicked on a small flashlight.

He shined the light on the registration book and found the name he was looking for. Emerson Moore was in Room No. 3. He had seen two hallways leading from the main lobby. He pointed the light at the entrance to one of the hallways and saw a small sign. It indicated Rooms No.1 through No. 3 were in that direction.

He motioned to the other man to follow him. Just before he entered the hallway, he heard the rear entrance door shut. The two men froze and listened. Not hearing anything, they entered the hallway.

"You stay here at the entrance and watch the lobby door," the first man whispered.

"Okay," the second man replied quietly.

The first man walked quietly down the corridor and past the first two rooms.

The second man took a couple of steps to better position himself to watch the front door. When he did, a floor board squeaked.

A table lamp turned on and Mazey sat up on the sofa. The back of the sofa was facing the main lobby.

"I've been meaning to get that fixed," Mazey said as he yawned. "Guess I fell asleep here." He turned and found himself facing the deadly end of a Kalashnikov.

"Quiet," the second man hissed.

"This here is my place and nobody tells me to be quiet!" Mazey said as he stood and faced the man.

"Sit down!" the man ordered.

"He doesn't have to sit down," a voice said from behind the man. "This is his lodge."

The man looked over his shoulder and found Sandie stepping out of the other corridor. In her hand, she held her .38. It was pointed at the man.

"Now, drop your weapon," she said in a firm tone.

"I'd suggest you do as she says," Mazey said. "She knows how to use it."

The man made the mistake of swinging the weapon toward Sandie. Sandie didn't wait for it to come all the way around. She squeezed off two quick shots. The first caught the man squarely in the chest and the second in the abdomen as he fell backwards.

"Nice shooting, Sandie," Mazey said as he jumped over the sofa. He raced to the bar where he grabbed his 20-gauge double-barrel, sawed-off shotgun. It was loaded with deer slugs and able to put a big hole in its target.

"I'm just glad I'm a light sleeper. I thought I heard some sort of ruckus going on between you and somebody; I came down to check it out," she said.

"And I'm glad you did." Mazey knelt down and began to examine the man. "Sandie, can you call 911 on that phone over there?"

"Sure can," she said as she walked over to the phone and placed the call.

Down the hall, the first man kicked open the door to Emerson's room and fired several rounds in the bed. He then flicked on the light and swore when he found the bed empty. He scanned the small room and didn't see Moore. When he heard the gunfire and voices down the hall, he ran to the rear door and fled the lodge. He ran down the path to his waiting boat.

Minutes earlier, Moore decided to get up and take a walk down to the dock. He had been lying awake for the last hour as the events of the past few weeks raced through his mind. Since he couldn't sleep, he went to retrieve his cell phone from Mazey's boat and check his voicemail.

He was sitting on the stern of Mazey's boat when he heard the first and second set of gunshots coming from the direction of the lodge. He realized the go-fast boat, which he thought belonged to someone who had checked in late, was probably connected to the gunshots.

Moore jumped off the stern of Mazey's boat and started to head back to the lodge. He didn't get far as the fleeing man emerged from the path through the mangrove trees and into the light. He stopped when he saw Moore.

Moore's eyes widened as he recognized who the man was. It was the Vuk!

"I found you," the Vuk said with unbridled glee as he pointed his weapon at Moore.

"I thought you were dead!" Moore exclaimed.

"That's what everyone was supposed to think. Just as I had planned," the Vuk laughed quietly.

"How did you survive the explosions and the fire?"

"Before I left my hidden office, I set the timer for the explosives.

Then I took my private elevator to the basement. I crawled through my escape tunnel to the building across the street where Zarkov was waiting for me, and we drove away. You people are so stupid."

Moore was stunned by the revelation. "But, how did you find me?"

"How nice of you to make the headlines in the newspaper. We Googled the stories and saw you were staying here. So, we made a trip tonight to visit you."

The Vuk paused as he heard sirens in the distance.

"I have unfinished business with you and it's long overdue."

"And I have unfinished business with you, too," Moore said as he faced the murderer of his wife and son.

The Vuk laughed. "And how are you going to finish it? You're unarmed!"

"I'm not!" a voice yelled from behind him. It was Mazey and he was aiming his sawed-off shotgun at the Vuk.

The Vuk spun around and saw Mazey emerge from the path under the mangrove trees.

"And neither is Zarkov," the Vuk said as he looked behind Mazey toward the path.

As Mazey turned to check that no one was behind him, the Vuk laughed at his ruse and fired two rounds. The first missed, but the second caught Mazey in the shoulder and his shotgun fell to the ground.

When the Vuk turned back to face Moore, Moore in a revenge-filled fury struck him in the face with a boat hook. The hook caught the Vuk in the eye, damaging his eye. The Vuk swore and pointed his weapon at Moore. Moore struck again. This time, he aimed at the Kalashnikov, but missed it and hit the Vuk in the abdomen with a sharp blow. In pain, the Vuk dropped his weapon.

"I don't need that to kill you," the Vuk said as his eyes narrowed and he rushed at Moore.

The Vuk moved in quickly to counterattack and landed a series of blows to Moore's solar plexus and face. Moore retaliated by connecting his right foot squarely with the Vuk's left shin. He followed his kick with a head butt, bringing his forehead down and across the Vuk's nose and face, causing more pain.

The Vuk recovered and jabbed the heel of his palm directly at Moore's chin as he tried to knock out Moore and potentially break his neck. Moore barely dodged the blow.

Moore twisted behind the Vuk and reached around the Vuk's neck as the two fell to the ground. Moore's thumb and forefinger secured a clamp-like grip on the horns of the thyroid cartilage above the larynx. Ignoring the Vuk's blows to his body, Moore firmly applied finger pressure as the two rolled until the Vuk's loss of air caused unconsciousness. When Moore felt the Vuk's body go limp, he released his hold and stood.

"Are you okay, Gary?" Moore asked Mazey who had pulled himself to a sitting position.

"Pretty much. Left shoulder is a tad sore," Mazey said as he minimized the pain he was feeling.

"Let me help you to your feet," Moore said, picking up the shotgun and assisting Mazey.

"Thanks," Mazey said as he stood.

"You better get this looked at," Moore said, staring at the wound.

"I'd suggest you look after your friend there and pretty quick!" Mazey said with a tone of urgency as he peered over Moore's shoulder at the Vuk, who had regained consciousness and was reaching for his weapon.

Moore spun around and saw the Vuk picking up his gun and starting to aim it at the two of them. "Drop it!" Moore ordered as he aimed the shotgun.

"Kiss off!" the Vuk said as he aimed and prepared to shoot.

The shotgun roared as it fired. "That's for my wife!" The shotgun roared again as the second barrel fired. "And that's for my son!" All of the deeply hidden emotions from the loss of his loved ones burst free as Moore fired. This had become an evening of redemption for Moore.

The Vuk's lifeless body dropped to the dock in a bloody mess.

"See. I told you those deer slugs can make a big hole. You really only needed one shot," Mazey winced in pain as he spoke and looked at the body. "I never took you as a guy bent on revenge."

Moore thought a moment, then responded, "Confucius once said 'Before you embark on a journey of revenge, dig two graves.' In my case, I had the two graves dug and filled. I didn't know I was on a journey of revenge. That just kind of happened here in the last week when I learned he was responsible for their deaths."

"You two okay?" Larry asked as he emerged from the mangrove trees with three police officers.

Before Moore could reply, his cell phone rang. He answered, "Moore here."

"Where have you been, Emerson? I've left you three urgent messages to call me and you didn't return my calls," Siwel said from his desk in the Human Trafficking Task Force's offices.

"Sorry. I left my cell phone in the sailboat."

"Well, you'd better keep your wits about you. They didn't find the Vuk's body at the warehouse."

"I know," Moore said.

"How do you know that?"

"Because the Vuk's here."

"What?"

"He tracked me to Kingfisher Station and tried to take me out. He's dead. The police are here now."

"Tell me what happened," Siwel said.

"If you don't mind, I'd like to get back to you tomorrow. I'm just emotionally drained," Moore said in response to Siwel's request.

"Sure, sure. I understand. Call me when you can," Siwel said as he hung up.

Moore looked toward the heavens and sighed as he thought about his wife and son. He felt a deep sense of relief and redemption.

The Next Morning
Kingfisher Station

It was late morning and Moore was seated outside on the wood deck, having coffee with Larry, Sandie and Mazey. Mazey's left arm was in a sling after his early morning trip to the hospital's emergency room. They had been replaying the previous night's event.

"Yeah. There I was. This guy had me dead-on and good old Annie Oakley comes around the corner with her guns blazing," Mazey said as he described Sandie's prowess with her .38.

Moore looked at Sandie. "Where did you learn to shoot like that?"

"I had a lot of practice," she replied in her deep southern accent.

"What did you practice on?" Moore asked.

"Her ex-husbands," Larry quipped.

"You don't mess with women from Tennessee," she added.

"I'm beginning to understand that," Moore agreed.

A movement on the deck caught Moore's attention. He looked around and saw the Vuk's python slither around the corner. "Where did he come from?" Moore asked.

"I found him this morning when I went to look at those guys' go-fast boat. I found the python taking in the morning sun. I figure he can help keep down the rodents around here," Mazey said, proud of his find.

"What are you going to name him?" Larry asked.

"He is a bit slimy." Mazey looked at Larry and said, "I think I'll name him Larry."

Larry took a swing a Mazey's head, but missed as they all laughed.

"I'd sure like to keep that boat though, but I expect the police will be around to take it away as evidence."

Moore's cell phone rang and he answered it. "Moore here."

"Emerson, how are you coming with that exposé?"

It was John Sedler, his editor at The Washington Post.

"I should have it wrapped up by tomorrow," Moore replied.

"Hurry up and get it done. I have another lead I want you to run down."

"Oh?"

"Ever hear about Jimmy Diamonds?" Sedler asked.

"The mobster?"

"The one and only."

"I'll tell you more when you finish your exposé. But, get it done." Sedler hung up.

"Bad news?" Sandie asked as Moore slipped the cell phone into his pocket.

"Nope. Just another assignment." Moore stood and spoke to his friends. "I'd better excuse myself. Got to hit the laptop."

Coming Soon
The Next *Emerson Moore* Adventure

Missing